EXTINCT DREAM

EXTINCT DREAM

MICHAEL BAXTER

Written 1981–1982

THE REGENCY
PUBLISHERS

ISBN: 978-1-959434-64-1   (Paperback Edition)
ISBN: 978-1-959434-65-8   (Hardcover Edition)
ISBN: 978-1-959434-63-4   (E-book Edition)

Some characters and events in this book are fictitious and products of the author's imagination. Any similarity to real persons, living or dead, is coincidental and not intended by the author.

Book Ordering Information

The Regency Publishers, International
7 Bell Yard London WO2A2JR
info@theregencypublishers.com
www.theregencypublishers.international
+44 20 8133 0466

Printed in the United States of America

CONTENTS

for Piera, Mum, and Dad

CHARACTERS - IN ORDER OF APPEARANCE

Gas Jenny Falcon
Moon Behemoth Magpie
Gesso Jawbone
Low Solid Rider
GoodBoy
Magus
Quake Quake
Fates - Fodfad, Trufus, Justine
House of Hethbad
Gabel the Heathen Dog
Elfawn
Faustlandia
Mr. Nicest
Mrs. Thankyou
Faustlandiagrad
Kazakastazakanaka
Beouwulf Tweedwulf
Pan
Amebus the Macrofaust
Doctor Greenwald
Dionysus Pentacle Pax

Petite Etoile Nysus
Idlegold
Dreyfusus
Captain Death
Marcip
Ben Hadira
Gilgagiggle
Drattle
Apotheascetica
Mofoto
Cara
Carat
Hadcuna
Crifta
Cara Endope
Quodope
Panic
Surplus
Rantana tree
Canto
Sasdad

Daniel 'JimJam' Snaps
John Sartorius
Capo
Jerry Travel
Betty Solar
Fol Mach
Suzie Beauville
Sulphuric Acid
Tess Infanta
Daniel
Humphrey

Eliot
Wallace
Carlo
Solomon
Guinevere
Marianne
Michelle
Berthe
Ariadne
Horace
Bartholomew
Melting Snow
Abacus
Griffin
Arthur
Janice
Rachel
Diana
Mildred
Agatha
Martha
Hercules
A.M and P.M
Duke, Earl, Baron, Count
Contessa
Flaubert
'Watchso'
Lapap
Tarot
Sat, Sit, Sot
Solid, Sad, Drail, Immich
Tell-Tale
Miss Longhi
Lord Abapple

CHAPTER ONE

GAS, MOON, GESSO, AND LOW INTRODUCED

It was the third time that week
He had grazed himself.
What does he feel like shaving on a Wednesday?
The second time that week, he had
Felt like cutting his wrists.
But he was not depressed, just lonely
In aggrandisement of nuptial bliss,
Burst song of a genuine fire.
He wasn't sure if the next six months
He would see him gain ground, bottom out,
Out of the red, into the black,
Decline the Good, or shift his perplexed
Shaving stick from shelf to shelf.
His old toothbrush reminded him of his
Fifth girlfriend, Menthol toothpaste
Forever his second partner.
He combed the bristles with the two-inch nail
Of his right little finger splattered the mirror
With toothpaste spots and thought of Munchkins.
A contagious episode. He made up his mind
From spots; on the spot, he thought,
Turning on the hotel tap. Hot water
Ran out. His wife became plastic in
Memorized verse. Work out. Aerobic.
Turning back to flush the lavatory,
Jive steps through a door.
Perspiration can beat the egg—learned homestead.
His wife was called Gas.
He had named her after their first coupling.

He called himself Moon and shone.
His teeth at the Sun. Gas resigned
Herself to the probabilities of questions.
Not sure if they were written.
They turned out to be unanswerable,
But titles that came to mind
'The Mushroom which grew into a Man.'
'The Cat that ate Fire.'
'The Buskers of Moscow.'
There were three falls in bed.

Crashing clothes horse.
Thrust and counter thrust.
Doorbell rings. Door enters.
Breakfast enters.
Buttered toast.
Hot as a volcanic crumpet.
Marmalade has written;
Overtime pupil of a sunny day.
Bitter passion has defended,
Knife-edge of taste untainted,
Untouched; Salt sweet.
A coffee dream cake,
They ate each other,
And disturbed Time's plover.

There are mists in underwear.
And humid growths, secret canyons.
Alive with creatures, exotic sculptures
From miniaturized artists who practice

In a universe pasted on the back
Of a cardboard harlequin operated
By children who dance with coins,
Smiling pennies and farthings.
Blotting their clothes came as a surprise,
Became conditional in coercive pattern,
Blanked optics of litany.
Shadow secrets; rummaging for these,
Only desires, in underclothes,
Thrown here and there, sought after by
Collectors of this present past.
"Get dressed. It's time to go out
And wish we were here."

They dressed up to the purple-pink walls.
He quietened his footsteps.
On the parquet floor. An abstract
Display of pedantic pattern,
Wooded rhythm, back-to-back,
Side to side; over to you.
Her footsteps sidled by sidled,
Node to node.
A faraway lift door,
At the end of a passage.
A purple carpet.
Tufts as tutored grass growing to fleece

2

Foot and show.
Drunken ranger, Pasteur of clean.
Press the button and burst with
Somewhere over the Same Rainbow.
They descended with a kiss.
They left a tip in the tutored
Hand of a bellboy. Happy Hotels,
Like the back of his hand.
He knew 'Welcome You' in the
The palm of his hand. Handsome lad.
He lusts. They left the key.
It was a large hotel the shape
Of the Taj Mahal; gigantism
In a desert resort. The New
Sahara welcomes you to a playground
Of special delights. A neon desert,
An African paradise that offers luxury,
Light, lust, erotic rocks, sacred
And profane companions, food
From News, perfect rest and
Perfect sweat.

At the door, a boy offers
A talisman to hang around
The neck. Sweet toil.
He offers a hand with the love
Of Jesus pie. There are no
Guarantees in this world.
Counting the steps down.
There are first-nighters and second-nighters.
Their hands are tight together.

A crab pinches their noses,
One claw to each.
Taxi in blue. Driver in red.
The desert blot of green,
And turquoise pools ricochet
The sparkle of smiling water.
Gas thinks this is an earnest pleasure.
She wishes for less and suggests
A camel ride to an oasis
Ten miles over the dunes
Kept out of Paradise by a wall
Of giant palms specially bred
To hold their own against
Drifting sand.
The oasis flirts with freedom.

But stays a green hole,
Forever its own boss and lover,
Or a lost card up the sleeve
Of a gambler, who isn't shot?
When he plays the winning hand.
They arrive heated, looking light,
Unstamped, telling tales as if
They hadn't met before. Without,
They sigh. Withal the vultures
Are hovering in make-believe.
They glide and wave goodbye.
Date palms, small huts trimmed.
With reeds and plastic flowers.
Welcome, melon, bitten with incestuous
Deprivation. "No signs." Gas rummaging
Her brain for metaphysical advice.

Moon contemplates her more, whispers
A piercing love word that falls
For itself and dies.

"You move me to dream,
And weave a soul dress
To cover your body
Whose curves are the burden of delight"?

"My love, I can conceive the mystery
Of your years in a moment's eating
Of rice. Do you fear the sun and
Soul of each sunray whisked in your
Eyes by ecstasy! Is it a salad of popery?
More to adorn your taste,
To tilt the edge of illusion,
In whose direction? Then enter
My mouth with a molten tongue.
Do not get gibberish in the sandwich
But shoot sparrows and watch the
Counting".

They threw themselves on gilt sand.
Show me delight. Scatter the scream
Of winter minds. Friends gather
And smother. Now they are four.
Untutored in law. Swop and swamp.

Gesso, a poet. Low, a writer,
A witch all-time moon trekker.
Precious peaches. Panegyric melon.

Fabled yogurt. Dazzling lemons.
Royalist figs. Dizziest pomegranate.
Honest lamb. Miraculous honey.

Talismanic bread. And they ate
To signs content. What bothers?
Washing dishes in the sand. Kisses of a union.
Beached on an island by a current
Whose origin is the fable?

"We are here for a hundred years."

Toast upon toast. They wrestle with
Life emerging from an eternal cocoon
Spun by worms we are.
There are no mosquitoes. Only cicadas.
Hummingbirds quantum jumping.
Monkeys carry young ones,
Begging, betting, and bickering.
No cats, No dogs, except Boyo,
A Tempest timeserver, who floated
Down in a balloon; cruel exile,
Served only to survive just enough.
Now a favorite pet of purists.
Gesso the Remarked backed a hunch,
Held his stomach, hurled regurgitated
Food into the sand. The desert sky
Cools into gas fire blue cremates the
Horizon with a sun of heraldic bloom,
Centering edifice to torture the eyes
Of onlookers. Low grasps the motion
Of coolness in contracting waste.
Four companions clear their rubbish,
Pack their wishes, dress, and climb on
Camels ride off to the sea of sleep.

Behind the grill, there is
A madman who hunts his shadow

In the shade of a dune.
Gesso talks in his sleep to Low
Who talks in her sleep to Gas,
Who walks in her sleep to Moon, who
Dreams of hunting the Elixir
Of Life. With waking, the earning
Of breakfast. Gesso fries each an egg.
They had decided to try out
This new resort, so glossily presented

In the travel shops.
Gesso, a peace-making poet,
He had been once around his cot
Which remained open until
He was old enough to be hurt.
Now he lives in New York,
Where he met Low. As a pair
They had learned Plato's dialogues,
Heartless. To recite themselves to sleep,
Whole parties to alcoholic despair
A party in a penthouse
Underneath a torrid sky, hung with collared
Ribbons and quaking tinsel, appetizers
Of the state of wealth; a marshmallow
Of a balloon floated through a glass
Door; Moon, an artist who became exquisite.
Gas, his wife. Her real name set free
When she was twenty years old; she youthfully
Floating through life's bubbles; when
A helpful angel of device mothered
Her invention. Whenever so quiet
They can be heard cooing.

They had moved beyond the speech.
Of day, through the tides of tears
Into a dew damp Diphtheria of emotion.
Their camels humped and bumped,
Exercising their grey matter,
Chewing and spewing the cud.
The day had hardly begun.
Camel prints became faint.
As a warming wind ricocheted off
Dunes, scattering trails across
Their path. A white-hot sun
Climbed to bear down on
Quadruple victimize riders.
After an hour had passed
Of spitting out sand, a rush
Of doom swept in from over
A deeply shadowed peak.
Gesso's Skin was grazed and sore.
Low had lost her scarf.
Protecting her mouth. Now the sun
Split the crystal. Gas' camel
Had blown a fuse and threatened
To wander off. Moon felt eclipsed

And sorrow for himself. He kept
His coolness and a diary in his
Head, wishing the entry was over.
In the blister of fear covering
Their traveling burn harbored
The feeling of being lost. It burst
And panic forced them to dismount,
Consider the option of staying put;
And huddle in a square of camels
Who could take being a marvel?
Of desert evolution. After three hours
Of mantra storm, in the drift of
Sleep. When they awoke, they dusted
Off their robes, shifted belongings,
Look for a compass. Gesso felt dated.
Low lit a cigarette. She wished she
We're pregnant.

CHAPTER TWO

FATE

The halfway oasis housed a Magus.
Or Guru or Witchdoctor. He wore
Head-dress fashioned from scrap metal,
Hardboard, mechanical parts. Like a
Warrior, a God, a museum fixture,
A relic badly reconstructed, a mad
An instructor who lived in a cave.
His favorite work was making rain.
A passion play with one player.
A mystery play with a dark hero.
He shuffled out with a vulture.
Hat stuck on backwards, a scavenger.
In full flow, flapping wings

And they are pecking the air.
He staged dance in circles,
Hopping every third step, two
On the right foot, two on the left.
Camels knelt by the water pool.
Moon approached the human statue.
Which suddenly jumped fifty feet
And somersaulted to land on
Top of a palm tree.
He threw down fruit, followed himself,
Spoken like a bat disturbed by
Light.

"You became stranded in a storm.
If I say you are lost in time
And not space I expect you
would feel I had no right
To make you feel unwell. You
Are sick, out of time. Don't worry,
A quest will help you recover
Your century of rags and pearls".

Gesso Jawbone Jess, a full
Name that could be played on
An accordion surrounded himself with
A blue aura and listened to
The advice of this recidivist raconteur,

This crumbling mountain of a mannequin.
He squinted an ear.
Low Solid Rider didn't want any more wrinkles,
Thank you. Being out of time,
She thought it might add an unnecessary

Choice. The quicker they find
A way back, a swift flight home
To write it up and sell the story
For a million bucks. Moon Behemoth
Magpie gritted his teeth, unsure
Whether to recite a poem, walk away,
Go crazy or confess his inadequate
Philosophy. He had no desire to leave
Whatever time he found himself in,
At whatever time.
Gas Jenny Falcon threw up her hands, sunk
To the ground, drew a mandala,
Recited a mantra, and shortly
Afterward went to dream but
Hardly slept. The mystery man
Told them, in solemn tones and
A sparkle in his eyes

"Listen; the surface of the sand
Trembles like skin. Hold your
Diaphragm in. Only exhale.
When I have finished your
Instructions, kindly donated
By a charitable house of Genii;
Follow the first bird,
Ask a dreamy virgin,
Eat a hollow fruit,
Swim in a shallow pool,
Endanger a species.
Call your coin."

Footman to the future faded
From sight. He had said enough.

This group of four lost from
Marked time, know not what.
They circled the oasis crisscrossing
The sand with footsteps in
Elegant arbitrary patterns. Palm trees
Shake off the sand in a breeze cooling
The face, drying perspiration.
The camels are growing old too quickly. Perhaps

Good for only one more journey.
A vulture's bird circles around
The oasis, larger and larger the
Circumference then heads east.
Low meets Gas searching the sky.

"There it is. We follow the leader,
Our cannonball is our crucible. Will our
Camels have enough strength. Or will
They die beneath us."

"If we had been instructed
To dig our graves, bury ourselves,
Resurrect ourselves, then proceed,
As a woman, I would have understood;
But to follow a bird of prey
Who flies so much faster than
We can travel seems a solution
I can't stomach it."

Moon meets Low, talking to Gas.
He interrupts.

"Fanatics don't lie.
That cool guru of a wizard
Made my flesh creep backwards.
Corpus of delight. The perfumes
In his recipe book. The erotic

Notes up his sleeves. Bravado in
The face flies fast. He
Managed a smile before a last
Laugh. What did he want from us?
Our time, our love and
Nothing. Got to get ready as soon
As possible, snatch the coin
From a beggar called Fate or
Else our tumescence will brief
Us for death."

Gesso meets Moon talking to Low
Talking to Gas.

"Talking to a camel
Would make more sense than following
A divining rod in pursuit of a bird
Whose characteristics are descriptive?

Closer to man-made than a Darwinian tantrum.
When nature kicks its legs,
We are suspicious and forsaken."

Camels snort and snort,
Kick dust over bundles of belongings.

"There can be no stragglers".

Moon signals a journey in,
Their backs are turned on
A sunset. They gulp in an iced
Indigo sky. Or mountainous night.

There are patients who hang
From trees, scratching their armpits.
Carpets wrap up tenors while
They sing. Artists paint in
Rubber gloves. Postmen deliver letters.
Doctors abort their feelings.
Intestines become rolled gold,
Mattresses collapse under starlets.
Time is melting equity,
Has bolted down its clown.
The worst is better now.
Solid lay dreams leach from
His mind crackled like a campfire.
Gesso loves cream cakes but
Dare not eat too many.
The sunset has reached its
Black-hole. The stars play
Ping pong in the earthier sky.
Camels lope and lump across precious
Sand. He would rather have a picnic
On a prairie, or kiss a nurse,
Then feel like a crab on a camel.
The temperature quickly drops to freezing.
The night's silent radar screens
Their presence for all to hear.
The bird they follow flaps elegantly,
Slowly, far away, but close enough.
They feel the damage to their
Spirits. The cold rivers, it's way.

Through clothes and flesh. A
Storm over the horizon, grumpy
Invisibility. They wish they could
Untangle the wires of solitude.

But they have no clues. Gesso
Thought back to his New York
Days. His thoughts could wait.
The bird they see glides
Slowly above, descending to the
Another side of a sand hill whose
Two craggy rocks strut like
A beast. A canopy of doubt
At five in the morning. Time
To bark. Time to grow. Not bad.
The quality of the day is a pirate
Patching his sails. Five thirty.
Lower the beasts. Push the feasts.
A scramble up. The eastern sun.
Damp eyes engraved by lush light;
Evermore, the sunrises cradled, crazed
Harmonic, a cloudless cast.
A small town ripples like Milton
Gold. Palm trees stare out starkly.
Houses look like honey cakes. Two
Dozen, to be exact. Slit windows.
Archway doors, storehouses in
The center. Trees scattered, unplanned.
Wells guarded and covered. This town
Is dive-bombed by the morning?
A bird whose suicide is noted by
The local lady of the night.
The only native awake. Quick

Off the mark. She welcomes the
Voyagers by herself. Her name
Is Quake Quake. Her eyes are black.
Her beauty is scarred.
The plan of years has only been
Unfolded once. There are no tissues
Of wrinkles. Semi-naked, autonomous
Experimental portrait. She extends her
Gold lust hand. Moon disembarks
From his ship of night. Embellishes
Her hand with a kiss. Bows
So slightly and beckons her away.

"Take me to a virgin
Whose dreams are fragile?
And fey"

Is there no sight sweeter?
And sure than this once

Possible encounter. She billows
His pride his footsteps crave;
The sand gives way to deeper
And deeper, until with each step
He is up to his neck. The
Damsel of blackest eyes sweeps
He up, in her arms. Poor Moon
Whose touching lips are?
Bruised and brave? He is
Bound in the bottle. She buries
It was in. Mr Gesso can't equate
The loveliness which approaches
With the worms, lice, leeches,
Slugs, scorpions, all clinging
To her legs. As a matter of fact

Low sharply rebukes him.
For turning away. Once facing
In the necessary direction Quake Quake
Takes him in her arms and
With stammering passion kisses his lips,
Ponders his tongue, sucks his saliva,
Crunches his balls and captures his heart.
His heart feels hot, and he has
No question.
He follows this archetype across
Warming sand to a well whose
The gallon bucket is gold. She draws
Up fates of the well. Fodfad,
Trufus and Justine.

"The asking price of a dreamy virgin
Is it a safe passage from here?"

Gesso starts to drink. He drinks
Like an artesian to no avail.
The vessel remains full. Challenged
To quit his folly, he asks for
A riddle or two. Fodfad in an
Eloquent mood recites her diddle-di
Dee.

"When a rainstorm meets a brainstorm,
What is the choice of the star under which
The meeting place is pinpointed, on
A map the size of a planet;
Of wit and rude inquiry,
Directions are free."

Trufus, gladly,

"Who has a backbone
The size of a bone of contention

Picked by Odyseus and Pantegruel
To the shape of a femur Fatale?"

Justine

"If a drowned carrot has
Its root in me what should a pear
Become if an alchemist bites on the
Cherry of desire before his deserts
Are served? If copulation is without
Remorse, what becomes of a blackbird?
Who perches on a rod erect, then
Sings an expensive princess to sleep,
Who munches pearls to sharpen?
Her teeth? If truth is a pity
On a soapbox, what are red and blue?
Bitten and wholesome, cute and
Spiky, elongated, and squeezed,
Diamond shape and watery,
Called above and below?"

Quake Quake caught Gesso as he fell,
Faint with knowledge and enlightenment,
Better than entertainment.
The formless Fates cried themselves.
Into the sand around the feet
Of a fucoid hussy who slapped
Gesso awake, then dragged him back
To her place. He found himself
In her womb. Low ran to the Town,
Searched every alley, pathway
And brick. Nailed by its wings
To a door, their airborne guide,
Alive and crowing about a dreamy
Virgin who could be detained in the

House of Hethbad. Low crucified
Her friend and cuddled him in her
Breasts, licking his wounded wing,
The feathers healed and shaped themselves
Reaching aerodynamic co-efficiency,
Being stroked with love and care.
The pecking order was over.

The hunt was on. Find a dreamy
Virgin or the journey is stoned.

A tree-high whirlwind
Excavates Moon in a bottle.
Flung into an alley, scattering
Three strays, the glass splinters,
Moon slithers like a snake
Saturated with sweat. He grows
Like a fungus to life-size.
He functions. The young witch had
Buried the bottle in her flesh.
She had become nauseous with desire.
She had wanted him for later. The
Free hero ran to the village,
Tapped Low and Gas on the shoulder

"I have survived an adventure
Unknown to Western man.
I returned to the womb,
A vista of pink warmth
Holding my breath for an eternity.
It all came back to me.
It all came back to me.
The body's aromas and perfumed juices.

However, it didn't last long.
She was no twin tub. I was
Buried in the sand and only by
Dreaming of our destination
And dreaming up an escape
Did a way out seem possible?"

The heroine gave him a kiss.
Gesso was still womb sound. He felt
Lonely. There was no hope for
His tiny self was magically tied to a woman.
He thought about what she could do in
New York, Chicago, or LA Films,
Chatshows, books, scandals. Perhaps
She could defuse those phallic
Totems ready to rape Motherlands
And Sisterlands. Then he realized
Her power was tied to the soil
Of her birth and life.
This desert hamlet of golden palms,
Whose fruit, concocted into potent
Drink became a hidden source

Of nourishment, the matrix of her magic.
Gesso felt scandalized, miniaturized,
Predestined, disestablished. He became
Born again of Quake Quake. He
Grew to manhood in a week. His
Love was direct. The others had
Given up. They rested by the pool
And began to learn the local language
By chatting up the locals. The House
Of Hethbad was the tallest in the

Village. Stark white, little square
Windows with ornate grills.
The entrance door is covered by a brown curtain
And it was hidden down an alley. A flight
Of steps led to an entrance chamber
With ten connecting doors.
Gesso had finished lovemaking.
And glumly wandered off to find
His friends. They heard his sighs.

At the entrance to the
Chamber, a large brown dog, sat
Growling at playful shadows,
Shadow boxing with his tail,
Deciphering night smells
Seeping through the smallest cracks.
Only his family, with or without
Friends could pass his guard.
Only somebody tried to poison.
It gave dog Gabel greater strength.
He tracked down his enemy within
Half an hour and devoured him within
Half an hour. Then buried his
Bones in the root of a tree.
Gabel turned up one day on.
The edge of town. Thin, hungry,
Looking for companionship. Quake Quake
Took him to the House of Hethbad,
Where he was fed, groomed and
Protected. Gabel's collar had no join.
It shrunk if an attempt was made.

To remove it. It glowed in the dark,
Grew spikes if in danger of attack,
Possessed the power of flight
And could explode with electrical
Bolts.

The bewildered four held each other's hands
approached slowly,
Wishing away the apparition
Whose grainy teeth grew more
Visible moment by moment.
The snarling caretaker stood his
Ground as the petrified intruders
Surrounded their musclebound adversary.
He disappeared, leaving only a paw
Marks in the house dust.
Each door opened and closed.
In turn, repeating the sequence.
Until guests had left the chamber.
From the single ceiling instrument
Music drifted down. Low entered the
First door. The others followed,
Feeling embarrassed by this ancient
Ploy. A large courtyard occupied
By a family and a beautiful girl
Seated on an inflated camel bladder.
Her hands were tied to a post.
She was clothed in a scarlet robe
Loosely hung around her shoulders.
Blindfolded and blind thrilled, this was
The dreamy virgin that they had had to find

Low approached the Head.
Of the family. He half-bowed,
Offered her a seat, took out of his
Embroidered red jacket and a black
Piece of paper, read out aloud a spell.
Then passed it on, lighting one
Corner with a match.
By the time it had reached Low the
Flames had climbed ten feet high.
But they didn't seem to be devouring
The remaining half.
They took the shape of an elongated body with
A large bald head. Its bulging eyes three
Times larger than normal.
This fluid shape remained a liquid illusion.

"As you can appreciate, dear visitors,
My genie is mighty powerful.
He will play tricks, design buildings,
Bring gold and jewels. I welcome
You with understanding, not friendship.

To listen to your story and tive
You the virgin."

Gabel, the dog
Flew down from the roof. Bit off
The cord punctured the bladder,
Crunched through the wooden post.
Elfawn, still unable to see,
Felt her way along the bodies
To her new friends. The genie
Sat amused in the air, waiting
For an order. Elfawn kissed
Each of the family goodbye,
Bathed in flames, she could now see.

CHAPTER THREE

ELFAWN FROM FAUSTLANDIA

Low wondered how
They could leave. Elfawn spoke.

"You have to ask my name
And number, my plane
And plumber, my last and
My first, my middle and
That is all."

"My name is Elfawn from Faustlandia
My number is one.
My plane is flat earth.
My plumber is Poseidon.
My last is a burial.
My first is to come.
My middle either a
Daughter or son.
You must come with me,
The genie and the dog,
Far away in a forest
Where fruit is abundant
Wholesome."

Holding hands and the dog
By its tail, they rose
Up on the magic carpet of
Cold flame, out of the courtyard,
Above the village, rising higher
Then birds hunt prey.
Dunes receded to the horizon.
Tiny buildings glowed in the sun.
And soon became dots of light.
Flickering across the sand.

As the magic carpet
Reached higher into colder layers
Of air and cloud, warm flames
Licked their bodies and curled
Around exposed skin. They had been
Quiet for fifteen minutes six seconds,
Spread out, not touching,

Playing statues. Only Gabel
The Heathen Dog wandered
Through the restless flames,
Darts of orange, ice blue,
Banana yellow and sunset pink.
The form continually being
Created out of cold fire.
It had a mind. It had grace.
They were skimming clouds,
Scaring birds, chasing towards
The shadow of night. Gas
Crawled towards Moon, grabbed
His arm pointed over the
Starboard side to the end of the
Desert. Trees dotted the grassy
Foothills leading up to mountains,
The sun slid down and down,
Last rays dissolving in the cloud,
Shimmering, simmering, fleecing,
Creasing, bloating, coating, any moment
Disappearing, settling as memory.
The dark cloud sculptures slowly
Faded to faint silhouettes.
Trees became phosphorescent,
Like lamps embedded in amber.

The magic carpet looped
Clouds lowered their sight
To a small lake high on
A plateau surrounded by
Crowding hills.
The flaming vehicle descended into an area
Of bare rock. The genie reformed,
His passengers landed with a bump.
Low twisted her ankle.
Elfawn enticed the genie into his
Miniature bottle which hung
Around her neck. Gabel
Splashed into the water and
Soaked everybody before wandering
Off. They were dazed from their
Journey. They had no idea in
Which direction to go, no provisions.
The Genie was near exhaustion.
Gesso looked for firewood.
Borrowed the genie who struck up
A light. Black water quiet
As a dead gorilla beckoned, Moon

Towards it with the gentlest of
Ripples stroking the waterside rocks.
The others were left warming
Themselves, preparing to cook
Some roots Gabel had dug.
Genie conjured cakes and soft.
Drinks. Meanwhile mesmerized
Moon dived from a boulder.
He swam breaststroke far out.
Into darkness. A little later

Gas alerted the others.
They stood in the wave of his strokes
And looked on the trail of unknowingness
They knew they had to follow.
Lowering themselves into cool ice water
Everybody felt like a shock absorber.
They maneuvered into a line,
Worked their way towards a low
Rumbling sound. Moon had been
Dragged into the orbit of a
Whirlpool. He had held his breath,
Relaxed, he allowed himself to be
Taken down the endless spiral;
His life spinning, grinning before
Him. He was aware of fishes
With long, lighted tentacles,
Touching his body, diving deeper
And deeper. On his arrival he
Felt very bruised, a bundle of bait,
A burden of a barrow, a brunt of
A bearer, doomed to swallow, gulp,
Ice cold water until his lungs explode.
The whirlpool carried him on to
A rock. It shifted with his weight
A few inches at a time, lowering
Him into a small chamber
Which is filled with water. He dragged
Himself off the stone, which shifted
Back to block the hole against
The powerful force. The water
Chamber emptied. Moon fell down

Seven steps, landing in an empty
Hall; damp, heavy with weed, algae,
Moss, and lit by phosphorescent rocks.
Small bushes grew in tubs.
Pink leaves, purple branches,

And large round green fruits
Twice the size of an orange.
Their skin was slightly
Transparent like small green
Balloons. Inside a seed was
Suspended in the center by
Filaments converging from the skin,
The seed is encased in a delicate
Cocoon. Each fruit hung singly.
When ripe, the hard skin split,
The seed ejected by springy
Filaments to the nearest soil.
Unerring accuracy: high in
The hall baskets contained
Phosphorescent rocks. Their
Qualities changed with breathing,
The flow of blood through the
Heart, with the dilation of eyes,
With dreaming and nightmares.
Moon woke wet and cold,
Astounded but not in bondage.
He raised himself onto a bamboo chair,
Then lay down on a bamboo table,
And started to study the room.

In the end.,behind him, three
Steps led to a highly polished
Black granite door. The effects
Of his swim wore off; blood
Flowed, skin warmed, clothes
Dried, eyes cleared, ears unblocked.
His reflexes sharpened as companions
Came tumbling down the stairs,
All conscious and shaken by degrees.
Moon shouted to them.

"There is a way out.
First, we eat the fruit.
Sow the seeds. Throwdown
The gauntlet. Explain the shape
Of our lips to the lips of each other.
Differentiate a kiss from a kiss on the
Cheeks of each other. Draw our
Likenesses with the excrement
Of each other. Channel our piss
Into the abyss called cracks in
The floor of each other. We are
No longer the heroes of each other.

Only pedigrees of our pasts. Ballasts
Of masts. Campfires drawing
Moths. Bankrupts of the bank.
Dare we live here,
In this paradise for more than a day.
To become its readers and
Blank verse versifies. Pleased
Detainees. I will lance the boil.

Of your communion, the risk
Of your levitation, show you
Finer marts of prayers and laments,
Backbones of joy, wax effigies
And donkeys tails. When we touch
Earlier works of our lives
Against a backdrop of joy and
Delineate mansions built only
To illusion, we ask
Were these capricious tides
Which left us on different shores;
The energy used, the slow decay,
Flotsam and jetsam;
Are these the string or pearls?
Are these tides the quantities of our present
Bending back to now?"

Gesso stood up. Shook himself
To warm up his muscles,
Feeling cramp after the crush.
The entrance chamber had held them all but
Only just. They had entered one
At a time. Most screamed their
Way down the spiraling water.

CHAPTER FOUR

MR. NICEST AND MRS. THANK YOU

Between the drumbeats of
Their heart, they heard footsteps
Approaching the other side
Of the door. It burst open.
A beautiful monster - half-lion,
Half human, half eagle, half rat,
Half hare, half sphinx, half unicorn,
Half dragon, half mermaid - stood

Transfixed reciting poetry in
An unknown tongue.
Its skin dripped a sweet perfumed
Oil. Its eyes reflected the phosphorous
Light and looked like it curled up
Chameleons. The lion's face frowned,
Lips slightly apart, saliva dripping.
Human arms and hands were crossed
Motionless. On its back, two huge
Wings of golden feathers, both folded,
Neatly tucked away. It had clawed
Feet. The fur on its legs was a rat.
Their shape, like the hind legs
Of a hare. The breasts came from
A sphinx. There was a unicorn's
Horn and a mermaid's tail. It breathed
Dragon's fire and had dragon's scales
On its arched back. The intruders
Stepped away. The monster they
Nicknamed Mr. Nicest and his wife
Mrs. Thankyou. Before this friendship
Arose, there had to be introductions
And a meeting. Mr. Nicest breathed
Fire across the room scorching trees,
And furniture. He roared with his
Lion's lungs and pieces of rock
Fell from the ceiling.
He hopped to the center of the room,
Creating turmoil by flapping his wings,
Settling to picking fruit, he chewed
Them one second. After ten

Minutes of huffing and puffing,
Seething and teeth picking, he said

"I know why you have come here.
To eat of the hollow fruit. You're
Not the first to brave the whirlpool.
I have met your type before;
However, you are safe.
You carry a genie whose
Energy I will help recharge.
You are lost in time therefore
Share my predicament. I only
Eat treasure seekers. They taste
So enthusiastic. In the next few
Rooms diamonds grow from floors
And ceilings. Precious stones
Litter pools. My wife lives
Deeper in this underground.
Come through to the living room.
With its magic crystal glass.
Magic mirrors, elixirs of life,
Love, Death, Ambition; mechanical
Birds that tell fortunes and
Dancing life-size dolls. Enter
And sit down. I'll serve you
A drink to relax, strengthen,
And wise you up. Your genie
I will place it in a platinum
Pyramid covered in layers of
Quartz and gold. Whatever you
Are thinking I will know about it?
Now make yourself at home.

While I call some fish from
The lake."

Gesso was puzzled.
They had all eaten the hollow fruit.
Kept a pip or two. Gesso whispered
To Moon

"Is this the species
We mustn't endanger. Perhaps they
Are the last of their kind?"

Before anyone could answer
Mrs. Thankyou burst through
A double-door. She was slightly

Larger than Mr. Nicest
She also recited absent-minded
Poetry but stopped on seeing her guests.
She looked young, moved gracefully with
Occasional flaps of her wings.
A bright green drink was offered around.
Made from Algae, fruit juice, and cultivated
Waterweed. This drink was a narcotic.
Low began to see beyond the walls,
Water and mountains, through
Fur, scales, and feathers. Her
Childhood came back home, the
Home of her brain. She looked in
A mirror. Her skin had become
Transparent. Blood pulsed through
Veins. Muscles spasmed. Her brain
Look like a storm of the tiniest lights.
Bones became the architecture of her
Being. Each is a masterpiece of design.
Her companions likewise grew visible
And functional. She could see

A large underground palace,
Room after empty room. Beyond
The lake they had fallen through,
With its ancient fish and plants;
A primeval life or a magical vision.
Gesso made somersaults on the table,
Reciting the Book of Books backward.
Gas undressed like a striptease.
Moon levitated, turning as if on.
A spit. Quake Quake couldn't stop
Laughing and put her arms around
Elfawn, giving her huge kisses.
Gabel the Dog did circus tricks
Then snuggled his nose between
Elfawn's legs. The Mistress Monster
Hadn't realized her immunity didn't
Apply to her guests. Moon felt reborn.
Now it was time to leave. The
Word was passed on. Mrs. Thankyou
Left for a moment. Low knew
Of an exit discovered with her
X-ray vision.

"We must be prepared
To leave now. To end our
Predicament, there is a passage

And a door leading to a ledge
Leading to a cave where fire
Is breathed from holes in
The wall. The cave will carry
Us to the top of the plateau.
We will be free to think out
Our next move."

All seven
Formed a line. Slowly stepped

Through the first door. Caught
Sight of the Monster Couple
In a large kitchen with a
Smoldering central fire. Over it
Turned a rainbow-colored fish
With huge spikes jutting from
Its side. On each spike a
Thousand barbs. Each barb
Contains a sack of poison.
A small waterfall was used to
Wash food. Large knives and
Hammers hung from the ceiling.
Bags of herbs dried by the
Fire. Trays of leaves and earth
Grew white and pink fungi,
Fleshy bodies asking to be picked
Squeezed and eaten. As the last guest
Went past, Mrs. Thankyou and Mr. Nicest
Caught her eye. Immediately their wings
Fluttered, blowing smoke everywhere.
Mr. Nicest spat fire through the doorway,
And chased after the fleeing seven
Who by now had got the message
From the kitchen. They ran into
A long hall covered by distorting
Mirrors. Above each mirror, a gaping
Mouth flicked in and out along
Thin pink tongue, which would sometimes
Reach and slurp over a face,
Leaving a stinging sensation on the skin.
After this more deal the last room
Of the palace had to be engaged.

Its floor of flagstones squelched when
Stood on, splattering a mild acid
Which burned and burned until
The pain produced death.

Suspicious Gesso wouldn't let anyone
Through until he had made a test.
He took a loose stone from the wall
And slammed it across the floor.
The gastric juices spilled out. This room
Digested its victims. The door on
The other side was the last link
In their escape. The monsters
Charging after their guests only
Wanted to return their genie to
Them and warn them of the
Dangers and pitfalls which awaited
Them if they left in a hurry.
The companions seven didn't know this.
Quake Quake noticed Elfawn
Had no genie. But Quake Quake
Knew a spell or two. She played
Around a while, with a few words
And signs in the air. Then shouted
Out

"Oom Oom Oomer. Um, Um, Ummer.
Dooperdash dooperdash. Let us fly."

Nothing happened. Her powers had
Run out. The monsters filled the
Corridors with smoke from heavy
Breathing. They understood the thinking
Of their retreating guests. Mr. Nicest
Handed the genie back. Gesso took

The bottle. The raised genie
Constructed a footbridge over the floor
Of the room. They thought it best
To cross one at a time. Meanwhile
Gesso talked to his hosts. The Master
Of the House remarked that although
They could have eaten them, put them
Away, he was unsure of retribution.

"We arrived here many years ago
In the same manner as you. We
Had not been taken from our own
Time but were put here to breed
By our owners. This happened when
We were young. As we grew older
And cleverer in the ways of this
Vast complex we became more

Difficult to control. Once we reached
Maturity with all our halves fully
Developed there came a time when
We had to kill this despot to live
Our own lives. This underwater kingdom
Belonged to an ancient magician who
Gave life to stone. The whole building
Thinks like a primitive organism,
Eats when food is available and
Slows down when starved. It isn't
All powerful and kills in only three
Rooms. Each room contains one of
Three exits. The palace has three
Levels. The intake level just
Below, the lake contains mostly
Work rooms and kitchen. Deeper down
Are living rooms and below that

The Brain of the complex. A locked
Room containing a fragment of
Something very ancient, which
Could be the magician himself.
It animates that which it inhabits,
A dead body, a tree, a building
Or even a toy.
We don't stay here all the time,
But hunt and travel away from
Man who would ill-treat us
As exhibits in freak shows,
Circuses and fairgrounds.
So we stay and hope to reproduce
Ourselves. You must go now.
Once across the room, the door
Leads to a hall and stairs which
Climb to the edge of the lake.
There are one thousand and
Six steps in all. So take
This algae food for energy."

They formed a line. Each
Would take their turn to count
Fifty steps. Three hundred steps
Would have been climbed after
A series of turns. The low ceiling
Meant walking with a curved back.
As the only light came from
Phosphorescent lumps in the ceiling
And walls, there was continual

Danger of missing a step, also
From slime caused by leaking

Through hair-line cracks. Moon
Took the lead, followed by Gas,
Low, Quake Quake, Elfawn, Gesso,
And last of all, Gabel the Dog
Who impatiently came last.
The first hundred steps were
Easy enough. Discipline. Each
Right foot, then each left foot.
After a hundred steps, they would
Nibble algae. Their progress was
Uninterrupted though timing became
Ragged. The last step. No light.
A blank wall. Moon felt around the
Edges. No luck. Under the steps.
The last. The second to last. The
Third step down. There it was,
A handle is hidden in a large slot
Disguised by the shadow of
A two-inch overhang. It was
Stiff, only moving after a few
Minutes of hard pulling. Slowly
A system of weights and pulleys
Began reacting and opening
Up the wall. A ray of sharp
Light cut through the darkness,
From the other side of densely
Packed foliage. Moon began pulling
Aside from vegetation until he
Reached a small clearing. A
Plateau continued for two or three
Miles on all sides. A blue sky,

A little breeze, migrating formations
Of birds, arrows to the future.
Distances home. Each traveler
Shielded their eyes as
They emerged from the dark
Tunnel. Last but not least
Gabel the Dog ran out panting,
Off into the bushes to hunt.

CHAPTER FIVE

EARS OF THE GODS

Stranded in Western Africa, lost in
Time, looking for a sign and
No way to go. They asked the
Revived genie. Once again, he formed
A magic carpet took them all aboard.
Gabel jumped on, holding a six
Foot snake. The magic flames
Flicked and feinted to the left
And then right, hovered three
Feet off the ground spread out
To accommodate its passengers,
Then rose straight into the air.

After a tour of the plateau
The magic carpet skimmed
Down over the lake towards
The whirlpool which increased
In size to two hundred
And fifty yards in diameter,
Causing a tornado-like wind.

The carpet charged upwards.
Out of reach. Mr. Nicest
And Mrs.Thankyou, macrocosmic
Monsters were being mischievous.

Only Gabel, the Dog, nearly fell off
In the escape. The sunset welcomed
Them, as they disappeared over the
Horizon leaving behind unsolved mysteries.

The magic carpet cruised at
Three thousand feet. Scattered lights
Below looked like dream beacons sent
From private worlds. A large cluster
Appeared to their left. The ship of ease
Hovered closely at two thousand feet
For the rest of the night. They
Slept through until morning. Gesso
Dreamed he was flying by himself
Over farmland in southern England.

Sometimes he somersaulted, other times
His arms grew twenty feet long,
His legs flattened, and his feet
Became like flippers. Once his nose
Lengthened, and birds rested before
Flying south. Suddenly he fell to earth.
He turned into a beachball and
Bounced along a motorway until he
Jumped into an open sportscar,
Next to a beautiful dark black-clad
Girl. They turned off towards a small
Town south of London. He changed into
A dog who laid his head on her lap
Nuzzling up her short skirt. She patted
Him on the head then disappeared.
The car crashed. In an ambulance a

The pretty nurse gave him the kiss of
Life. He put his paw up her skirt
And pulled down a huge slug which
Started devouring their clothes. The ambulance
Arrived at the airport. At thirty thousand
Feet two women hijackers made all
The passengers strip and kiss each
Other's arses. The pilots opened the escape
Hatches. Everybody was sucked out, changing
Into pigs which became roast pigs on the
Way down. Gesso caught a roast and
Found himself eating at a table in a
Vicarage; in front of him, a nude woman
With open legs. He proceeded
To crawl inside. He woke
At this point, feeling suffocated by
The sunrays of sunrise. The lights
Below had vanished. A wide dark river
Meandered lazily between small evergreen
Hills. A small riverside town stood out
On a left bank. Others were awake
Now. The magic carpet hovered over
The town. It was the source of their
Next quest. Each flame of the magic
Carpet turned into a starling. The carpet
Transformed into a bed of feathers.
The shrill mass approached the market
Square and landed chaotically. Each
Bird rose and vanished before bewildered
Natives. The genie returned to his bottle
Like a good boy. The hard floor was

Made of compacted red clay, a local material
Brought in from the hills by donkey carts
And Goat trolleys. A leader-like person
With a complicated multicolored feathered
Head-dress appeared out of the tallest building
In town. He was accompanied by two
Warriors. The chief headed towards the
Heroes and Heroines lazing around a well
Surrounded by flies. The genie made
His friends speak the local language, a
Rare dialect based on Phoenician. Gesso
And the others lined up. He stepped
Forward to meet the spokesman.

"You have entered our territory without
Invitations. Therefore you must be put
To the test."

His feathers rippled in the wind, looking
Good for a take-off. Outside a large
Circular mud but with a palm leaf
Roof hung with skeletons and dry plants,
A six-foot and six inches man stood with folded
Arms. He was naked except for an
Embroidered skull wore across his chest.
Above the skull is a sunset with a large
Star appearing out of the darkening
Sky. To the left is the moon. Around
His neck hung the teeth of children.
He had a shaven head. An overlong
Penis. Behind stood two beautiful young
Girls, are also naked except for loin cloths.
The uninvited guests ambled over to the

Great Witchdoctor, their guards' prodding
Them with spears. The great Cocker
Smiled on seeing Quake Quake, Low, Gas
And Elfawn. All lovely ladies. He
Immediately had a huge erection. His
Two girls came on either side of him
And licked his penis until he
Ejaculated into a bowl. The semen
Was mixed with goats milk and
The juice of small white berries. The
Resulting drink was offered to his guests.
Behind them, guards prodded until
Eventually, Low supped one mouthful,
Followed by the others.

After this sickening ritual they
Entered the mud hut, the headquarters of
Magic. Their heads swimming.
Quake Quake collapsed onto a stool. Low
Nearly fainted. Moon and Gesso felt
Sick. The air was full of heady incense.
Low started to speak.

"Halfway house, Halfway home.
The pleasant request on my
True love's shelf.
He lit the taper and burnt
The candles. A hot experience,
A not experience, a wishy-washy
Realm of darkness. But a creature
Is born too soon when its brain
Has bounced happily,

Goaded by sideline players
Who dreams of the chequered moon.
Wax mine. The curious are
Tectonic. The hilarity set.
The map and pen. The quirky
Bend tied in knots.
I sing of my cot. Oh lend me
A life and a penny for a piss,
Except in the garden, the wayward life,
And learn from experience
A duckpond can be crossed with
A hound.
Give me a punchbag of wisdom,
Truth, futility, privacy, and much
More than I can tell, tell, tell,
Well?"

They all slept, including the witch doctor.
Snoring was at its peak—a bell rung.
A monkey had pulled a string
Attached to its tail. Guests woke
With a hangover. They were taken
Outside, put on to donkeys, and led
Into the hills. Their destination
A temple that covered the entrance
To a cave, entrance to another world.
Inside, guests were stripped, bathed in
Pigs' blood, washed in a cool ice stream
Which flowed through the temple from
The cave's interior.

The witchdoctor offered a choice
Of seven passages from his Time to
Their Time. Each method had a
Different timescale, a different period of
Hope, illusion, parody, and finesse.
The methods were as follows
Journey into the cave.
A ride on a donkey to the tallest
Mountain.
An adventure into a well.
A flight on the back of a
Giant Vulture.
A dance with a monkey.
Sexual union with a witch doctor.
An adventure with drugs.
They tossed for their selection.
Moon went first. Going down
The list he would gradually
Eliminate each choice until one
Remained. Tails, yes. Heads, no.
After his thirteen turns he
Ended up with a Flight on the
Back of a Vulture, Low
With Drugs, Elfawn with
Journey into a cave.
Gas was landed with
Adventure into a well.
Gabel, the Mighty Dog, would ride
On a donkey. Quake Quake tossed for
Sexual union. Gesso danced with a
Monkey. The great magician kissed

Each participant on both sides of the face
And smiled the great smile on the
Face of the moon. He is the man
In the moon on the day we are
Born, who charts our chances
With the permission of the planets,
Breaks our luck, brings us a fortune;
Fashions the curtains which hide
Our stages plant the audience and
Writer of dreams, who copies our
Stories for the ears of gods.

CHAPTER SIX

ELFAWN'S FAMILY AND FRIENDS

Elfawn from Faustlandia, a fearless country,
Where tall spires shine with gold.
Peasants toil mercilessly. Aristocrats make
Magic with carved stones.   Elfawn had
Been born into a peasant family in
The depths of a very large forest
Comprising one-tenth of the Land.
Her father was a hunter and sometimes a
Gambler. Every Friday, He would get
On his horse and gallop to a local
Village to drink and gamble. One
Evening his meager earnings were
Lost to a man better dressed than
The others. He was an envoy from
The capital. Elfawn's father lost his
Daughter with an I.O.U. He lost his

Only daughter with a bluff that
Failed. The envoy asked for Elfawn
To be a servant for one year, after
Which she would be set free. Elfawn
Was sent off to the tavern to join him.

Faustlandiagrad, the capital punishment
Of a country ruled with kindness and vigor
Bewildered Eflawn. The envoy whose Power
And threats persuaded her father to let
Her go diminished in importance and color
In the mix of different peoples and behaviors,
Markets, processions, dances, fairs, and royal
Gatherings. At first, she resisted his
Sexual advances. The day before
The envoy was due to visit his estate,
The strange couple went riding in a
Royal park. Together their horses trotted
Along hidden paths and open spaces.
After an hour's riding, they dismounted
Near some bushes and trees. They talked
Of their lives, loves, and dreams. In his
Enthusiasm, he edged closer and closer,
Putting his arm around Elfawn, touching

Her right breast. She ran off towards a
Thicket and fell, twisting an ankle. He
Followed, knelt beside her, and began
To lift up her skirt and petticoat.
She wore nothing underneath. At this
Point a large white horse crashed through

The undergrowth reared over the about
To-copulate-couple and kicked the envoy
On the head, knocking him cold. Elfawn
Struggled to her feet, climbed on the
Horse, which carried her away into the
Depths of the park. She hid in a copse
Surrounding an artificial mound with a
Greek Temple on top. Here she met a
Wizard who pretended he was a poor man.
She took food and drink, slept, and woke
As if in a dream. All this passed through
Her mind as she prepared to enter
The cave. A possible way home to
Father and country. Or would she choose
Another time and place, with her new
Friends. They were all free to choose
And not so free. If decisions were
Wrong their paths could crossover and are
Lost forever.

Elfawn kissed everyone goodbye.
The cave loomed over her like the Great
Bear of Kazakastazakanaka, which she'd read
About as a girl. Bats hung from the
Ceiling, the burbling stream echoed into a
Torrent the deeper she went. Rocks scattered
Here and there, covered in ancient ferns
And mosses that had survived history.
All daylight had gone. Elfawn lit
The candle lamp she had been given.
It cast giant shadows of herself and

Stones and the water looked like oil.
She clambered over the boulder and fallen
Rock, grazing her hands and legs.
Water filled the cave floor in puddles,
The stream creeping its way through
Least resistance. The cold began to find her
Weak spots. Damp made breathing difficult.
The slope became steeper every two
Or three yards. The cave noticeably

Narrowed. Elfawn heard a continuos
Crashing, water thundering, pounding
On rock. The cave curved around a corner.
A spray blocked her path.
The lamp nearly went out. She
Placed it on a rock a few feet back,
Throwing just enough light for her
To turn the corner. There, a
Streak of water falling sixteen hundred feet
From a small hole in the mountainside.
The cave carried on behind the waterfall,
A vertical tunnel penetrating
The mountain rock and cave ceiling. Elfawn
Picked up the lamp
And partially covered it with her jacket.
She crept along a ledge around the water
And though getting thoroughly soaked,
Losing her light and almost slipping into
The churning cauldron of black froth,
She managed to escape the liquidizer.

On the other side, a small gap

In the rock, enough for a thin person
To squeeze through. A faint glow seemed
To emanate from this new darkness.
Elfawn wriggled through Into a large
Cavern, which greeted her with bright white
Lights of animal and vegetable origin.
Some of them shifted from place to place.
A manmade table or altar surrounded
By seven figures completely covered in
Fur sat in the center of the cavern.
One light landed on her hand.
The creature, a large fly with a planet
Size eyes, sparkling phosphorescent hair
All over its body and sticky pads on
Its feet.An inch long in all. Elfawn
Screamed, hit the fly onto the floor
And stamped on it. A splodge of light
Was left behind. Immediately Elfawn
Was bombarded by flies who fixed themselves
To her hair. Her head was a mass of
Flickering light. She screamed, clutching
Handfuls, throwing them hard on the floor.
Just as she became weighed down with
Light flies a figure scampered across
From the table, and with his fur

Beat the rest away. The Guardian
Of the cavern pulled Elfawn over
The shiny floor. She was laid on the table.
Behind the fur, dark butchered voices
Cranked out a sound. Elfawn understood
The Lingo is still under a spell.

Between them, they philosophized over their
Find. Elfawn couldn't see her hosts but
Felt cold, weak, suspicious, and helpless.
From behind the fur, hands appeared,
Slowly reaching out to touch her; their
White hands, four fingers, and long nails
Had been partly tattooed with dragons,
Mouthless faces, patterns of intricate and
Endless mazes. The disembodied hands
Removed her clothes and left a shivering
Naked body, which one by one, the seven
Wise men mounted. Each time she was
Covered with fur and felt the keen lean
Boney flesh cutting deep between her legs.
All seven fed her their semen.
Then they poured a powdered drug
Into her mouth. She felt her body
Dissolving, her mind floating. Flies started
To land on her in thousands. The mass
Lifted her into the air to the roof, through
A wide crack, high into the open air, higher
Still. She could see nothing, count nothing,
But felt loathing and felt dying. Then
Well above the trees and grass
The flies dispersed into the bright atmosphere.
Elfawn fell and fell and fell to earth,
Into long grass high up on a mountainside.
Her naked, wounded body
And drugged mind slept through the early
Day. She was no longer herself but at
The moment of falling had conceived,

At two o'clock, pm. Soldiers picked up
The poor body and took it back to camp.
Their surgeons tended wounds and fly sores.
They spoke her native language. She had
Come home. She remained drugged for nine
Months. They took her to a convent in a
Town near the border of Faustlandia.
Border patrols were on the lookout for
Bandits, brigands, and wildmen. Elfawn was

Cared for by a good local woman who spent
Many hours listening to stories that made
No sense in that time and place.
After a few months had passed and
Her pregnancy was still not obvious; a young
Officer who had helped rescue her wished
To meet her again. He enjoyed her
Company, even though he couldn't decipher
Her mindlessness which had disguised itself
With language. They were married in
A local church by a very old priest
Who could see inside souls? He blessed her
And exorcised any remaining malignancy.
Her spirits renewed, Elfawn settled down
To married life as a soldier's wife. He
Didn't mind her baby and would ask later
Who was the father? After six months
They traveled to the capital for a large
Parade and Fair celebrating the founding
Of Faustlandiagrad as the capital city. They packed
A cart with necessities and with a small

Troop of soldiers made their way out of town.
The journey would take seven days, forty miles
A day over difficult terrain. Changing horses
At each inn. Sleeping in each other's arms
For the first time, they had time to talk.
Elfawn related her best story. But unclear
Where her return journey began, confused
If she wasn't still dreaming. Married but
Pregnant with an unknown. The husband
Couldn't break the spell of her mystery.
He watched her day and night with awe.
Breathed the scent of love into her mouth,
Caressed her skin and hair till his
Being felt dissolved in the texture of Eternal
Woman. He mapped the lines on her hands
And face. He had no ordinary woman with
Him. In every inn, she would see faces she
Knew and one belonged to the envoy she
Had belonged to in the vague past. He
Didn't recognize her but even so stared
As if a puzzle had to be solved to save
His life. Later that evening, he became
Very drunk and felt like dying. On the
Fifth day they passed a forest which
Elfawn knew it to be her home. They made
A detour so she could see her father,

Who lived alone in a small log cabin.
With white smoke.
A vegetable garden and an old man
Hoeing. Horses halted by the gate. She
Recognized her father. But he was slow

To see her. He had become depressed
On losing her. Now gradually, his mind
Trickled recognition. His face lit up,
Blanching at first, then smiling, then
Crying, then reddening with excitement
And self-defeat. He moved over to his
Long lost Elfawn, daughter of the tallest
Trees in the land. He embraced her.
She told him she couldn't stay but that
He must come with them for the
Celebration day. Her father packed his bags
And threw them on the cart. The blood
Pair had much to say. The journey continued
To the capital city. The road became more
Crowded. They had lost a day's travel,
So Elfawn's husband went ahead to report
For duty. Day six, Father was now filled
With facts, but feeling uneasy about the
Birth. Day seven. The city towers in
Sight; gleaming gold, rivaling the sun.
Flags of all nations fluttering in a gentle
Wind. Hot air balloons, dozens and dozens,
Colorfully floating over the land with
Messages of peace and goodwill trailing
From them. The woodsman, a brave and
Natural man saw all this with increasing
Vigor. In the city, they met her
Husband at a prearranged site, outside
The Cathedral. He took them to his parents'
House. There they rested. Celebrations
Began on day nine. From a tower

In a city of towers, they saw some of the
Kingsmen marching in full traditional dress.
Archers, foot soldiers, cavalry, special forces
For water, forest and mountain. Weapons
Designed by clever men and warriors invited
From other lands. The crowds threw
Flowers. The sun shone its brightest
For weeks. Clouds had scurried away.
Celebrations continued long
Into the bright night.

Fireworks sparkled over the carnival
Filled streets. Children stayed up late,
In fancy dress, dancing and playing.
Faustlandiagrad experienced one of its most
Happy days.
Elfawn and her husband
Whose name, according to records, was
Beowulf Tweedwulf was free and headed
For a village two miles from town.
They hoped to rest before deciding
Where would baby be born?

Past the last main gate.
Fading noise, fading lights.
Light of the moon.
The shadow of trees.
Blue horizon behind blue hills,
Paunchets of Mother Earth.
Silent, mysterious pleasures
Pounce from shades and
Dark shiftiness. These carry
In her eyes, the gravity
Of a gravedigger, the wisdom
Of a witch and the cunning

Of a fox.

Beowulf Tweedwulf, a soldier,
But not at heart,
A time server from youth,
A busybody, a whoring young man,
A part-time drunkard, a hunter of note,
Had become reformed on first
Seeing Elfawn naked and wounded.
He became convinced hearing
Her apparent gibberish turn
To sense, to sensibility.
He couldn't sleep that night.
Creeping out of bed, he felt
Like a walk in the garden.
A contemplation of his life,
A dream of his world.
Stars of the clear sky struck him
As beautifully alone in their multitude.
Beowulf sat down on a cold wooden seat.
He drew his coat tightly around him,
Wishing he had put on his vest and leather
Waistcoat. He felt there was no heat left

To extract from surrounding objects.
Slowly words parted his lips,
Smarting the mucus membranes of oral desires.

"There I am.
If I imagine myself out of me,
Standing there beside that oak tree,
With no clothes on,

Even pissing against it,
Or shitting by it,
The old oak tree.
My age, I could carve on it,
Say forty.
My birth certificate lost
When I was a baby.
Mother died soon after.
Father, a carpenter, put
Me to work early in life;
I could make a coffin by
The age of ten.
But the army needed drummer boys
For the local camp, I was
Given to soldiers and have
Remained one since.
What do I look at?
A courtyard with large granite
Flagstones, three feet square.
Hand cut from a famous quarry,
Partly polished and cold as
Jack Frost. Along a curb, where
The lawn begins, and a hedgehog
Is hunting insects. On the
Lawn marble statues of women
Carry water in jars, baskets of fruit,
Cats and dogs, placed where a

Gardener fancied. The moon is bright
Now. I can see to the furthest
Gate guarded by two carved wooden
Dogs. Children tell how, on a full
Moon, they wander off, howling,
And snatch bad children from
Their beds, dropping them into
Quarries to be crushed to death.
An owl hunts mice. His hooting
Scoots with the wind into distant fields.
The one most magical time in

My life, a visit to an alchemist
Who worked above my father's
Workshop. It was late at night,
I couldn't sleep. I walked upstairs
To the roof. There was the old boy
Gazing at the stars, drawing
Star maps by lamplight. Through
A trapdoor. I saw this and
One night. The old boy had
A huge beard he tied around
His neck. He threw over himself
A white powder and immediately a
Transformation overcame the alchemist.
Into huge bird-white feathers,
The hookiest of beaks and talons
Large enough to grab a small deer.
Some of the powder drifted over
To me. I found myself flying through
The air, as an owl hunting
The night trails. This lasted for two
Hours.

The alchemist never returned.
From that day until this, I have
Found life unfurled. Throughout
I have occasionally sat quietly, hoping
The world could go away."

Beowulf Tweedwulf finished his ramble
Through the garden, lit a cigarette,
Wandered over to a statue, kissed
A marble breast burnt his lips
On the cold. He was found dead
Next morning. It had been a shock
For the innkeeper, who rose early
To clear up the place after a hard
Night's eating and drinking, finding
A naked body hugging a womanly
Statue.

Zip Zip Zip.

Guests found the angle of their poise
Shot through.

'Dead bodies indeed':
'Hanging in a garden.'
'Arms Around a statue.'

'No clothes. No life.'

The world is askew, and trees are running away.
Walls warping, clouds leaden with
Acid rain. An undertaker was
Summoned. He did his job.
Police were told, and suicide was recorded.
Guests stood gossiping about possible
Motives. The distraught wife, pregnant
And near birth.

'Was he the father?'

'Perhaps she's a witch.'

But they had no evidence,
No learned thesis or
Facts at hand.
Elfawn was told by the innkeeper's wife.
Elfawn moaned, sighed, and whispered 'death,'
Then fainted. And put to bed,
Her father held her hand.
She sighed, and he sighed.
Their journey home was postponed
For a few days. They heard
The clatter of the hearse below,
Pulling away out of the yard
To the village mortuary down the
Road. As the sun moved round
Direct rays struck Elfawn on the
Face. She found their strength
Gave her speech.

"Journeys past,
Journeys to come,
The world is weary of me.
Can my child find a haven
Once gone from me.
Failing to swim, I drown,
Failing to dream, I snore,
Failing the love within me
The child will turn away.
I can't burn the carousel
Which holds my past
And parades it around.
A penny drops.

A smile erupts.
A smile to take away
The smile of death.
Show me a mirror,
There I find an image
To turn aside.
To entwine the claws
I best design.
Shadow of a snout,
Horns of a devil,
Eyes of an evil.
The seductress punched the huntress.
Punctual mistress of bliss.
The sign I failed to see.
Science fiction of a blind muse.
Will I fail to find
A way out of the maze?
Dim this camouflage.
Dent this armor.
Crunch the arms
Metal fatigued.
I remember,
As a slave in Africa,
The muting of my senses,
The prosecution of the mind
Tuned in to wipe clean
But dithering, losing
The fix on it.
That pattern of experience
Preceded by travel.
A cavel of cushions
Plumped up to soften gravity.

What do I get but mystical
Experience, Rape, knowledge,
A living dream pounded on a drum.
And a father who sits there
Watching my hump
Expecting a tree to sprout.
His hands transpire work,
His veins shout louder
Than his mouth.
His skin is thicker thank bark
His hair is spindly as pine.
And he smells like old ozone.
I feel I could auction his body
To doctors. A body so old, wise,
Wizen, rooted in nature's infinite

Infancies. The burden of my complaint
Isn't. I can't lie;
Not that the silkworm is smarter,
The elephant more memorable
But that l'rn a mother to be,
And baby is big.
When I travelled in a caravan
Behind a veil,
Unimpaled and sturdy in my virginity,
Cupid proved a bad cause,
A truly missing link of a lost
Cause, a side of me unrailed;
I was like a lone vixen unhunted,
A pheasant unhung,
A hare uncoursed.
I had a view from the front

Of life and wore blinkers.
Now I'm on a track
Listening to servants praising
Their servitude.
I hope to be fair
And far away,
Show the child an absurdity
Or two.
Before he earns his victim's badge."

Elfawn's father remained asleep
His nervous flesh assembled
Into upright lines.
Elfawn slept for twelve hours, then
It was time to pack her father
Dear. A half-full cart in the yard,
A borrowed horse pulled them along.
The package of their minds
Signed and sealed.

CHAPTER SEVEN
AMEBUS THE MACROFAUST

Eagles hunt over the wart of earth.
High on a hill, a tower, where
A great magician with his glass
Spies the power,
Maps the hour,
Delivers his potages to fire
Crux of hope,
Crucible of divination.
The tower can be seen
From over thirty miles
Around the plain of life,

They have been led.
The horse bolts down a lane,
Happy to chaseth nose of fear,
Up the gravel to the caution of a gate,
Which swings open,
The hand of a stable boy
Catches the reign.
Poor Elfawn. Her bewildered father
Is loading a gun.
No light. No chance.
He tries to explode, but
The dampness of age
Has dissolved his fuel.
Where are we? Who are yu
He shins up his rope,
Tieing a knot to heaven.
There saints prepare his chance,
But he slips and wakes tall,
Devoid of wantoness.
Elfawn slaps a face.

"Take us to the owner of this tower.
Whose spells turn heads dizzy
At suppertime."

Steps worn deep by years of work.
Creaky locks rust when it rains.
Woodworm-rotted banisters,
Railings, gateposts, and frames.

At the top of the outside stairs,
Crumbling at the edges,
A short, thin, mustached,
Ragged man, wearing cast off

Clothes from duke and earls.
Burnt offerings gleamed in his teeth.
This wizard of rumor and
Piloted magic had formula success
In his younger days.
Now he had to try and try
Again or recipes became tainted,
Doubtful, apologetic.
This part-time Pan unchained
Himself, slowly descended towards,
The bemused pair; they stepped
Back: the magician breathed fire:

"I have had you brought here,
A special concession from above,
I know of you and your efforts
In life. My spies are few but
Efficient.
Here you will give birth.
I will be a father while it grows
Into a strong man who will rule
One day. Come upstairs and
Leave behind the weary world.
Enter this tower which holds vast
Secrets, simulations of paradise.
Many rooms whose functions none
Know. You will find your
Quarters overlooking a pond and stream."

They were scared, didn't want
To go in. A strong force drove
Them through a double door
Covered in open-mouthed masks

With almond-shaped eyes, representing all the
Races of humankind. The central hall
Contained a library, a large fireplace,
Wall lamps with colored glass shades,
A versatile polygonal table which
Could seat up to twenty people.
On the ceiling, maps of the stars
Surrounded by murals of faraway lands,
Deserts, hermits, caravans from

The east. Elfawn's father entered
First; the prisoner or guest of this
Wondrous man? He smiled about-face,
Weighted his feet, found his pockets
Full of fortune. Elfawn followed and
Was led to her room on the second
Floor. White walls. Hand-painted flowers
On the ceiling. A hard mattress,
A gallery of musicians to soothe
Her nerves. A medical corner with
Potions and ointments to cure all.
A fierce fire burning in a cast iron
Stove, which boils water for a minutes
Grace. A deep-pile carpet which sucks
In sound. All the colors of a rainbow
And many more. Climbing plants
From far off climes perfume, the air
With flowers.

"All this is more than I hoped for.
Here my baby will be born
With joy; kick over the toadstool
Of sorrow and come to know his

Way through this cruel world.
No more will I stand alone
Badgered by the male of the species
Whose taste in living is deathmasks
And effigies of hate, confidence
Tricks of progress, catchpenny phrases
To fill our minds, philosophies of bruised and
Bruising conceptual guilt, religions
Of male divinities unearthed from
Love, monies which refill the fullest
Pockets and pollutions which soil
The fabric of life. My womb in
A womb. I know spells to keep me
Here. Intruders beware, or Death will
Lick his lips."

The wizardy, magicy man
Who lived in this towery tallness
Became most alarmed.
Here was a powerful woman,
The goddessful woman he dreamt
Of the night, he found a meteor
In his hanging gardens. Now his
Troubles would begin. The baby

50

King fully born. A mother whose
Housing instinct had tricked him
Into this move.

Far into the distant fields
Light flicked its way between trees;
Imperceptibly shifting parallax,
Motion internecine, color patina,

Peasants dotted like statues; still-life.
Golden corn piled high on carts
Trundling along little tracks,
Lines of sight mapping out a
Pastoral pish, a powdery of
Pechral meandering. A salad
Of confusion. Little ideas and
Lambs pull grass, chewing the
Whole day long. Their shadows
Mottle the grassy hillocks, their
Fleeces pick up color and speckle
The canvas is cupid-like.
To the left, is a river with no virgin water.
Fish full, fish-faced, gleaming
Highlights a painter might think
A must. Banks trimmed with willow
And reed. Birds scooting, darting,
Chanting. Fishermen flick their lines
Lazily over currents and secret still
Spots where lurk the life of pike,
Perch and trout, even the famous
Rainbow boater fish; a rare sea and fresh
Water fish. It almost flies up from
The sea with its wing-like fins.
There's a small village built on
Stilts to be one up on winter floods.
A waterwheel treading circular steps,
Going nowhere, except by a calculus of
Heraclitus, losing time and form,
A clock of shadows ticking over
Washed out glory; bubbles are beautiful.

Past the pending village and high
Over the trees, distant mountains
Make mauve the horizon, match
The music of aerial perspective to
Kabalistic symbols above the window
And scattered through the garden.
Down to the right, bickering shadows
Of bushes and walls, red run with

Green mosses, lichens packing their prairies,
Building structures with painstaking daubs.
In the garden, a mechanical man points
Out the wonders of nature. His eyelids
Flutter. His stomach rumbles.
His ballet takes twelve hours to
Complete. Elfawn's father sits in a
Rocking chair lights a pipe,
Muttering his thoughts, tidying his
Life.

Dwarf man of Magic leaves the mutating
Pair in their capital room, in this house
Of coming joy. His name Amebus the
Macrofaust, a portent of a grim age, a remnant
Of a silver sage, his master who taught
Him all unrolled the cream of knowledge
Into his digesting mind. A balance achieved.
Weights fixed and well placed. He was cast
Off to explore our darkness of the heart.
And the world had no chance to counter
His must. So the achieved had plans
To balk at the facts. Too late, Amebus

Stitched fame to his silk, a fashion
Unseen, un-named, undrawn. Creative powers
Had blown on the course his place in society
Close to the top. The background
Of success was no handicap to him.
The playground of fortune, where
He wore his fame, made way
For his applause and pay. Once
Proven, his spells, healings, and potions,
Dealings snowballed, and Nemesis was
Flattened. Amebus walked wearily to
The roof, climbing hundreds of steps.
Sure he felt puffed out. All
Those steps, night in, night out.
Those stars, infinite numbers, endless
Mapping, endless movement, and discovery.
All for Noble's horoscopes. He felt
More could be said, yet he didn't
Know how. For a change, a visit
To the Earthly scene, a voyeuristic
Pan across a blessed surface.

There's no danger to the joints
Of Earth. Mountains in place, holding
Still. Trees all around, not walking away

Or crashing down. Rivers and ponds
Keep their courses and places. Soil
Of the fields lies
Soaking sun and rain,
Not often blown by checkered winds.
As for animals, they take their places
As rightful characters in a drawn out

Play, which outlasts seasons. A blackbird's
Singing is a delight and saving grace.
In long grass, a couple undress and
Copulate. Her face fills the lens with
The image of passionate entrails. His buttocks
Are the image of fungoid fat. Amebus
Continues his telescopic voyage. Cruises
Along a country lane, then flips up to a
Tree top where boys are watching
The enjoined couple. Laughing boys look
Like prunes. A flatulent solution to a
Question. Yellow pond reeds follow their
Career in a scurrying wind. Ducks,
Moorhens, wild geese, take their leisure
On the surface; quacking, pecking, packing
Lunch. A watery western of symmetric
Fantasy between the waves of design
And arbitrary pattern. In the town,
Blackboard of civilized behavior,
The telescope spots a barren woman picking
Up coins, children playing in gutters,
Splashing passers-by. Windows of butcher
Shops gleam with red flesh blobs. A
Mortuary of taste. Veg shops, Cake shops,
Ale houses, where shapely serving
Women occasionally lift skirts
To show their legs and collect a
Few coins to feed their brats.
Or they strengthen the beer at the
Landlords expense. This way his
Telescope purchased the purity of a vision,
The mystery of land whose guts

Were happy to be opened out for a
Sunlit inspection. Therefore prophecy
And the quick richness of nurturing
Sight. He now felt it best to
Twiddle the knobs back to the Heavens,
A peaceful place, a patch of paradise,
A berth of beatitude, a branch of

Battle, a portent of peace, a royalty
Lost. He felt tired. He closed the dome.
And sat down heavily to ponder the
Tarot. And drunk a heavy draught
Of elixir and dreamed of the possible
Life, hard on the heels of sleep.

His head slumped on his left
Shoulder. Despite an afternoon glow,
The room shaded through purple to
Brown to black, balanced against the
Outerworld, in his mind's eye. A
Semblance spirit parted from his body,
Flew against the four walls and ceiling
And disappeared through a ventilator.
For a moment, brightness bled through
The phantom, almost making it disappear.
An opaque molecular membrane developed
Instantly to shield the spirit, which
Flew first to the nearest cloud, a
Fairweather nimbus hurrying away. The
Spirit of Amebus bathed for a few
Seconds enhanced its transmutability,
Talked silently with the cloud. Then
With the ability of a swift, he dived

Down in a swathe of red light,
Streaking towards the tower. He hovered
Above Elfawn's balcony window, wishing to spy,
But not to hint at his presence. Through
The flattest of glass, clean as purest ice,
Clear as mountain air, and he noticed the old
Father playing patience while Elfawn boiled
Water. Spirit Amebus flew to the nearest
Village. Addressed himself as a prominent doctor
Who on his cart charged through
The village scattering women and
Children. The white tower sparkled
On a distant hill. Doctor Greenwald
Arrived in an hour.

The tower's surface cracked,
Crumbled, held together by moss, lichens,
Trails of ants, centipedes, woodlice, millipedes,
Solitary wasps, honeypot bees, ferns who have found
Tiniest cracks to spread their roots. Ivy trails
Also had colonized many parts but had
Been controlled. The tower's surface was

A wildlife paradise for the tiniest of insects
And to swallows that nested under eaves
And windows. Amebus glided up the tower
To his observatory window, charged
Through the glass, halted at his body,
Evaporated into mist, circled at speed the
Sleeping corpse, then funneled into an ear.
A slight stirring, a finger twitching,
A nose running, an eyelid flickering
Nostrils flaring, lips pouting,

A knee reflexing. Up gets
Amebus is whole once again.
He yawns and stretches, sprays
His moldering clothes with perfume.
It's getting late. Downstairs
A trusted servant opens the gate
For the good doctor directs the cart
Into the yard. Doctor Greenwald, best
In the county has a short, smiling
Moustache, blue eyes, black hair,
Which covers his ears. His lips
Are thin and white. When he talks
Words spin from his mouth.
Somersaulting, diving, twisting their way
To the hearer. By the time they
Reach the receptive ear they have
Performed more tricks than a stage-full
Of conjurors. He has dazzled the
Mind into believing things it wouldn't
Think about it all year. This enlightenment
Wasn't readily available, only when he
Was deeply moved. When he listens
The heart and mind of his
Patient becomes an open landscape,
In bright clear air. Details emerge
For the keenest eye. Songbirds trade
Their music is from tree to tree. These
Notes are picked up as pieces of a
Musical puzzle. Clouds sweep across,
Higher and higher, lower and lower,
Always changing, inspiring best thoughts,
Saddest thoughts, even the most secret thoughts.

These are all brought in to add to
The building of a solution which will save
The troubled soul.

CHAPTER EIGHT
DIONYSUS PENTACLE PAX

"Come in Doctor".

Elfawn called out. She was about to give birth.
The room was prepared. Clean towels,
Hot water. Her father had left and
Paced up and down the passage.

"I want to give birth squatting."

"That's O.K. by me. Take this
Potion to help you relax."

With a final heave, the head appeared;
Elfawn's legs wide apart, knees taking
The strain, hands holding a bar
Chained to a ceiling beam. On
Her face perfect calm, though her
Eyes watered perfumed tears. There
Was plenty of blood as the Doctor helped
Baby slip out. No need to cut, or use
Force. Once slapped, the boy gave an
Enormous yell. The afterbirth was
Specially stored in an icebox and taken
Away by two dwarfs. Once Elfawn
Had been cleaned up the washed down
Baby snuggled against her breast. The
Doctor walked out smiling a fixed
Unfathomable smile. The baby had
Golden eyes, slightly pointed ears and
Little hair. Eyebrows raise up in an
Expression of surprise. His long head

Had a pointed chin with a deep dimple.
According to ancients, a favorable face
Kit. Doc slipped down the steps in
A dream. He knew the babe was
No ordinary babe. No chip off the old
Block; no like father like son; no he
Has her eyes, his nose, her lips, his chin.
More like a changeling he once
Came across at the back of a cobbler's

Shop. It turned out to be a little monster
Like the one he found in a castle.
Most upsetting for the parents as the child
Grew six fingers and toes. He had the
Sharpest claws and the biggest brain in
The country. He beat up small children
And could outclimb and outrun ten
Year olds. Both came to bad ends.
Once their ugliness and sexuality got out
Of hand they were dumped in darkest
Forests, left to wolves and bears. Of
Course being in their element they
Found their way back to parental nests
To adoring mothers and grandparents
And were fed on finest human flesh.
Elfawn's baby, at present a bundle of
Innocent gurgles, against his mother's
Breast, had, to any expert's eye, the
Potential of a monsterish child or an
Avenging angle of unhappy distortions. On
The other hand to his all-powerful
Mother's eye this darling little one would

Be a handsome man amongst men,
A hero like Alexander, a man whose
Actions were effectively best, whose competitive spirit.
Wouldn't fade out these daydreams,
Uncharacteristic or characteristic; he
Wasn't sure.

One road at a time. Make it to the
Tower's gate. The doctor's cart clattered
Away down the iron chip road. His mind
Full of impossibilities. Reins slapped
Gently against the horse's pounding muscle.
He gave one look back towards the Tower.
A heartache hurried through his body.
He wasn't sure if he would ever return.

A full moon following the visit.
The great wizard, Elfawn and baby,
With grandfather tagging along, walk
Through a field, with the first sign of
Mushrooms. Baby is going to be christened.
In a stone bath, some ancient
Rock, with dew gathered by spreading
Cotton cloth over grass. The bright moon
Shines in its halo high above. They

Walk through a gap in some trees
Clustered around holy stones. They
Reach high into the air, in a circle, some
Up to forty feet. Their colors change
By magical powers that live beneath the surface

In a palace of elves. Around each stone
Are gathered enough people to form a
Circle by joining hands. They chant quietly
And in unison, hoping to contact the powers
That be. Baby arrives. It has grown so
Fast, outstripping siblings of a similar age
Who have been brought here, also to
Be dipped in the magic dew to save
Their lives the troubles of disease and
Injury. The naming of names. Elfawn's
Child will be called Dionysus Pentacle
Pax, or Nysus for short. Three
Naked women and three naked men
Dance round the stone bath; they breathe
Quickly, in corybantic style, wearing
Out onlookers as much as themselves.
When they finish, sweat glistening, they
Lick each other dry. They copulate, each,
Three times. A large Oak stick
Struck against the tallest stone signals
The bacchante activities to end. A tall
Priest covered in goat's hair advances in
Short steps; his mock phallus strapped
From his shoulder, bobs up and down.
Nysus the Ungodly, is placed in water.
The priest squeezes baby's phallus;
Mother's milk spurts
Over the baby who is lapping it up.
Elfawn then washes him in dew and
Dries him out with her hair. The congregation
Line up and in turn kiss the child on
Its feet. The stones have now turned

Deep Orange through to sea green. This
Sight can be seen for miles around for
Those lucky enough to be awake the
Few minutes the show lasts. They all
Chant Nysus: Nysus: until their lungs
Are hoarse; in a slow-moving circle
Around mother and child. Participants
Dissipate, Magician, Elfawn and Nysus stand
Alone. The moon filters through hazy

Cloud. Stones have turned to deepest
Blue. A quickening wind. It was time to go.
A falling star fell for a minute, then
Burnt out just above the horizon. Petite Etoile
Nysus, was growing fast as bamboo. He
Had drained his mother's milk and local
Sheep and goats. Often on a sunny
Afternoon he could be seen lying under a
Goat sucking at the udder. Neighbors
Who dared would watch this strange babe,
Only a few weeks old, strutting about
With a stick in its hand.
Nysus was now two
Feet tall with lots of ginger hair hanging
Down his neck. He spoke his mother's
Tongue fluently and a smattering of far
Off languages heard in the local market
From traders and gypsies. Two months
On the man-child wanted to know who
His father was. This was difficult.
One morning while Elfawn was hanging

Out the washing, a storm broke from
The east. Lightening struck close by
And knocked her out. Although unconscious
For only a few minutes, the impregnation
Of her body by hairy ghouls came
Back to her. Helped up by a handyman
She stumbled across to shaded seat. Nysus
Came waddling over shouting 'Help': in six
Languages. He guessed straight away the
Traumatic effect the near miss had had on
His mother. He saw by the guilty
Expression in her eyes that she'd remembered
Something very important. He jumped on
Her lap, told the handyman to clear off,
Unbuttoned her blouse, took out both breasts
And sucked them dry in five minutes.

"Who is my father"?

Elfawn replied telling
All that was revealed while she was
Unconscious on the grass. The rapidly
Developing child of darkness jumped off her
Lap,ran away laughing and shouting; demon-
Like; echoing where there was no reason
For one. In Nysus time, there are

Three, perhaps four, seconds in his
Minute, about eight minutes in his hour.
His day and night is about an eighth
Of ours. His impossible growth had
Promoted wild rumors down among the villagers.
Dr. Greenwald recognized the signs. Soon
They would want to march on the Tower

And either burn it down or destroy what
They thought was the cause of every recent
Mishap, dead child, mutilated lamb or calf,
And bad omens in the sky and in the cards.

CHAPTER NINE

NYSUS

Six months had passed since
The fathers had been revealed. Nysus,
Fluent in so many languages,
Advising Amebus the Macrofaust on
Planetary paths, astrological projections, while
Writing small musical pieces for the local
Church. Nysus's looks were changing fast,
Now four feet tall, long dark red hair,
A pointed, hooked nose, sharp ears, flat
Against the head. Considerable muscles and
A long penis which became erect at
The slightest sign of a female. Village
Girls would sneak away on warm days
To chase and fondle him in the cornfields.
They would partially undress or just lift
Their skirts. His energy was such that he
Could mount six or seven in a row. Of
Course, some girls talked and parents
Were very angry that their daughters
Were changing character in sinister ways.

One evening a meeting took place in
The village hall. A priest and headman
Called for the extermination of the monster child
Of a prodigious universe. Dr. Greenwald
Testified that their were few virgins left
Over twelve years old. What they didn't
Know was that Nysus couldn't reproduce.
He was genetically sterile. A one-off

From evolution's 'individual' shelf. The
Aggrieved marched to the local shop
Led by the priest. An ironmonger
Provided tar for torches, stumps of wood
With straw wrapped around one end. Also
A rope to tie up the victim before
An exorcising fire. Torches noticed by
A passing jackdaw made him swoop
Down and perch on a gutter's edge.
The crowd jabbered excitedly, alcohol
Had been passed around to buck up

Doubters, faint hearts and the general
Esprit de corps. The jackdaw, Idlegold,
Mimicked the sounds and flew off. He was
Hit by a stone from a catapult, but
Managed to fly home bleeding. Word got
Around about the bird spy. Better to
Start now. Idlegold squawked to Amebus
His conversation. The happy trio listened
While eating their vegetarian meal at a
Long oak table. They laughed together
Drinking deeply their own brew. A mixture
Of herbs, straw and spices from the East.
What could peasants do against their
Combined magic. Nysus, baby love, had
Been through all the manuals, potion books,
Spellbinders. Had digested them, reformulated
And experimented with their formulae.

Up the lane or down the lane,
They heard crackling torches light bales
Of hay on top of a cart. Around
The Tower they piled sticks, branches

And old scarecrows. The laughter of
Nysus reverberated down, putting a certain
Fear into the arsonists. So loud did
It became they blocked their ears with
Wax. Elfawn had rescued her father
From the lower level. Books had been
Prepared. Up in the observatory room with
Its open roof and circular balcony a
Balloon was being inflated by magic
Machine. A monkey statue's mouth was
Attached to a tube leading to a large
Bundle of fabric. The arms moved up
And down in time to the inflation rate
Of the balloon, which drifted above the
Tower within minutes, flames reflected
From its underside. A basket was
Attached, large enough for five adults
Squashed together. Flames had crept
Upstairs and around the building.
The balloon was ready for take-off.
Books threatened by fireballs of heat, grew
Legs and walked to a balcony on their
Level, grew wings and flew into the
Orange black night following the balloon
Higher and higher over the crowd which

Shot arrows, threw stones, shouted,
Swore and charged about. Flying books
Followed each other in alphabetical order.
Soon the white balloon and tail had
Disappeared through clouds which had
Drifted, since evening, over the whole land.

The priest stood on a tree stump and calmed
The mob.

"The flaming phallus behind us will no
Longer harbor despots of magic, immoralists-come
Lately, seducers of children or Elvan vibrations
To disturb our true feelings."

Some weren't so sure that things were
That bad. Hadn't potions healed? Hadn't
Lords and ladies visited the magician.
Hadn't Amebus in his younger days given
Entertaining parties and fairs with
Pyrotechnics of endless variety. It was only
That woman's arrival that had turned him
Inwards. The birth of the child had
Made him a recluse and a servant of it.
Its ugliness and fast growth were distortions
Of nature, not to mention its absurd learning,
More advanced than the cleverest of men.
Their necks strained upwards but the balloon
Had gone for good, lost in the patterns
Of stars seen between the drifting clouds.
All had been emptied of emotion or frightened
To the marrow of their bones or drained
By the exhilaration of alcohol or turned on
By the fiery tower. They wandered away
Wiser, not sure if all that had passed
Was a nightmare, a storm from the heart
Of a demon or a punishment from an
Angel of God or a warning from a
Mundane spirit that greater cycles of power
Had begun. Their participation a lubricating
Cause and effect.

"Have I ridden over the darkest hills
In search of a soul to call me in
Choose food and drink to nourish seeds
Presented by a bearer
From a world apart
For a reward of isolation?

This banishment in a basket
Hanging over the earth,
With its dots of light
And mysterious stillness.
For even though I play notes
On a flute smuggled in,
They are lonely sounds
Whose wings are frail?
They won't reach the moon,
That is where I hoped
They would go,
For fearless love tills the moon,
Never failing the tides and poets
Whose echoes rebound,
Intermingling;
A confused reception.
No-one knows if their thoughts
Are their own or cross bred
Musings which surprise the mind
Or hand which spills words on to paper.
Who has picked my tune,
Forlorn patient of doctor heart?"

So thought Nysus, Monster of the Moment.
Burning torches faded into sparks.
The balloon drifted with the Easterly wind
Far from the place they knew so well.

Their balloon ship like a planet or moon
Intrigued shepherds, vampires and lovers
Who lived through silent nights,
Excepting sounds of bleating, sucking,
Kissing and sweet nothings.
It traveled at ten miles per hour,
The trail of flying books faithfully behind.
These would be useful ballast at the
Time of descent. Elfawn, Nysus and
Amebus huddled together for warmth.
They were approaching Faustlandiagrad.
A myriad lights like a sea of fireflies.
A warning had gone out to this city.
Three hot air balloons on patrol
And six hang-gliders prepared to intercept.
A bath at night gave Elfawn
And friends an advantage. Nysus
Could see far into the dark with
His third eye hidden below a lid of
Skin. With the magician, he recited

A spell to leave behind, each
Minute, an after-image to confuse
Their pursuers. They had left three
Images when a hang-gliding man
Fired shots at each from a gun fixed
To his left shoulder. He was also blind
To the flying books which he couldn't
See, because they were an impossibility.
One shot grazed the real balloon causing
A very slow puncture. Nysus bored with
This pot shooting levitated out of the basket,

Flew underneath one glider, cut a cord
Which meant a slow descent to a
Broken ankle. Nysus wasn't mean. He
Circled behind another, snipped a string
And down he fell to a broken leg.
The third tried to out-manoeuvre
The deft demon. He wasn't lucker
Except for a brief thought, he'd
Shot Nysus in the arm. Wrong.
He received a punch and tumbled
Down, down, to land in a haystack.
Next, the balloons which had intercepted
Their Westerly path. Nysus armed
Himself with fire and placed on top
Of each balloon, a small fireball which
Burnt through the glazed cotton. All
Three drifted safely to earth.

CHAPTER TEN
TRAVEL AND STRIFE

Now they were free to travel
Over the border; over lands with
Stark mountains, dark rivers, white lakes
And endless forests. Many days
Passed before they landed in poppy
Fields by the sea. Stunted trees
Leaned with the prevailing winds of
Summer. Fields were busy with peasants
Who hardly stirred when a white
Balloon landed. Books which had
Been signed up as a ballast, fell off on
Impact, into neat piles, hidden by
The poppies and camomile. The
Travel some four, in exile, walked off

To find a village, hire a horse
And cart, collect books, buy a house,
Set up home and inhabit their thoughts.

Outside a large village, with two
Gothic spires, there was an old
Rundown monastery belonging to a
Local congregation. The purchase
Pleased the few remaining monks
Who welcomed the money. They
Decided to become pilgrim priests,
And brothers. Gardens had become
Overgrown. High walls had been breached
In many places enabling the curious
To prowl the grounds. Nysus was
Hidden during negotiations. After a month,
Repairs had been completed, and the
Monastery safety patrolled by geese.
The chapel was left for the use
Of local parishioners, in an effort to
Appease them. Elfawn was still thinking
Of the balloon trip, especially the large
Towns and cities passed over. How their
Patterns, some radial, some grid-like, others
Concentric, trellis, or jumbles of history.

There were towns so densely packed it
Seemed no rain could seep between buildings.

Locals were suspicious of newcomers
Who never went to Church, who were
Building a tower planned higher than
Their spires. Nysus, now five feet tall.
His handsome ugliness invited fear. None

Except his mentor saw him. His three
Shortcomings, a tongue stretchable to seven
Inches. A gold and brown hairiness covering
Enormous genitals which stood erect at
Fourteen inches. Clothes disguised details
And exaggerated his form. Wearing a cloak
Made him into an acceptably bulky figure.
For all his musclebound body he had
A supercharged brain which fed on books,
And continual observation. He now commanded
Paths of action, plans of his mentors who
Used their experience to temper his fate.

Three years passed in the mysterious
Monastery, converted, courted and won over
From the locals who coveted it as holy
Ground. Nysus had grown to his monsterish
Maturity. A metamorphosis the like of which
None had seen or heard of since time
Began. Now seven feet high; the splitting
Image of his fathers and some spitting
Of his mother. Something like gnarled
Wood polished by a sculptor; like a Greek
Statue encrusted with barnacles and coral;
Like Pan when young; Like a film star
With elephantiasis. He kept hidden away,
Working at wonders of philosophy: the questions
Who am I? Does matter exist? Is an
Apple more real than a star? Is water
A magic substance? Are shapes of faces
Reflections of character: Do animals have
Souls? Is an ant as intelligent as Plato?

Why is the earth round? What is sound:
What is what? What is? What what? or
Playing with maps of stars, finding out what
People will do. Just a bit tiring studying
Alone with nobody to discuss these things
Of the mind. He also used to paint and

Draw sketches of underworlds and fairylands
His third eye could see to. They seemed
To many the places where he belonged.
Elfawn the caring looked after this
Threesome as best she could feeding,
Washing, cleaning, shopping, foraging,
Mending and occasionally appeasing the
Curious. Amebus had fallen into a quietist
Frame of mind. Most of his days were
Spent alone studying his flying books.
The grounds were large enough to hide in
And daydream under the sun or shelter
In shade reading runes and secret
Books of the dead collected from bazaars
Around the world. His assistant
Collected herbs from hedgerows and field,
As well as pursuing his own hobby
Collecting moths and butterflies. Also
Chasing milkmaids. Elfawn's father was a
Tired man. Dragged from his forest,
Taken to the tower. Made to escape in
A balloon. Now stranded by the sea
Which he didn't like. Most days for him
Were quiet, spent making fires and furniture
To fill empty cells and reflectories.

One day in late summer,
A melancholy time for some.
Trees are mature green,
Blossom is seeded and
Turning to fruit.
Sunflowers are over six feet tall,
Each with its spiral face
Staring at the sun
Without going blind.
Young animals, mice, rabbits,
Birds and domestic creatures
Are learning roles,
Learning the ropes;
How not to get entangled,
How to run away,
To run after,
To lie still in the long grass,
To float higher than clouds,
To dive at a speed that deceives
The human eye,
To find a mate and reproduce
So the story goes.

A troop of soldiers march and ride
Through the village. They call for supplies,
Women and shelter for the night.
Most women had gone to hide, except
A few young ones who fancied to look,
Even though they knew they would experience
More than a sight for sore eyes.
The village was usually off the soldier

Route and unharmed in a war for many
A year. Now times were changing.
Rumour had it that a war was spreading
From the center of the continent. A
Land called Faustlandia had been invaded
From the east. A great army marched
Westwards slaughtering and enslaving whole
Countrysides of people. These soldiers,
About a hundred, marched northwards to
Join a Marshall, a General and a Colonel
Who were gathering an army from all over.
It would march to meet and halt the
Invaders. The troop marched past the Abbey.
They stopped to pray in the chapel.
Elfawn saw them and warned the others
To hide. Some troops, inquisitive at
The emptiness and silence wandered
Along corridors which seemed insolent
In their formality, cleanliness and order.
They weren't men at arms trained in
Chivalric codes and martial arts, but
Recruits from towns, ports and fields.
Not given to feeling with insight the nature
Of things, but to feeling perversities towards
The unknown. When they glimpsed Nysus
Sleeping under a tree, three soldiers stopped
In their tracks, rubbed eyes, dropped jaws,
Scratched hair, felt sick, anger, self-righteous,
And violent. They ran off to tell the world.
A hunt ensued through the whole complex.
For monsters, demons, witches, wizards.

Swords were drawn, guns loaded, ropes
Noosed. The assistant was found, gagged
And castrated. Amebus turned himself
Into a statue. Nysus hid underground,
Digging himself in like a rabbit.
Father was decapitated by an eager young
Farmhand, Elfawn was raped by twenty soldiers,

Then tied to her headless father. All was
Not lost, in the wild storm taking place.
Confusion mounted as more men ran
Through the buildings, kicking down doors,
Scattering papers and furniture. They weren't
Sure what they were looking for,
Just something inhuman, unpleasant and
Slimy. Elfawn had fainted. The flowing
Blood had subsided to a trickle. She
Did not dream.

CHAPTER ELEVEN
NYSUS, GENERAL OF THE WORLD

One soldier noticed disturbed earth
In a cloister garden. Nysus had buried
Himself there. Fear made him mature
Quicker. He was ready for all and any action.
A group of soldiers started digging. A fire
Had been started nearby. It was spreading
Out of control. Smoke billowing in the
Draughts, driving out soldiers, dampening
Their violence. Nysus was almost uncovered,
One sword blade away from death.
A soldier nicked Nysus' flesh.
The next moment Nysus punched up a
Fist through the remaining earth,
Levitated the speed of a bullet,
Spat acid in the faces of soldiers,

And continued to spin in the air
Spraying acid over the heads of the enemy
Who was running amok. Nysus, now
Eight feet tall and still growing shouted
A deafening scream which penetrated
The thickest stone walls. Soldiers ran
Deliriously out of the building back to
Their commander who called for a bugle
Retreat and battle formation. Nysus landed,
Ran off to find Elfawn. He untied her
And licked her wounds. Father was
Buried in a cloister garden. Amebus, by
Now, had dismounted his plinth, and
Hovered as a kestrel over the scene,
Watching in case he was shot down.
Nysus carried Elfawn outside, placed her
In the shade, against an elm tree.
Nysus had reached full maturity
At nine feet. A monster with a battery
Of deadly weapons. His acid saliva. His
Infra-red eyes. His rasping scales and
Dagger teeth which grew replacements. His
Contagious laugh that made people die of
Breathlessness. His telepathic sadness that
Made people so low they went to bed

And cried until dehydrated.
In front of him a frozen staring
Troop of soldiers; their disbelief
At purple pulsating scaled flesh. Rippling
Muscles. Dark red eyes. Extra fingers
Which twisted three hundred and sixty
Degrees. Bright orange hair and thin blue lips,

Before them, Nysus, future General of the
World. And here was the kernel of his
Army. He made his immediate plans
Known to the officer in charge. He would
Lead and train this gang of men,
Sharpen their wits and tactics. He collected
More men on the way to battle; up to
A hundred thousand marching behind him
Ready for the great war.

Elfawn, awoke; silent, thoughtful,
Reclothed herself from a straw bag
Placed beside her.
Today her child faced his destiny.
Nysus led off his embryo army
Watched by mute peasants.
Some tearful at the Abbey
Burning down.

"Elfawn from Faustlandia Amebus chided,
Perched on her shoulder"

"What you see before you
Is an illusion.
Now breathe deeply.
Inhale this liquid.
In the palm of your hand.
This world is too slow
For the likes of you.
It is an octopus of minute,
A tin of caviar,
A basket of shrimps.
It's clear you are a destined
Woman, a rare breed
Who will come to their past

Through adventure after adventure.
Wave goodbye to Nysus,
Ultimate power of the new world."

Elfawn cried one tear. Dusted herself.
Straightened her rags. Walked over to a black
Stallion called Dreyfusus, summoned by Amebus,
Once mounted he cantered off the
Highway down a country lane which
Led to the sea. Elfawn with Amebus
The kestrel on her shoulder gave
One look back at the abbey smoke.
Swirling in a contrary wind; one look
Back at the road shrouded in dust
Settling on trees, bushes and peoples' faces;
Clogging their tears.

They rode a brisk canter
Along a nobbled path.
After jumping a hedge
And riding down a steep slope,
To a cliff top, Elfawn dismounted,
Outstretched both arms,
Raised her head to the sun,
Stepped once to the left,
Once to the right,
Showed her breasts the sky
And sang a hymn to the place
Where she stood.

"Earth: how tired you look
At the end of each day.
You have felt the sun and rain
Grappled with the unquietening wind.
In the night, kindness will fall

Allowing dreams to work their stories
Into the pages of understanding
Spreading a translucent surface
Across the mind which stampedes
Back into day, when woken
Without recall.
But Earth remains its changed
Unchanging; a mammoth of delight.
I stand here with open arms
Embracing the desire of sight,
To capture and release
Each color of hope
Which traps and spreads over
The sight of which I cannot believe."

CHAPTER TWELVE

ELFAWN'S NEW ADVENTURES

Dreyfusus nudged Elfawn in the back of the
Neck. Time to fly away. Where to? She
Wasn't sure. But the horse knew if
Anybody did. Well, let him lead.
Let him take her where he wants to.
No doubt Amebus the crafty kestrel knew
Of the destination. She remounted, glad
To rest on the muscle sculpture called
Horse. A steep path to the beach. No,
Not this way. Dreyfusus galloped to
The cliff edge, launched into mid-air
And flew higher than the highest pink
Cloud. On they flew until a black sea
And star studded sky made Elfawn feel
More lonely than for many a year.
She was cold. The kestrel
Gave her a cloak of feathers. The
Horse's legs powered through the air.
She became sleepy. When she woke

They had landed on a large ship that
Had sailed every sea, yet had no crew
Except a captain and his dog. The tall
Black cloaked figure called over the intruders
And asked them for a forfeit. This ship
Was a carrier of souls for Captain Death
Whose four eyes, two at the back of his head,
Sought right round the earth those
Ready for departure. The ship could travel
As fast as necessary to reach every port
Where departing souls gathered in crowds,
Eager for the next world. When full the
Ship would rise into the sky and disappear,
Leaving behind a ship in its image to
Carry on the good work. Amebus knew
More than this, that Dreyfusus carried
New souls to empty wombs. Elfawn, too,
Realized opposites at work. She spat out
Spells and dived into the sea and found
A dolphin who carried her to the nearest

Shore. Dreyfusus flew far away, not
Staying to find out what the forfeit was.

Exhausted and wet on the nearest shore
Elfawn had pulled herself on to the seaweedy,
Stony beach. She breathed deeply from the
Seaweed. Vapor which revived her.
Amebus had flown to shore and changed back
To a man. He asked what was next. The past
Had been too difficult. They were tired of
Leaping time to an unknown where and when.

Elfawn picked up some flat stones and
Skimmed them over the waves. One stone
Skipped sixteen times before plopping into
The salty depths.

The landscape forms shore to shore looked wooded.
And complicated. Hills rose gently to a steep
Escarpment, parallel to the shore as far as
The eye could see. Copses, grazing sheep,
And clustered farm buildings snuggled together
In little valleys. There seemed no obvious tracks
Or footpaths. Bushes along the beach looked
Impenetrable. Selecting hefty sticks from driftwood
To use as weapons, they forced their way
Through bramble and hawthorn to a more open
Forest of yew trees and moss-covered ground.
Quiet as a graveyard. Quiet light. They sat
And rested in a shaft of sun. Amebus felt
He had no magic left, that it had been
Lost at sea. Elfawn felt wrong
And that none of this should have happened
To her. Smoke drifted from some trees a mile
Away. Making good progress, they came across
A blue five-barred gate. The farm was called
Norsewood. It was painted black.
No animals,
No mess, no smells, and no straw. Windows were
Cracked or broken, barns empty sheds spotless
With no sign of dung. Puzzled, they opened
A blue door to the farmhouse. Inside
Everything was spotlessly clean. Fresh food on
The table; a fire that burned, not needing
To be refueled. As Amebus and Elfawn

Began to sit down, the chair spoke

"Do not sit on me."

The fire said "Do not dry yourself in front of me."

The food followed with "Eat me and you'll be sick"

The floor squeaked "Don't walk on me".

The whole house hummed with every part
Wanting to deny its usage. In fact the whole
Farm wasn't to be used. The unwanted
Couple ran outside and lay in the sun for
Two hours, dreaming of what they shouldn't
Be doing on this farm. Both felt homesick
For Faustlandia, even though they knew a
Great war gripped the whole continent.

The next morning, after sleeping
In a hayless barn they walked to the
Nearest village, found by following a track
Over a hill. People spoke in negatives.

"I don't feel well today."

"You mustn't speak so much"

"The sun isn't so warm as yesterday."

"You aren't any younger."

"Don't use my carpet."

"Don't buy so much food."

"Don't study at school."

"Don't loaf around"

"Your looks aren't young anymore."

Sometimes it became complicated.

"The other day I went for a walk but
Didn't walk as fast as I could have,
And I didn't enjoy the sun and sea
As much as the next person who
Didn't say much because there was little

To talk about that wasn't boring."

Elfawn and Amebus left this village
To look for a town.

"Don't walk too fast or you'll not reach
The town feeling fresh."

It was ten miles away.
Things were worse there.
The Mayor spoke.

"No. No. No."

The woman said -
"Yes. No. Yes. No."

Or any number of permutations of the two
Words.
The mens's vocabulary was limited to

"Not, never, nohow."

People lounged about looking into each
Others eyes with one hand on a knife.
This medieval town looked spanking clean.
A pleasure to look at, out of the corner
Of one's eye. People were relaxed and
Smiled a lot when not speaking. Children
Played childrens' games - hopscotch,
Skipping, tag, postman's knock, and sing-song
Games whose eloquence astounded their
Parents.

"Chapter, chapter, little happy chappy,
Out with his nanny
Ran to a girl
To pinch her pretty happy"

"Elephant, Elephant
Why did she lose her pants?

Because a boy came along
In the middle of her pong
And stole them right away."

Elfawn needed a place to rest and wash
And sleep. After some awkward questions

They were given directions to a small
Boarding house on the north side of town.
A little old lady opened the door

"I don't have many empty rooms
But come in and look for yourselves."

Elfawn found two suitable rooms, small,
With one window, a jug and bowl, a wooden
Bed with straw to keep warm. And a
Brown woolen rug. They slept nineteen
Hours finding the dreams of lost sleep
Captivating and memorable. In the morning
They both felt the realization of never
Being able to return home, of being
Stranded in an island country where
People spoke so differently in each town.
A maid enters. Fills the bowl with water.
Provides a towel and soap. Elfawn undresses
Washes herself all over. Amebus, up since
Dawn, is outside brushing down two
Horses he has brought using his magic ring.
Breakfast. A boiled egg, slices of ham,
Hot mead and plums. Off to the capital.
Details of the journey, courtesy of a local
Broadsheet. Three stops to rest and feed
Horses. Two stops for meals. Three stops
For the body's wastes.

In the capital city, split by a
Wide murky river, poor people outnumbered
The rats. A tall red castle surrounded
By thin black towers emitted soldiers
Dressed in chain mail, who marched
Continuously through alleys, street and squares.
Like ants flowing from a central nest.
Occasionally peasants would be arrested and
Hauled off in closed cars. Elfawn and
Amebus began to feel themselves out of place
Riding horses among the poor. Their feelings
Turned to fear as they were bundled off
By soldiers, grabbed by the hair and
Trussed up in a car called 'never returns'
Or 'nevers' by the street dwellers. The cobbled
Roads shook every bone, every chain of mail.
By the time they arrived at the castle
They were very sore and had to be lifted
Off the floor and onto the ground. At

This point Amebus's ring was taken.
Elfawn suspected rape. However, they were
Walked to a large hall with dark ominous
Looking heraldic shields around the walls.
Under each shield portraits of Kings and
Princes. Under these round rose tinted
Windows. Below displays of swords, lances
And other fighting weapons. The roof was
Constructed of parallel arches, the ceiling
A grid of beams. From them hung
Shrunken heads. From the heads bones like
Femurs, hipbones and phalanges. From the

Bones hung feathers. At the end, a bell.
When this was rung, another death
Took place. The prisoners were untied
And sat on two chairs over a trap door.
Question time. They decided telepathically to
Play innocent travelers passing through,
Journeying to see the Northern Light in
The Land of the Endless Sun.
They weren't believed and were sent
Tumbling through the trapdoor onto a
Filthy floor. Two jailers jostled them
Into jail. Could Amebus possibly save
Them from a damp dying. His ring had
Gone, but he had one magic tooth
Which had been overlooked even though it
Was made of gold with a diamond at its
Centre. Amebus asked Elfawn

"Who do you know who could save us
From this dead end?"

"Mr. Nicest; a great monster who could
Devour this castle in one go, or
Dreyfusus the stallion who could kick
A wall down with one blow.
Nysus, but he's unavailable.
I'll toss a coin concealed under my tongue.
Heads the horse, tails, Mr Nicest."

Mr. Nicest won. Elfawn lay quietly in the
Straw rubbing her ankle where the chain
Pressed tightly against her flesh. Amebus
Placed his magic tooth on a cleared patch
Of floor, blowing away the last speck of

Dust, polishing the stone with saliva and
The cuff of his shirt. The tip of the diamond
Shone through the gold root. Amebus rubbed
His hands three times, kissed the palm of his
Left hand and spat on his right and
Spread the spit. He whispered into his
Cupped hands close to his face magic words
All beginning with X or Z. Finally, he placed
His right hand, then his left hand over the tooth,
Pressing down hard. The tooth appeared
To travel through his hand, sat on top of it,
And grew to ten times its size, ending up
The shape of an egg. Amebus put this
Bright yellow pulsating object under straw.
And waited. They fell asleep. Two hours
Later there were raging sounds somewhere
Outside. Standing on her friend's shoulders
Elfawn could just see through the bars into
The square. Arrows and spears were flying at
Mr.Nicest; monster of much class; at war
With hundreds of soldiers. All parts of him
Were fully mobilised. Since the days under
The lake he had been divorced from his wife
Who now rode out killing and roaming in whatever
rovince she fancied. Their underwater kingdom
Destroyed in a marriage battle. Mr. Nicest
Wounded here and there were devouring soldiers
With fire, the bearing of wings, lashes of a tail,
Teeth bites, and slashes of talons and claws.
He was a hundred feet high. Traveling
On a magic carpet picked up cheaply
In a bazaar his daydreaming homed in

On Amebus's bleeping tooth egg. He decoded
The message and came as soon as he could.
Nicest had fought his way over to the
Dungeon grill; with a flick of a finger the
Bars were off. He stuck his forefinger
Down into the cell. Both inmates
Jumped on board, slowly maneuvered out
On to the ground level. Overawed by his
Size and a new wave of troops with cannons
Bearing down, the escapees nearly fainted.

They were lifted by the giant into a
Pound which smelled of human excrement.
Mr. Nicest charged through the outer walls,
Over the moat before barging down the central

Tower. His magic carpet, the size of a
Ballroom waited in a town square. Nobody
Was in sight. Folks were cowering in basements
And under beds. Before embarking the monster
Picked up his two passengers from the
Excrement pound, and the carpet lifted off
As easily as a leaf in a gust of wind.
Before long the city below looked more
Complicated than any carpet. The enemy
Had been defeated, and that land was
Never the same again. A people's uprising
Put in a populist Government. Tyranny
Stamped out wouldn't return.

CHAPTER THIRTEEN
ELFAWN PASSES

The carpet carried Amebus to Western Lands. Elfawn
Jumped from the carpet and gracefully
Glided down to earth, landing in the forest
Where her father had lived. His wooden

House still stood, though scarred by fire.
Elfawn looked sadly up at the carpet
Realizing that she would never see
Mr. Nicest again, nor Dr. Amebus. Both
Would settle deep in the mountains.
Adventurers and explorers would bring back
Tales to tell of strange kingdoms ruled
By a giant and a magician who couldn't
Remember his name. Magic was the only subject
Taught in their schools. Elfawn lived alone
Till she died. She cut wood, collected fungi,
Entertained as a storyteller and as a gypsy
In local fairs building up a reputation
For prophecy. But she didn't become too
Clever, allowing chance to rule her words.
She lived another sixty years, only in
Dreaming did she travel. She died in
Her sleep after a dream of planets and
Outer space and all its wonders. She died
Feeling less lonely. Passing her house in
Subsequent years visitors dropped in to pay
Homage to the prophetic old lady. The forest
Had become much smaller as the great war
Ended; prosperity returned and wood was needed
To rebuild. She had ghostwritten her
Life story which became a bestseller.
In her dreams the adventures of
Gabal The Dog intrigued her most. He
Won second choice in the temple.

'To ride on a donkey!'

No self regarding
Dog would do such a thing so he
Trotted behind to begin his adventure.

CHAPTER FOURTEEN

THE ADVENTURES OF GABAL THE DOG

Gabal began life in an overturned
Dustbin in a small town on the coast of
Tunisia. He was one of four pups. Two died
Just after birth. Gabal turned out mostly
Black with two white spots under his eyes.
A mongrel. His mother a stray hunting
Dog from the desert. His father a passing
Hound belongs to an Arabian prince, who
Camped on the outskirts one night near
The end of December. The Afghan
Hound was allowed to roam before nightfall.
And came across a bitch on heat.
He mounted her without delay,
There was little time for foreplay. A quick
Sniff, and up he jumped. His keeper
Chased after him as soon as he saw
What was going on. He didn't want
His master's prize dog catching foreign
Fleas or disease. Still, the Afghan stayed united
About five minutes before he was dragged
Off with great difficulty by his keeper.
Whom he bit in the hand to show
Anger at this coitus interruption.

Gabal grew up on scraps from
Port-side rubbish tips. He grew up in rough
Streets. His mother taught him where to

Look for food; in the alleys behind
Restaurants, shops, large houses, and mosques,
The quays where ships from all over
The Mediterranean docked, grain spillage,
Dried meats and fish left unattended. And
The struggle with other dogs, cats and
Poor humans, a subsistence war, to stay alive,
Strong enough to win the next meal. The
Packs of dogs encountered, pined, battled
For leaders. The best fed usually won;
The best hunter with the most local knowledge
Always came to lead. Gabal as a young
Dog learned fast. He fed well and outran

Kids with stones and sticks. Fought pet dogs
With vicious ease and soon headed a ten
Dog pack which under his leadership
Dominated the town. Not being large this
Seemed a greater achievement than in fact it
Was. In Tunis, for example, they would have
Been eaten by packs of large hounds with
The mixed blood of Alsation, Afghan, Boxer
And Great Dane. But Gabal had learned
More craft than these apologies for wolves.

One fine day coming to an end, Gabal
Sleeping under a wooden box near a handsome
Sailing ship from Genoa. It had three
Main sails and cannons pointed
From port and starboard. The ship was being
Loaded with rations, slaves, sheep, rabbits
And chicken. Activity had been intense all day.

Gabal, now three years old, had had
Enough of small town life. Fed up
With routine of petty thieving, fighting
And defending his top dog status he
Sniffed towards the portside activity. Waited
His chance, chased a rat that fell out
Of a crate of fruit, snapped its head off
And swallowed its body in two bites. A
Sailor saw his efficient craft, passed
A word to the captain who fancied having
A smart dog to clear his ship of rats. Two
Seamen chased after Gabal, who gave them
A little run around to make their effort
Seem real. He then slipped into their
Clutches, with a cord around his neck. He
Didn't bite but growled deeply, shaking from
Head to tail. Once aboard he was put
In a whicker basket tied to a rope, and
Thrown overboard, ducked a few times to
Wash out fleas, mites,lice, dust and any
Other crawlies that hold tight to dogs.
Gabal nearly drowned. A sadistic sailor
Who didn't like dogs was relieved of his
Duty and Gabal was given to a cabin boy.
He dried the dog, brushed him, talced
And perfumed him,making a stray into
A pampered pet. At night they slept
Together and the boy came to love Gabal,
Who became the most efficient rat catcher

Ever seen.
Most days passed routinely on the open
Sea as the ship headed east to Alexandra.

In port Gabal was allowed to roam under
The charge of his boy keeper. On the second
Day they searched out a fairground, leaving
The almost restocked ship early in the morning
Working their way through hurrying porters, dockworkers,
Repair men, pimps, soldiers guarding military
Equipment and beggars always in danger of
Being kicked into the water. And the
Food stalls, flower sellers, trinkets, cloth, shoe
And booksellers, all jostling for golden hands.
After this melting potage, the good friends
Arrived at the entrance of a back alley
Leading behind a large hall where
All sorts of pets were sold, from tame
Lions to sparrows. Through a large arch
At the eastern end a partly walled
Square filled with tents and many people
Accompanied by children. Each tent was
Occupied by a sideshow. There were magicians
Of the type who could read minds, draw
Rabbits out of hats, turn grown men into zombies,
Little girls into crows, little boys into toads
And parrots into princes. Magicians of the
Kind who could make persons and
Belongings disappear, or only their belongings;
Or only the persons with clothes left behind.
The types that could saw a woman in half,
Chain her up and lock her head in an
Iron mask and release her with
The wave of a wand. Some tents were full
Of trained animals; lions that could pull

Out of grey hair with their front teeth,
Tigers who could roar to tune,
And Minor birds who could woo your
Wife with a love poem from the Orient. In the
Games tents, shooting the hump off a cut-out
Camel, the beak off a vulture, the fez off
A Turk. Throwing loops over swords, slack
Rope walking over a bed of nails, sharing
Snakes with bare hands and scorpion racing.
The most popular tents were full of food.
Sherbet drinks, sweetmeats, candies, biscuits;
Not to mention a new discovery - iced cream

Which seemed the most magical substance
Of all. At the end of the day Gabal
And friend arrived at the ultimate show.
A packed audience stood in silent awe.
A black hooded wizard's eyes roam
Over a naked woman who slowly disappears.
First a faint image, see through, then an
Outline, then a halo which dispersed
Into a cloud which drifted over the
Crowd who immediately became drugged
With delight and handed over handfuls
Of money when the collection came
Round. The woman didn't reappear. The
Wizard asked for a volunteer for his next
Trick; turning a woman into a dog or
A dog into a woman, all with the aid
Of a magic sack and three drops of mysterious
White potion. Gabal volunteered, barked
His way to the platform, parting the

Bewitched crowd. The boy and dog climbed
Into the sack and were sprinkled with
White droplets. The sack was tied with a
Golden thread. All lamps were turned out
Except for one hanging over the center of the
Stage. In deep shadows, the magician
Moved swishing his wand side to side
As if cutting down invisible demons living
On corn stalks. After five minutes
The magician facing his audience
Bent low over the sack, spat on it, kicked
It, struck it hard with his wand. The audience
Gasped. Lamps relit. He pulled away
The golden thread, out jumped a dancing
Skeleton of a dog's body and a boy's skull.
The audience in an uproar. The magician perplexed.
He threw the sack over his monster, which
Collapsed into a pile of old doggy bones.
Out of the sack, second time round, sprang
Gabal and the boy, except Gabal was now
The boy, and the boy Gabal. Proof of this
Was that Boy remembered his life as a dog
Very well and Gabal could recite his
Tables, to the pleasure of arithmeticians
Who dotted the audience. General applause.
People shook hands with each other
As was the custom after a good show.

CHAPTER FIFTEEN

GABAL, BOY AND DOG

Now Gabal and Boy were kept
Back by an unaccountable force or pull.
They couldn't leave the stage. The

Magician, after everybody had left,
Bundled his two victims in a sack
And swapped them for silver from a
Trans-Saharan slave trader who dealt
With Arabic rulers and minor despots
Along caravan routes. Novelties were
Useful to appease potential interrupters
Of traffic.

By now Gabal the boy thought
It was time to ditch this spell,
Spell out certain facts to his captor
And bite a few heads off. Boy the
Dog wasn't amused with his furry
Cover and wished to dump this
Disguise and leave Africa for good.
After their capture the muddled two
Were caged in a box cart with no light
Except for one small air hole.
This slight prison, pulled by two camels,
Joined up with a large caravan going
South, heading straight for a midpoint
Town deep in ambivalent territory.
The caravan train, over a hundred carriages,
Stretched to a mile long. Some pulled
By horses, others by camels. Children's
Carts were pulled by ponies alongside the
Main line. Escort soldiers rode in short
Columns either side. Cavalry were needed
Against marching tribes, who often picked off
Stragglers. At night a general camp formed.

The front third carriages staying still as the
Second and third sections drew parallel.
Soldiers encircled the three
Columns as best they could.

Individual carriages had painted cloths
With brightly colored birds, horses, landscapes
Or geometrical motifs. A caravan train provided
A theatre of life. And the shapes
And sizes of captive beasts defied the
Encyclopedic. Some carts and owners
Provided for soldiers who number
Five hundred. They were paid half in
Advance by the traders. At journey's end
They received the rest of their money
From the recipients of this vast store,
Rich tribes craving for exotic luxuries.
Gabal's car tagged on to the children's.
His captor, a trader named Marzip
Felt none too confident about this trip.
He was small time, dealt in curios, freaks
For more idiosyncratic clients. He constantly
Ran into raiders on his individual journeys
And saved himself by the weirdness of
His wares, which scared off superstitious tribesmen.
Such a large caravan train was prey to
Attack, sandstorm, dry oasis, disease, squabbles and
Unruly soldiers. Stories of bloodshed, rape
And maiming horrified even hardened travelers.
However, at present, it looks magnificent,
Colour and shape serve up rainbow

Feasts which would liven any painter's
Jaded palettes. Marzip looked for
Omens. He wasn't sure of his cargo. Didn't
Know its potential. Wasn't sure if he could
Deliver his prize.

Marzip looked down both
Vanishing lines.
Intense blue sky,
Ten in the morning.

The caravan leader had ridden from back
To front, telling stories, giving good news.
After passing a water truck behind
His leading troops he waved his lance three
Times. Marzip woke up in a daze
From his daydream doze
To see three columns
Lurch forward with a delayed reaction ripple
Of a slow motion fire cracker. Before Marzip
Moved off he fed his donkeys hay.

In the distant dust priests chanted prayers
Of protection for wealth of mythic proportion.

Gabal and boy escaped their confines.
Fangs sunk deep around Marzip's neck
Doing irreversible damage. Boy tied Marzip's
Hand behind his back and dragged
Him into the cart. Gabal sat at
The front. Boy took the reins. They
Had decided to stay with the caravan
To see where destiny took them.
As the journey passed the first week
Groups of travelers attracted to each other, stayed

Together especially at night around campfires.
Soldiers acted as night watchmen.

Dog wanted to be dog, boy to be boy.
Gabal the Boy dug a hole four feet deep,
As if digging out a bone. Nearby
Folk were very amused and laughed to
Each other at these strange goings on.
The boy jumped in, curled up as if
In a womb and let the dog cover him with sand.
Growling stopped interference.
After ten minutes Gabal the Boy
Burrowed his way into the loose sand until
His tail disappeared. Five minutes later
He came out backwards, paws had changed
To feet, dog legs to human limbs. His right
Arm dragged out Gabal the Dog. Boy was boy,
Dog was dog. Onlookers gasped and didn't
Understand these strange reversals. Two soldiers
Weren't happy and threatened Gabal who
Stared and growled; they backed away.
Their eyes full of fear learned in the space
Of two seconds.

Who knows what the space of two seconds
Can contain in the most secret corners
Of Time's anamorphic universe buried
Between the eyes of every individual
Whether human, insect, bird or snake.
What is known of the Creator of
Misanthropic bye-ways set-up with traps
To catch out functional habits -
The mental bunkbeds and hammocks

Of day to day living. Who is the
Captivating goddess shooting beauty into
Our eyes, blackening our souls, mirroring
Our desires, masturbating our passions,
Feeding our childish dreams bleeping like
A lighthouse on a lost continent found in
The heartland, the heavyland of myth
And nostalgic gardening.

CHAPTER SIXTEEN

GABAL, DOG OF GOD

Nobody seeing these two soldiers
Could be unaware that they had seen
The Divine strike at their soul's chord
And shivering in terror worked their way
Back from Gabal, Dog of God, who having
Tasted humanity realised his transformation
Was a miracle of body and brain. Gabal
Trotted over to his cart, curled up underneath
With one eye open. Boy was also remade.
Not only had he seen the face of man
Through a dog's eye, his mind had
The ways and means and infinite passage
A dog's universe brings. He ran over
And curled up beside his dog and slept
With the sleep of an angel.

Overnight temperatures drop.
Fires go out.
Soldiers catnap.
Stars swim the ancient sea of night.
A town on the move
Hums, chortles, chirrups through
The meanest hours until
A faint light drifts
Above the dark horizon.

The first night people made many celebrations
But as the journey wore on, early to bed and
Early to rise became the weary desert travelers'
Rule. Their wares: spices, glass, damask cloth,
Silks, Persian carpets, gold, silver, and jeweled
Objects, ceramic tiles, clocks, statuary and slaves.
Copies of the Koran. Spies belonging to desert
Raiders who lived in the mountain infiltrated
The camps and caused mischief to wheels
And harnesses. Raiders attacked when the
Caravan train's organization seemed most slack.
Pits in sand were dug and disguised. This
Halted the train which became prey to
Sniping day and night, until soldiers'

Numbers had been reduced enough to make a full assault Successful.
Only the useful were spared.

One night Cabal became aware of
An atmospheric molecular change. He knew all the
Odours of the caravan people, having sniffed
Around each group and been kicked, hit
And occasionally stoned. These people weren't
Fond of dogs, especially one too clever by half.
Beyond a mountainous sand dune
A group of tribesmen were preparing
For a sortie, quiet as the star they
Crept over the highest dune slowly drifting
Their way down its slopes. Sand sprayed
Into the air reflected firelight.
Cabal spied this speckled wonder floating
Free. He smelled bandits' odorous bodies,

Their sweaty clothes, their horsey flesh.
Boy, nuzzled in the ear woke and quickly
Summed up the danger. He told
The nearest soldier who raised the alarm
By juggling three torches. The
Word spread and two hundred soldiers
Were ready, in silence, unsure of where
Fighting would start. Travelers herded
Themselves together. The battle was
Haphazardly fought. Bandits were more
Interested in making noise, creating
Confusion than killing soldiers, inducing fear,
Worry, uncertainty and general alarm.
The raiding party, after a twenty minute
Skirmish ran off to their horses to ride
Back to the main force of two thousand
Horsemen. Through the rest of the night
Traders loaded guns, sharpened swords and
Knives. They knew the horde would
Follow through the next day.

The Commander's name was Ben Hadira.
His face was covered with many scars.
From many battles. Women were greatly
Attracted to his dark skin, fine bone
Structure and fierce black eyes, all which
Added up to a mysterious bravado, an
Underlying worldliness subdued by physical
Battle. Gabal, Dog of God, conversed
Telepathically with this soldier scholar.

To outfox these desert rats, Gabal thought

It best to take a party of two hundred
Men and circle around the main
Body of tribesmen. As they slowly advance
Increasing in pace to a crescendo of
A charge, this main thrust would
Be met head-on by the remaining soldiers.
With mirrors women of the camp could
Blind the horses with sunlight. The
Original two hundred, by now having
Veered off away from the battle would
Circle back and attack the tribesmen
From the other side. Ben Hadira followed
The suggestion and successfully defeated
The enemy with only a quarter of
Their numbers. However, they hadn't been
Destroyed and would return for more
Sneak assaults, depleting one by one
The number of caravans. Soldiers found
Night warfare enervating and spirits
Seeped away. Gabal knew this and
Knocked on wood, a better plan had to be.

Ben Hadira opened the flaps of his
Multicolored, striped, pyramidal
Caravan tent. This formed his headquarters.
Inside, seated around a large glass
Diamond-shaped object set in glowing
Bubbly volcanic translucent stone, were
Four magic dwarfs wearing plain
Grey cloaks and little two inch high
Pillbox hats. They had big black eyes,

Red lipstick and
Rouge on their cheeks and the
Star of Bethlehem on their foreheads.
What Ben wanted was power to turn
His enemies to dust. To pulverize them
With mind power. To wipe his trail clean.
The dwarfs sat there, passive icons of
Man's aggression. Not only had they
Been involved in every major war since
Civilization began but had brought
Disease and famine into their
Repertoire of ills.
They couldn't speak and relied on
The crystal to change color to reflect

Their approval. A petition in the
Form of questions was usually
Required. Colors changed from bright
White through to green to red and then
Black. Ben asked his way through
Three hundred questions hoping for
The final color of approval Lapus
Lazuli blue. Transfixed at the sight
Of it he knew his unrhetorical approach
Had worked and he knew what must
Be done.

He took a two-headed sword and
Crushed each of the dwarfs to pulp.
Extracted their hearts and ate them.
Ben Hadira found himself growing
In size like a genie just released
From a bottle. He quickly left his

Tent running into open space. All the
Time he was growing, reaching fifty,
A hundred, three hundred feet, stopping
At four hundred feet. That was it.
He now had the power to hop,
Skip and jump across the sand dunes,
Gather up or piss on his foes, and
Drown them. This was easier thought
Than achieved. The tribesmen not
Without their own smart shaman
Scattered with the wind. Ben soon
Caught the slow horses, lame ones
Or those trapped in sand. He ate
Them. After all, it was hot and hungry
Work; a body his size could consume
An oasis of water a day.
Two days passed, and nearly two thirds
Of these parasites of the desert had been
Devoured or squashed. The energy required
To complete his task left him
Exhausted on return to the caravan train. It looked
Small, petty, worldly but somehow Holy
And sacred. Of course, he now had
To shrink back or commence to expand
Forever. Gabal watching with a wry grin
On his cheeky doggy lips watched
The enormity-of-it-all striding from
The south kicking up a sandstorm
In his wake. Only Gabal knew the

Secret word to reduce this man ballooning,
But the word was conveniently lost

In his Sub-Conscious mind,
Ben Hadira breathed in once too
Often and started to float into the
Blazing blue sky. Lungs had become
Overlarge and acting like balloons
Carried Ben closer to the edge of the
Atmosphere, where he exploded, scattering
Over the whole area, bones, and skulls,
Of horses and men. It rained blood for
Twenty minutes. The desert bloomed.
Travelers said their prayers.

CHAPTER SEVENTEEN

CITY OF THE MORNING SUN

Gabal the Dog became the
New leader of the caravan train,
By popular vote, after proving it
Was his strategy that saved them
From destruction. He would take them
Through many magical adventures.
Three months passed and soon they were
To arrive at the City of the Morning
Sun. Gabal had only lost two trailers
To bandits. He was patted and stroked
Until his fur shone like a black mirror
But his muscles ached. Close to journey's
End he began yearning for a rest.
To lose his identity, become a nobody,
Just a dog to be given a bone,
Patted, brushed, a chance to chase
Intruders and sleep in the midday sun.
But there was one adventure left.

In the depths of the Saharan
Sand lived three wise worms who
Swam in underground water which
Flowed and shifted according to the Moon's
Cycle. Not only could they scan all the
Books in all the libraries of the world
With telepathic telekinetic ancient winds
But could search and find in the
Hearts of people all their smallest desires.
They honed into the caravan trail and
Picked up Gabal's mind which had so
Many confused desires the worms of the
Desert looked for a simpler case and
Settled on a young woman, a slave,
Being transported as a gift for a prince.
She was seventeen, saw her future
In a flash of a sunset. A guard
Assigned to her had large brown eyes,
Black hair with long curly strands
Falling down his neck. The more she
Saw of him, the more she wanted
Him. Now with the help of newly

Found energy, words encapsulated
With power, visions of destiny,
Sight boosted by the will to change
At all cost; these gave her towering
Confidence, a breach in the cryptic
Prison of cultural reality where she found
Herself marooned. But tides change,
Thank God. One evening she climbed
Down from her wagon. Everybody else

Was either eating or gossiping. She
Stole over to her love who
Stood silently gazing at the stars,
Unaware of the rustling of cloth
Approaching him from behind. Some
Night watch. He was composing a verse
For his beloved back home.

"When I leave this sparkling
Sand of night,
To look elsewhere,
At ground,
At people,
I am reminded of the journey
I make, through the deserts of life,
Looking for, finding
An oasis of beauty, love and goodness,
And you are that oasis
My loveliness
Whom memory of, speeds the time
Of desire but slows my life
To a snail's pace.
Of all these stars the furthest
Is nearer than you seem."

At that moment the young girl
Touches him on the left shoulder.
He spins round startled, nearly stabbing
Her with a knife he kept up his
Sleeve. She falls into his arms. He didn't
Know what to do next. Yet he also had
Great desire. An empty caravan used for
Storage was parked amongst the deep
Shadows of a group of camels and horses

Munching hay. He lifts the girl in his
Arms, kissing her lips quickly. He looks
Around, his heart beating like jungle drums,

His hands shaking like an earthquake,
His eyes dilating like a crimson sea
Anemone, his penis as stiff as a piston,
His skin as sweaty as a turkish bath.
Nobody noticing. He hurries off.
Runs up four steps into the wagon. Places
The girl on the floor. She is passive,
Waiting. He kisses deep into her mouth.
Their tongues slide together like mating
Snakes. He kneels beside her, blushing
Face and holds her sweaty hand.
The young soldier slowly lifts her
Coat and undergarments. As slowly she
Opens her legs as he puts his head
Down to explore new perfumes
Sweet juices and fresh flowers
In the secret garden of this young desiring
Maid. He unbuttons her blouse to cup
In his hand, firm round breasts.
Resting from sublime moistures he
Drank in the hot currents, she breathed.
Now he could no longer wait.
He undressed his lower half. Her
Knees were placed against her chest
Revealing the paradisal valley he was
The first to discover.
He lowered himself, entering with
One thrust. From now until morning

He empties himself of all his juices,
Making up for all those lonely nights
On duty when lust burnt into his very
Bones, when he felt he could split the
Earth with his penis. The girl experienced
For the only time a man who could
Stay in her all night. She quaked,
She shivered, in fever, in ecstatic
Dreaming. Fought like an unbroken horse
To rid herself of his entry;
Scratching, biting, spitting. He used
All force to stay in, or occasionally entering
Her anus when she offered it inadvertently.
Sometimes she cooed for an hour or so,
Mindless of his copulation. Sometimes she
Shook, and shrieked through the
Convulsions of orgasm as if her flesh
Would fall off, her eyes fly out to join

The stars, her breasts challenge the Moon's
Roundness, her juices flood to irrigate
The desert. When all this was over
They both felt like man and woman.
The three magical worms had covered
The wagon with an air of forgetfulness.
Nobody could remember it was there,
Even when the strangest noises
Which they immediately forgot about
Seemed to be coming from somewhere familiar.

He was back on duty by the
Time the sun rose. She crept back

To her caravan feeling like a woman at last.
Her father looked at her with new eyes.
Her mother knew her eyes weren't
Necessary to see something as old
As the hills. At this change they
Said nothing. For their minds had been
Safely untuned, flying into the abyss of
The outcast where those having failed
The straight and narrow wait for
Ridicule, spite and fear. Nevertheless
They cried and screamed at their girl
For the first and last time. The next
Day three old women hobbled over
To her as she lazily drew pictures
In the sand - of warriors, cats, dogs,
Pyramids and mosques. They tied her
Hands and led her away. She wasn't
Seen again by anybody in the caravan
Train.

They were nearing the golden city.
A halo seemed to circle it high above
Almost rivaling the sun in its
Intensity. Lines of people waving and dancing,
Intricate patterned cloth and plaited hair.
This city seemed near; in fact its
Nearness was a mirage, its people
Projections from worldly wise worms
Ruminating on the fantasy of Utopias,
Those inbred kippers belonging to
Smoked areas of the brain.
These dreams passed through every
Infamy of travelers, now tired

And in need of supplies and rest.
All they got was a sinking feeling;
Into sand they sank, deeper and
Deeper, over their wheels, camels
Panicking, struggling to breathe. Children
Suffocating swallowing mouthfuls of golden
Particles, soldiers fleeing but getting
Caught, ever deeper in sandy graves,
Breathless. Within an hour mass
Destruction. Camels survived and odd
Pieces of cloth blown in the sand -
Leaden wind which now crept up
To smooth over the ruffles of death.
Gabal the Dogged and Boy had left
This scene sometime before. Only
Such a masterful dog who knew his
Place in the world could switch to
The wave-length of three mighty worms
Who paraded their talents for all to see.
Gabal had wandered off in sheeps
Clothing with Boy dressed as a
Shepherdess.

They traveled through many nights-.
Until a small settlement was found which
Seemed to drift in a haze of elliptical fits
Like a planet which had lost its
Sun. Gabal and Boy cleared the mist,
Found a home in the sun with
A family of favored fortunes. This is how
Gabal arrived, later to begin a new adventure
With Moon, Gesso, Gas and Low. He was

Now following a donkey away from the great
Temple, into the sea of the unknown.

CHAPTER EIGHTEEN

A DONKEY CALLED GILGAGIGGLE

Gabal called donkey, Gilgagiggle.
He trotted beside his friend over pebbley
Ground. Mosquitoes, flies and bees circled
Incessantly over their heads. Pinnacle-like
Mountains towered two thousand feet above them;
Covered with rock, clinging trees, creepers,
Lliana and giant ferns. Birds of Paradise
And hawks shared the air of these
Sky-bound gardens. The quiet path they
Trod along featured trails of ants, swiftly
Crossing snakes and leeches hanging from
Leaves. Gilgagiggle knew his purpose.
High above the center of his brain
In the memory cells of his past sat
Thoughts which count as the story of his
Life. Brought up in the temple from
Earliest days; born in the middle of summer,
Under a fig-laden tree. His work included
Pulling carts carrying priests, visitors, fruit
And general supplies needed
From the village. When Gilgagiggle was
Five one visitor not only became the
Present witch-doctor but in effect
Carried out a revolution in the neighborhood,
With his bad manners,
Foul breath, free for all sexual drive,
Unwashed hair, long dirty fingernails
And the habit of defecating
In public. Powerful magic. He could

Deflower a virgin at thirty yards. Whip
Coconut cream with a fart. No-one dare
Touch him or drive him away. His
Powerful body odor kept people at a distance.
Animals wouldn't stay in sight. Although
Tall, thin and stiff-looking he could out
Contort a local contortionist, outdance local
Girls, outrun young bucks, outswim crocodiles
And outclimb monkeys. He was called
Drattle, also the name of the dialect
He spoke. Gilgagiggle's first trip with Drattle,

Up to the local temple nearly finished him
And afterward he made his way to the nearest flowering
Bush to breathe its perfume with all his might.
Before a week was out Drattle had the temple
To himself, the village worshipping
His new god, a tubby statue carved
From Ivory. Its eyes huge rubies
As big as the eyes of a leopard.
Gilgagiggle, a curious donkey who
Knew much about his small world
Rather than a little about the world at
Large, walked into the temple one day,
Drank from the holy pool,
Licked the statue all over - falling immediately asleep
He dreamed of life after death, the
Facts of after life, the facts of life
Pertaining to his continent born when the
Wife of God tripped over His nose and
Fell to earth giving birth to Africa before
She died. Her blood became the River Nile,
Her urine turned into Lake Victoria

And skin cells became sand of the deserts.
In life after death Gilgagiggle learned
One golden secret which would enable him
To converse with any animal, insect or
Human. Another trick he turned to his
Advantage consisted of embracing every afterlife
Being and licking their ears. After
A few hundred embraces he had
Absorbed enough listening power to
Know all sounds celestial ether carries.
There is always a waking time.
Gilgagiggle isn't happy to wake.
He aches but immediately his mind
Becomes a cosmic radio. At first
He jumped and kicked wildly, salivating
At the same time. Locals thought him
Rabid. One young novice witchdoctor
Slowed Gilgagiggle down by throwing
Ashes over him. This calmed him
Down and enabled Gilgagiggle to
Learn how to switch on and off
The huge inflow of noise channels.
All that was necessary was the
Registering of an act. If he walked
He could hear insects. If he sat down
He understood bird talk. If he brayed

Once and stood still humans could be
Heard going on and on. Replying to
This one-way traffic took longer
To learn and required one more
Dream. After hard work under
A hot sun Gilgagiggle's keeper,

A young boy eager to learn the
Ways of men was pushing Gilga
(His nickname) because he was
Walking slowly listening to grasshoppers
Talking about the clouds. He began
To dream while supporting this
Reverie. High on a cloud over the
Celestial plains laughter rang out
From the mouth of a lost god; that
Is, all was lost except his mouth.
It whispered sweet words, hummed
Honeyed music, laughed like crashing
Sea. When Gilgagiggle approached
This isomorph of natural depiction
He jumped inside, and covered
In saliva, was baptized, so to speak,
In the tongues of man and animal.
When he woke prodded by a boy
With a sharp stick, he said "Forget
It", and walked on. Later the boy
Understood Gilga and his ways.

CHAPTER NINETEEN

GILGAGIGGLE AND GABAL

Gabal was enjoying his sortie
Amongst the jungle green. Before
Long they hoped to reach a rest house,
Before night, that sleep tight rest for
Aching muscles. Soon they found a cave
With a tall and narrow entrance
Fringed with creepers and ferns.
This seemed the right place to spend
The night. The sun had just reached

The mountain tops, throwing deep jagged shadows
Over the land. Large fruit bats were
Out nibbling at figs and nectar-full flowers.
So dark was the cave it seemed
As if it was a piece of a world
Untouched by light. A darkness which
Penetrated skin, eyes, ears, displaced
Blood, added to one's weight, made
You feel obese, a fatted pig in
The slaughterhouse of existence. And
Time stood quietly murdering hopeful
Thoughts in this black pod of hellish
Name. Gilga and Gabal stood on
The brink of this bastion of negativity.
Behind them the sun shot rays through
Clouds splitting the sky in rosy segments
Of a giant scallop. Mountains flattened
Out into forbidding shapes like giants
Just woken from sleep to roam night
In search of food and fornication.
Coping with the silence of dusk moths
Fluttered over webs of spiders who
Showed small bright lights on their
Abdomens. Snakes sneaked their way to
Peace. Gabal fears his path and future.
A surprise. The black cave doesn't
Lead deep into the mountain but up
To the top. Crude steps cut by aboriginals
Reach the summit where a sacrificial
Altar of granite hacked into a rectangle,

With a groove for blood to drip quietly
Away, waits a victim. To find these

Before long Gabal and Gilga were
Steps the wall of darkness had to be
Passed through. Courage, fortitude,
Forbearance, adrenaline. A luminous
Moth floats past Gilga's nose, doubles
Back to sit on it then leads them
Through the curtain of darkness to the
First step. Moth proceeds as a meandering
Speck, rising out of sight. Gabal decides
To wait no longer. Climbing the steep
Slippery steps is difficult for Gilga
The donkey. Gabal is behind, pushing,
To prevent a downward tumble.
After twelve exhausting hours
First signs of light. Gabal now
Close to exhaustion, stumbles more and
More. Gilga has worn his knees red
Raw. Through an exit they see dawn
Light about to reach the altar. From the
Top they could see deep greensome
Valleys snaking away in mist. Other
Mountains ranged higher disappearing in
Cloud. But the sun found a way through
Striking the altar red. Both
Travelers breathed heavily. Gilga sat on
His haunches, lowered his head and
Slept. They were thirsty, hungry,
Not knowing which way to go. They
Dreamed of finding a haven.

Before long Gabal and Gilga were

Surrounded by squat muscley primitive
Men with huge skulls, hairy smiley
Mouths full of worn-down teeth. They
Hummed together with swaying heads,
To the beat of flames from their campfire.
Were they apparitions or real illusions
Or ghosts of the mind's eye, ancient
Adversaries paying a visit? There was
No time to lose, as one on the
Left with the biggest brain growing
All the time said "I am the Christ."

Another said "I am the Devil". Others,
The Buddha, the Madonna, High
Priest, St. John, St. Michael. Swollen
Heads. Except one whose head shrank
A millimetre a minute. He just spat
Out ritualistic words like blood, time,
God, sacrifice, victim and carried on
Until his head was gone. Another
Who had shouted obscenities turned
Into a ten-foot phallus. Gabal charged
And tore to shreds six of these
Putrifying phantoms spewed from the boil
On a devil's arse, a devil who had
Passed this way and farted over
West Africa. Hence the monadic
Spores were attracted to this mystic
Place, attired themselves with old
Psychic forms which float in places
Where they had best times or worse
Times of their lives. Gabal made short

Work. One fiend remained with eyeballs
The size of melons, eyes which saw
Deep into the recesses of matter,
Past the smallest particles, past
The smallest charges, through sub-
Particles, through black holes into
Rebounding, mirror haunted,
Inverted, infinitely dimensional universes
Called matter of factuals. Gilga raised
His weary body and kicked those
Hyperactive eyes to pieces, shattering
Them into small fragments which floated
Off the mountain top and re-assembled
Into a dodecahedron, fifteen feet high.
A traveling vessel to be magically used.
Gabal and Gilga jumped aboard
As it floated to ground. It was
Propelled by sound and Gabal barked
As he had never barked before,
Leaving behind a scene of carnage
Which as they receded seemed to
Fade like misty memory. The great crystal
Air ship sped towards the sea, Gilga
Eee Awing, when Gabal got tired of
Barking. Natives pointed to the wondrous
Sight, a flying dog and donkey.
Birds weren't afraid and seagulls,

Sparrows, even eagles hitched a free ride.
The sea, once reached, looked calm
And lapped around midday fishermen's
Legs. They were about to pack away

Their catch when one looked up and
Ran in terror as a strange crystal
Object traversed the sky. Reaching
The border of land and sea made
The celestial machine dither. It
Awaited an order.

Gabal thought

"To a dream island please"

Five miles offshore waves grow
Before the coming storm. Crystal ship
Starts to break up, dropping fragments
Here and there. Gabal petrified thinks
Back to 'when'. Gilgagiggle counts
Backwards from infinity.

CHAPTER TWENTY

A SEA DRAGON

A Sea Dragon, conqueror of the world
In a great age long before man,
Rears above the waves, churns the
Sea into a maelstrom.

"So this
Is what you want" he roars,

Scales flying, belching smoke,
Fire and carbon black. He swallows
The unfortunate pair, shattering their
Fragile craft. Down they slide to his
First stomach where they are caught
In the skeleton of a shark. Meanwhile
The Dragon thrashed around in
The sea creating even
Greater storm effects. The only way
Out was on a surge of blood from
A hemorrhage to a vein which pulsed
Through the floor of the stomach.
The Dragon had six hearts with
Enormous pumping power, which was

Needed to overcome the pull of the
Moon creating tides of blood through
The enormous bulk. Gabal gnawed
His way, very slowly, through
The inner linings covering the vein
Beneath them. After much scratching
Chewing and stamping by Gilga,
A green jet from the vein hole
Shot high into stomach space
Carrying Gilga and Gabal
Through the stomach entrance up
The neck to the back of the
Throat. They landed on some cartilage
Ridges and hoped the Dragon would
Spit them out with mouthfuls of
His salty blood. The Dragon's
Mouth was full of ancient teeth
Cracked, chipped and darkly stained.

He was long past the age of self-renewal
And made great commotions for self-
Expression. Gabal and Gilga worked
Their way through Stalactites and
Stalagmites of rock-hard enamel. Suddenly
A powerful rush of air pushed
Them forward out of the mouth into
Open space and blinding daylight. They
Landed in water near the Island of
Dreams a place and time every person
Knows about, because they sleep and
Go there whether they like
It or not. Gilga was still counting
Backwards from infinity so thereby
Maintaining his hold over the reluctant

Dragon which now followed his prey
To the island and lay quietly
Off shore unable to land on an island
Whose domain included death. The silver sand
Was so fine that once disturbed it
Would stay in the air for hours.
There was no wind, breeze or charm
Of air on this island whose beach
Seemed to stretch away to the ends of
The earth. This island had no center
And looked very flat with a delicate
Covering of flowering shrubs inter spread
With palm trees. Wildlife limited to
Monkeys and butterflies. The island traversed
The ocean ribbon-like and had no
Beginning or end. Gabal and Gilga
Began to explore and their pawsteps
Left little clouds as they walked over the beach.
The Dragon had swam off, bored,
Into the deepest valleys under the sea
Where others of his kind lived on,
In their golden past.

CHAPTER TWENTY-ONE

THE ISLAND OF DREAMS

The Island of Dreams wasn't
On any map. It had shrubs, grass,
Thickets of luxuriant flowering jungle,
Butterflies, hummingbirds, nesting birds,
Quick sands, treacherous to man and
Beast; sandcastles, sand-dunes, honeycombed
Sandpits where large clawed crabs lived.
Ready in waiting for prey to slip

Over the edge of their sloping death-
Traps. Some parts showed signs of
Human habitation; foundation stones
Laid by some honorary person, shipwrecks,
A variety of skulls used as nests by seabirds, plastic
Cups and rubber contraceptives. Gilga had
Given up his infinite counting. Gabal was undecided.
They were stranded. Gabal ate birds'
Eggs and was dive-bombed for his
Pleasure. Gilga ate grass.

The Island of Dreams perishes
At the end of each great cycle
Only to be reformed out of the sea
In a new configuration. This process
Happens overnight in midsummer, the
Height of psychic materiality. Gabal
And friend had arrived when the
Island had reached the peak of a
Perfect cycle. Before they could begin
To explore a thousand thousand
Thousand dreams from people of every
Culture a slow disintegration overcame
The length and breadth of what
They could see. Sand began to
Flow into the sea. Trees withered.
Birds flew off in flocks. Crabs died
On the spot, turning into empty
Shells piling up knee-high. An
Electrifying blue sky came lower
And lower. Then an enormous explosive
Flash; a sheet of light, in an

Instant of a second, stretched from
Horizon to horizon. Dog and donkey
Were temporarily blinded. And the
Island was no more. Gabal and Gilga
Found themselves on a makeshift raft on
Tree stumps and reeds floating towards some
Honest land.

The Island of Dreams started
To grow once more. Gilga thought
His dreams could have formed the
First sand to flow back. They had
Missed the true experience available
On that island. If they had arrived
Earlier or a little later then they
Could have seen layers of images
Filtering down from the sky changing
Into finest sand at the last moment
Before touching sea-level. Never-ending
Ideas, confusions, limitless associations
Which almost breathed with energy
As they criss-crossed, interweaved,
Reproduced themselves as
Fast as light. What was seen? Only
Flashes of color falling like water.
Even dreams evolve. Life began on
The Island of Dreams before anywhere
Else. Cosmic dreams of Gods fell
And left patterns matter picked up
And used to make a basis for life.
Even mountains, stones, rivers, waterfalls,
Marshes, glaciers dream. And theirs all

Helped with life. On the Island
Overcrowding takes place and falls
Of color cease. Birds, trees and butterflies
Multiply. Each embody a dream genie.
And magic sand so fine can penetrate
Into bodies through the soul, cleansing
Both. Creatures take on, like hosts,
The life of dreams. At the peak of
A cycle the normality of illusions has
Reached a stasis. Travelers, of land, mind,
Or soul, find this paradox a comfort.
Some try to settle down, build houses,
Collect things and wildlife, but before
They even start on the foundations there is
The giant explosion. No more.

Gabal and Gilga grooming each other
Thought they were safe, unaware their
Raft was being lifted by a wave which had
Risen to fifty feet in thirty seconds.
It sped towards the mainland amid a
Darkening sky of swirling grey clouds
That spiraled, pitched, crashed until
The sky seemed unable to support itself,
And heading for a collapse, threatened
To devour the sea once and for all.
As the mainland approached they
Heard cries of terror, so loud against
The wind. As the now hundred
Feet high wave crested down onto
Villages and farms combined magic
Helped Gabal and Gilga's craft fly

Into the air high above the apocalyptic
Roar. In the aftermath, bodies picked
By vultures floated on choppy lakes;
Crocodiles feasted as never before.
Gabal and Gilga high above the carnage
Flew their craft far away into the desert
Whose dry waves rippled motionless in night's
Peace. They headed north across the
Mediterranean hoping to reach a Scandinavian
Forest and live by a restful blue lake.
The only other exceptional air travelers
Of those days were angel-like creatures
Called Muses who contrary to popular
Belief were numerous and very reproductive.
They exhausted themselves in this activity
Against their will. The method,
Simply described, consisted of
Two ethereal bodies flying higher
Until the atmosphere barely survived.
Then in an embrace, the two bodies
Merge and start a slow fall which
Gathers momentum until the speed of sound is
Reached when the sonic boom splits
The conglomerate body into four younger
Ones that fly off at right angles to
Float until their muse souls recover.
This reproduction continues most of the
Year only interrupted by solar flares.
Meteors burning up in the atmospheric,
Comets and general cosmic disturbances.

The way to escape this cycle is
For a Muse to find a human mind

To attach itself to. More sensitive
The mind the better, more thoughtful the mind
The better, and the longer it can stay
To inspire the longer it is free
Of the sky and reproduction. Sometimes
They leave to reproduce, just to taste
The exquisite embrace which lasts
A week, sometimes a month. Young
Muses flit over heads of humans
Flirting like Cupid with mischievous
Intent. Many a person has fancied
His or herself inspired but the feeling
Subsides the next day. Sometimes
A muse is imprisoned in a mind
Whose power is so great it uses up
All the energy of a muse who doesn't
Live for long after its inspiration dies.
Some are destroyed by shadows of doubt
Which leap from waves and forests
To devour soul-flesh which tastes
Like honeysuckle nectar. Some are
Destroyed by dark thoughts which
Hide under wings of birds and fall
Like stones through the heart of a muse.
The greatest threat comes from Cupid's
Arrows which crisscross the sky at
The speed of light. Enough are launched
To enable every man or woman to
Fall in love. Many are lost in
Collisions over the sea, desert, mountain
And plain, but enough pierce muses
To smite their hearts. Once in love

The muse will travel to icey lands
To die in the snow to preserve tears
Of joy or broken hearts. Their true
Safety is in the human head though
Many a muse will never find a
Suitable home but pines until the day
It dies. There are mutations of Muses
Who have evolved into Goddesses who rule
Quadrants of countries where muses
Are specially employed in the cultivation
Of the genius, becoming more
And more historical.

CHAPTER TWENTY-TWO

MEET A GODDESS

Gabal and Giggle cruise by
A Goddess who jumps aboard and
Meets their minds head-on. They are
Hers. She takes them down to a
Island in the Aegean where they meet
A fate worse than death. A white
Temple gleams high on its pinnacle
Of rock. Flowers and herbs surround a
Cool pool. Gilga chews his way through
A patch of grass. He feels happy and would
Like to stay. Goddess had entered their
Minds. They felt as she felt. Their own
Thoughts became clearer, like melting ice; -
Just as fluid, just as drinkable; possible
To flavour, possible to poison. Human Beings
Lived nearby. They worshipped their
Goddess with sacrifices. Her two historical
Names Extremeter, Mummeter, had been
Reduced to Mer which evolved into Summer.

She didn't herself, care for sacrifice
And preferred spectacles of dance, feasts,
And orgy. Her people were dark, hairy
Short and muscley. Excellent fishermen,
Clever carvers of stone and capable
Of self-defense. A group approached
To tidy up the temple and surrounds
After a night of revelry. Fish-skeleton,
Broken glass, pots, chairs, linen, clothing
And fire-ash were scattered everywhere.
They saw two strangers grazing and
Resting in the sun. A woman from the group
Walked across and asked Gabal
His origins. By courtesy of Goddess a
Language link was established. He replied
That they had flown in from a heavenly
Isle in the capacity of servants to Goddess
Who wished to see what went on in her
Name and if it was worthwhile staying
On, when there were so many undefined
Places with new populations and interests.

Goddess wanted a more down to earh
Account, even though she knew most
Of what was going on. The woman
Wasn't surprised by this. She shrugged,
Walked off to tell the others. They
Too, knew there were plenty of
Goddesses waiting to move from
Colder northern climes where people
Were less able to give so much
Of themselves. The women cleaned the temple
In two hours.
Gabal and Gilga faced a dilemma.

To stay put or rid themselves of
Their paradise spirit. To travel north
They needed a quickly achieved plan of action.
Shadows of giants lay across this land
Even though their bodies were dead.
And decayed. These shadows remained
Attached to the earth for centuries
And accounted for barren land and
Women. To erase their influence the
Right magic is needed. The enormous
Amount of energy released could be put
To many uses, including, Cabal thought
To refuel their flying raft. To find
The correct spell they would have to
Leave one stone unturned. Under
It would be the spell written on parchment.
There are stones and stones. The
Island was four miles long and
Three wide. It contained as many loose
Stones as hairs on a donkey's back.
Boulders as big as houses, fist-sized
Fragments fallen from mountains, benches
Of sea-worn rocks ,and stone walls built
Over centuries. Gilga kicked over a
Stone and didn't expect a miracle.
The task seemed impossible. Cabal
Went to sleep and half-an-hour
Later woke with the answer. He
Picked out a lonely stone behind
A tree. If he turned over all
The stones on the island and left this
One unturned it must conceal the

Spell. A theoretical approach. It worked.
He felt power stream into his paws.

His hair grew an inch and silky soft.
His teeth grew sharper and whiter.
His ears heard the faintest heartbeat.
His eyes spied the farthest sparrow.
He could spring the length of the island.
He felt strong enough to levitate
Their raft into the high air streams.
Strong enough to empty Gilga of
An alien mentality and set his
Own mind at rest.

Island people, curious by nature,
Became more and more interested in
Their visitors. Although used to passing
Wizards, magicians, pagan priests, magical
Animals were quite rare. If they could
Be caught they would make fine circus acts or
Performing animals once their powers
Had been neutralized. One islander
Fancied his chances. Gabal had
Been renewed in body and soul.
Goddess had to vacate her host. Her
Power was less than before and by
Mutual consent they departed. The
Islander planned his attack. He brought
Friends and a large net. Organized a
Trap near the raft. Gabal smelt
Smoke and ran to his craft, found
Himself surrounded with his back to
The flames. He leaped into the flames

And kicked pieces of burning wood
At his hunters. The islander looked
Even more impressed at a dog who
Could defy fire. He knew this dog
Must be his alone. Gabal rushed away
To find Gilga, who was under attack
By men trying to jump on him,
Muzzle him, tie his legs and tail. Gabal
Lunged at the throat of one, snapped off
The nose of another, a finger,
A thumb. Six men carrying a net
Led the attack. Four lunged
With Tridents. Gabal and Gilga, now untied,
Face the net and waving prongs.
Four years from captivity, no retreat.
They freeze, then leap a metaphoric
Leap high over the enemy, who drop

Their weapons in disbelief and insignificance
At the acts of this mighty dog. The
Story spread over the whole island before
Supper. Gilga grazed by a stream
When a rush of air overhead
Distracted him. Looking up, Gabal
Was flying at two hundred feet.
Then made a sudden landing by
Dropping straight down, right beside
Gilga. He crawled underneath the donkey
And took off with a donkey on his back.
This sight constituted the world
Picture for Islanders at that period.
The burnt craft had turned into
A unique fireball which had risen

To a hundred feet above the Temple.
Gabal entered with his passenger.
Islanders, who had gathered, gasped and
Cried at the miracle before them. The apparition
Moved forward slowly, then with a
Loud explosion shot out of sight leaving
Behind a hysterical crowd who ran to
The Temple to pray to their new Goddess.
The old one had left for the mainland
Bored with the fishermen and peasant
Attitudes. The Temple looked lost.

CHAPTER TWENTY-THREE

SAFE

Traveling at a thousand feet
Following contours, climbing mountains,
Terrifying ships, scarring eagles, lighting
The night of shepherds, this flaming
Star became a legend of hallucination.
The final landing in a great forest
In present-day north-east Poland
Was as spectacular as a meteor
Crashing, of lightening striking twice
In the same place. More than a few
Trees were knocked down. Forest hunters
Hardly daring to return to that area.
As soon as the flames subsided
Gabal and Gilga left the craft and
Walked to find a home. They were
Startled by cold and dampness, but soon
Acclimatized themselves by growing fur.
The clean air and untroubled trees
Gave them great joy. They walked, ran,
Pranced and jumped around in this
Beautiful new world. Here they lived

Together, untamed, unmolested and
Mostly undisturbed. Sometimes Gabal
Would lead a pack of wolves out
Of interest. He would win leadership
Without killing the old leader who
Would then take over again once Gabal left.
They lived in a cave under a pile
Of rocks. Gilgagiggle became a source
Of magic and magical stories for
Forest people. It was rumored he
Could cure warts and ugliness, blindness,
Sterility and lameness. People brought
Hay bundles from outside the forest as presents,
Sometimes milk, sometimes merriment in their
Eyes. In time understanding of the moment
Dog and Donkey had passed through
Their lives. Peace had been chosen,
The biology of passion overturned. They
Had run through a fearsome gauntlet,

Found it a false parade of power.
Their pension was a proud reward,
A gift from the fire they'd borrowed,
The carriage of spells which had
Housed their ambition. Fleeting lives!
A tandem path which had become
A spiral then a maze then a single
Line to a wilder place.
Singers made audiences cry, shout
"More",
Stamp feet until actors once again
Paraded the story from beginnings to ends
And the means of minds who watched

The show knew it was better to live,
Not hurrying to die, than carry themselves
From morning to evening, thinking of
Shallow truths in graves where patrons
Prayed. What dogs our days? Chaperones
The donkey of spirit who guards
The early warning limit? They lived
Their lives beyond a normal old age.
Gabal was very old before he gave
Up hunting with wolves. Gilgagiggle,
A legend at death had a ghost who
Kicked down doors at inns. Gabal's
Ghost led lost children home.

'At the moistest hours
Of turmoil tribe,
Dig deep into sleep
To wrench the ladle
From handiest man,
Woman or child
Who bangs the can
And biffs the cradle.
In a drastic dance,
Holly dolly,
Who gets the kiss,
The music macabre,
The burning bliss?
What are the chances?
Who shares the answers
Cannot know.
Certainty was a curiosity
The look of an hour
A sad affair.
Gabal and Gilga

Had met ends meet.
Apotheascetica, their guide in the after-world
Had the mark of an angel. A delicate
Creature who threw out phonies, a
Hundred at a time. She loved these
Two animals of time and made them safe.'

CHAPTER TWENTY-FOUR

GAS JENNY FALCON

Gas Jenny Falcon watched alone
Gabal and donkey leave the Temple
For the green high ground of jungle
Cover. Her escape home to the Nineteen-
Eighties started with a descent into a well.
The high priest took Gas by the
Hand, pulled her roughly to the
Hole in the ground surrounded by
Grass and spiky straggling bushes.
She waved goodbye to the remaining
Four who seemed like statues waiting
For pedestals, so they could take their
Place in the world.

The well had a ladder tied to
Its side. Gas soon felt cold. She
Found descending easy. She had climbed
Down a hundred feet, and there was
Still no sign of water except drips
And flows from cracks. Light above
Was now no bigger than a silver
Coin or a thimble of snow. At last
Her feet came to the end of the ladder.
What next? Very warm water.

And a strong current swirling at the
Base of the well. She held her
Breath and dropped in. Immediately
Swept under a rock along a
Corridor and into a cavern that
Stretched as far as the eye could
See. Illumination was very faint, mostly
On the end of entangled tree roots, living
Nodules of light. Gas was a good swimmer
In warm water. Easy survival. Occasionally
She would hang on to a branch to rest
Until the even current dragged her away.
Lightly dressed, she wasn't weighed down.
The longer she stayed, the safer she
Felt. The well was a natural
Formation of volcanic origin and had

Been adapted by man. Gas felt
She had traveled about eight miles
When the water stopped flowing
With much strength. She trod
Water and looked around, noticing
That hundreds of pipes from the ceiling
Of the cavern were drawing up water.
Except for a small exit about
Two foot square the water was
Dammed but not building up.
Gas swam to the side, and found a ledge.
She levered herself onto it and rested.
Her eyes, sharper now, could pick
Out thousands of pipes drawing water
Either for irrigation or drinking.
Across the eddying water Gas spies

A stairway. She swims to it,
Against the current, more dangerous
Now it has nowhere to go.
The stairs are small and seem made
For pygmies or little people. Her
Clothes are in rags. The outline
Of her figure in the modular light
Seems potent of a magical creed.
A metaphysical paradox of evolution.
A twilight of creation whose death
Meets the eye. A serpentine line
Drawn with parallax artistry by
A creator hidden from his prejudiced
Hand. She rose step by step in her
Glory. Higher up she looked back.
Her eyes felt very tired. Reflected
Lights on water made her dizzy.
She sat down and rested five minutes.
At the last step a locked door.
She banged on it and shouted for help.
Then fell asleep. When she awoke
The door was open. A short black
Man stood there almost naked.
He beckoned with his hand.
Gas followed him into the warm sun,
And humid air, through a long
Flowering tree grove to face
A city built of gold.

'Beyond the golden gates of her eyes,
Her true body spelled out,

Like a blizzard,
Gifts of sight,
What prince of the golden city
Wouldn't fall under the spell
Of passion, spelled out
Like change of seasons
Or phases of the moon.'

Gas was born hard at work
Screaming and kicking into a room
Where all sorts of adults stood about
Looking pleased. Her parents, North
London upper-middle-class, intellectual.
Gas Jenny Falcon was thought to be a
Beautiful child with the intelligence
Of a panther or a leopard: the way
She walked so early and talked
Spoonfuls at mummy and daddy.
She was early in saying 'please,' 'thank-you,'
Opening doors, opening books.
Later she went to a private school for
Junior education and showed much promise.
Later still, a public school for girls
Who dreamt of handsome boys and
Rich men. Her friends came from
All corners of the globe, from wealthy
Families. Then came puberty; blood,
Breasts and boys; a fanciable face
And figure, an electric brain.
Late teens: school rebel, archetypal
Anarchist of gilded legend. At
Sixteen, on holiday in Switzerland,

She met a university professor whom
She fancied more than the man
On the moon; they went to bed in
A field of spring corn. He took her
From behind and then in the missionary
Position, and thought her as hot as
Six Indian curries. Their session lasted
All afternoon much to the joy of a farmer
And his hand. Gas became pregnant
By mistake, having forgotten to take
Her pill. Abortion in a clinic high
In the mountains. Afterward her holiday
Progressed successfully and she never saw lover
Boy again. Back at school work
Required for university entrance, Oxford

Or Cambridge. By now her talents
Dominated the school; magazines,
Stories, debates and gossip. Oxford was
A waggle. Gas took three degrees
In English, Philosophy and Psychology.
At twenty two an associate professor
In New York; in a winter she wrote one short
Novel and nine short stories. She met
Moon in London, in a pub. After
Sex, they teamed up and married
Becoming a celebrated couple on the
New York-London axis. They became
Hot property in the dinner guest
Market. No children yet. They
Took a Saharan holiday in a fashionable
Resort in a reborn desert, shrinking

162
In the last decade of a formidable
Century. Then the adventure began
Now she faces a golden city whose
Spires and domes and mud huts blind a
Newcomer's first sight. She followed
The short black man on a red earth
Road beaten hard by decades of use.

CHAPTER TWENTY-FIVE

TO PLEASE ETERNITY

"My name is Mofoto - first guide
Of the Ancient City of Cara, founded
By migrants who came through forests where
Now there are deserts. They were
Giants who defeated a tribe of monsters
Who guarded the goldfields this city
Was built on; the source of its wealth.
It is a city that has gone beyond
History and now exists to please Eternity,
Whose inhabitants stay here on visits
To see old earth. Their rooms have
Furniture wholly or partly made of gold.
Every building of importance is gold
Clad. The giants died out as the
Climate became hotter and descendants
Of their slaves took over. My sort.
We are a short people but well
Skilled in knowledge of the universe.
Although we can't see our guests.
We know they are there because the gold
Is worn away so quickly. Even
Woven gold sheets sometimes go
Missing. We built our city, as
It stands now, over two thousand years

Ago. Our early enemies failed
To defeat us and passed into
History. You are the first visitor
For a hundred years. You will be
Highly sought after by princes and
Chiefs of various tribes who will
Either try to buy you or fight
In tournaments for your favors.
They each have harems and
Constantly try to embellish their collection
Of women. Princesses have kennels
Of men whom they use as they wish.
The Emperor of this city is
Never seen. He lives his life as a
Monk and scholar in an inner temple.

He is elected for life by all those
Over thirty, and he must be
At least forty. We have a warrior
Chief and a council of government
And committee for each segment
Of the city. Functions like water
And waste are dealt with by
Separate groups who co-operate
With segment committees. There is
No money here. Only words are
Considered currency. Individuals who
Speak well, who play with words to
Create ideas; these people appeal to
Us most and are honored in
Every home. Construction work is
Carried out by every able man
Who must complete a period in

Each area of necessity, like making
Roads, repairing buildings, farming,
Collecting food. Women look after
Children in groups and write
The books of records of visitors
From eternity. They also design
Our houses and furniture, paint
Our walls and tell stories. Men lead
The way in the physical. A woman
Can be Emperor".

"I'm glad to hear it
Where are you taking me ?"

"To meet the council. First they will
Clothe you in a golden
Robe. Then you will eat and
Listen to music and songs in
A great hall. After that you will
Be expected to tell your story
And where you are going."

"I hope to go home,
Actually. I was only on holiday.
It seems like an eternity
Since I was swimming
In a hot pool thinking
Up the plot of my next Novel."

"People are beginning to gather.
Note we dress naked except
For loincloths. Our climate
Is most congenial and our
Skins deepest black. By now
One or two visitors from eternity

Will be following us. They can
Exist here because of the property
Of gold which allows them to
Be here without harm in the material
World, which after all is a charade
For senses, a play on veils, a ritual
Of Gods rehearsed every moment.
One will see the true play of
Things probably after death. Our
Visitors don't give anything away.
They don't talk but listen and
Signal approval by tapping our
Knees which jump with reflex
Action. This causes much amusement
To children."

"I have no children but
When I return, I will have
Many."

"If you leave! The last visitor
Had to stay till the end
Of his life. A golden world
Makes us long-lived and I
Am over ninety."

Gas was a center of attraction, people
Walking behind her, through narrow
Streets with high golden-walled
Houses. People leaned out of the windows
Smiling and laughing. A happy people
Weaving ivory jewelry and plaited
Hair. Cara wasn't large: about half
A mile by a quarter. The focus

Seemed to be a large domed hall
With tall, perhaps two hundred
Feet towers on four corners. Other
Buildings consisted of towers or rectangular
Houses. And they shone so brightly

Birds wouldn't fly near them. No
Doors. Such trust. Gas asked about
Thieves and punishment.

Mofoto.

"Any person who harms
Another member of our city
Out of anger or greed is punished
By deprivation of food. After a month
Or so when they are close to death
They are slowly brought back again
To normal strength and released."

CHAPTER TWENTY-SIX

GAS IN THE CITY OF CARA

Mountains called 'Teeth of the World
Dragon' overlooked Cara from the West.
To the east dry dusty hills,
Waterless and beyond them, Mountains
Of the desert. Gas entered the
Glorious Hall of this ancient world
Where people shone delight in living
Which infused a forgetfulness of
Things past.

'There are many wild purples
To bring in the beauty of a day
When stones as heads
Bury the box of woes.
Go on, tell the mansion
Of a dream, tell its many

Doors that standing there,
Looking in, will enter the major
Of an eye, dance of a coy
Skeleton. Act on: more among
The very things which twitch
And twiddle the faces you might.
Cannibals are pretty in the face
Of hunger. Eat your own,
The flavor is right.
By a stream, you pitch
An ornament, a palace
Of bears who dance blind
And slain. A meteor burns
Itself out. You wonder who
Is coming too; A godsend.'

Gas felt powerfully pretty.
Her hair loved its golden
Light. Her body now revealed
To all was applauded by men
And women. And when she
Spoke their language, a miracle
Occurred at hand. It was
Solely that she was mighty clever

And had learned it while
Walking up the strand.

Gas was asked to sit down
On a sculpted redwood chair,
Cushioned with bundled
Hair taken from dead people and
Monkeys. Light shone through

Coloured glass filters placed in the
Dome, spiraling from the apex to the
Base. The glass crudely made in
Varying thicknesses. Animal bones had been
Embedded in a mortar frieze below the
Dome. All around, people stared,
Chatted, smiled, laughed, smoked, chewed,
Waited for the examination of the guest.
A recorder, with paper and a quill
Pen, entered, followed by the head man
Always called Carat. He approached
With speed, sat down on a golden
Chair. The scribe sat on the hard
Earth floor. Carat asked the first
Question.

"You arrived by an underground
River which carried you for
Some distance from a particular
Place. Can you describe
A Night on another planet
After its life is half over?"

Gas thought for a minute, unsure
Of her feelings, but she overcame
Them and answered

"There are three stockings
I fill for Christmas
Three, four, many
Associations.
Airs of tranquil sheep
Bleat over the grass of doves.
Damp excuses bargain away

The error of sleep.
Dance on the floor's latent
Scattered names.
Top-up tanks of savage dreaming.

Where there are flowers in
Eyeballs, leaves babying their earth,
Sure is the night, blackbell
Of a bean feast, patriot of a trump card,
Cash and woe,
Explorer of images,
Explorer of chains
And claims to a landscape
Of hatredness, punch drunk
Painter drunk,
But night can hide
From itself except
Where it begins and ends."

Carat understood and waved his hand
By his ear. Gas's speech received
A standing ovation.

"My next question. Your body is
Most beautiful and much admired
By women hunting princes of this
City. Tell me about the Nature of
War!"

"When I was a child
The children next door
Hunted in droves, like
Doves chasing butterflies
Over poppy fields in the aftermath

Of a harvest. I chose my friends
Because they had dirty faces
And sticky hands, walked in
Cartwheels and sold the
Produce of person
To a lazy teacher.
We were young at the gates
Of heaven.
When older legs stamped
On the message of good
We waited, hoping to bless
A new beginning but couldn't,
Like a child eating a beefsteak
Sure to break some teeth.
It was news. When I was sick
In the ears, a drummer would
Drum home his message.
I learned it fast and

By heart. I wasn't sure
If the next line equaled day.
It began again. To this minute
I remember when and look
No further than the nearest
Lake to float hopes like dead
Sparrows into its center,
For the pike are always hungry."

Gas received another applause and
Began to feel tired but tried not
To slump in her chair,
Deliberately kept her back straight

And chin up. Carat's next question,

"You are obviously very clever, learned
And experienced; creatively productive.
Could you explain how you see
The shape of clouds?"

"When I am old
I'll sit on a chair
On the highest mountain
Known to peoples of the plains
And watch like a quiet, alert cat.
As a young woman, now and
Then, face like a burnt cake,
An apple pie or a roast lamb,
Sure as an arrow, as tree bark,
Or the Garden of Eden,
If I wish to pass water on truth,
Smother the only fire of a man's
Heart, I shouldn't wonder
You ask me questions
That removes the skin of an orange."

More applause. Gas rose and walked
Out, feeling she deserved a break
She was escorted to a rest house
For women, where she fell asleep.
Ten hours later she woke feeling
Washed out. Two youthful assistants
Offered her food and drink, then
Themselves. It was a custom in rest
Houses for young girls to offer their
Bodies to older women. The threesome
Cavorted and laughed for an hour

Tasting the sweetness of desire before
Father time finishes Life. This sensual
Playtime revived Gas, who was washed
With fragrant water by the two girls.

Taking stock of circumstances,
Gas thought it best not to pursue a
Thorough investigation of this dear city.
She had no intention of becoming someone's
Prize or a philosopher performer.
She wanted to get away.
A knock on the door. In comes
Chief guide who bows and pulls
Both earlobes, first the right, then
The left. An anticlockwise rub on
His stomach and then his forehead.

"You must follow me to spent the
Next few days in Carat's palace.
There to meet his family and friends
And perhaps to hear of your future.
Also, this is the hunting season.
You will probably be asked to accompany
The princess in a chariot tomorrow."

Gas wasn't too displeased at being
Obliged to follow and felt a chance
To leave the city legitimately would
Enable her to make a quick survey
Of escape routes. On the street she still
Attracted the curious but a new oratorial
Star had risen overnight and crowds
Flocked to watch him combat

Older professionals who did their
Best to make sure new styles
Didn't catch on. Gas was led to
A circular space, a sort of seven
Dials containing horses for hire.
These trotted out of the city
To distant villages and landmarks.
This horse hire business was run by
The army such as it was. Cara had
No formal army, or police only bands
Of volunteers who served for a year
After six months of tough training
In jungle-covered mountains.
Men and women came forward

For this work. The essential defense
Force being unknown. Chance Strangers,
Adventurers, explorers were either absorbed
Or killed. No major expedition for centuries
Had found its way to Cara. It had
Remained a legend, a rumor of
Incomplete mythologies. Gas and
Guide traveled in a northerly
Direction past market stalls selling
Jungle fruit, river fish, brightly
Colored clothes and flowers. Today
The sky was clear, the sun blazed
Like mystical fires of the desert forge
Known to turn people blind when they
Happen to erupt, not too often, thankfully.
Gas traveled, hopefully. She wasn't
Sure how to take these deeply black,
Anciently civilized people. There was a
Brooding that underlay the happiness

And eagerness of the prevalent lifestyle
She would be surprised if there wasn't
A skeleton in the temple. A left-
Handed god that demanded sacrificially
Virgins or children or herds of sheep
And goats. Her guide said nothing
To her even though he rode along
Side all the way. Although outlying
Buildings were ordinary dwellings there
Were no signs of slums or poor
Quarters. People smiled and waved, children
Handed sweets covered in gold foil.
Gas mused that streets were hard
And unpaved. She wondered where
Their gold came from. Perhaps they
Were particularly successful alchemists.
But it seemed unlikely. They were involved
In language and not science in any profound
Way. They loved decorative rugs
With arabesque designs based on leaves
And fruit. They painted the inside
Of buildings with stories and fables of daily life.
Clay sculptures, hardened in the sun, were
Painted and some were fired stonehard.
They had no watches other than a
Rudimentary sundial or weapons above
Spears, bows and arrows. Gas
On her dark red horse with a white

Patch on its forehead saw that Cara city
Had ended. She turned around, gleaming

Domes and towers clustered like friends
Against a background of purple-green
Mountains, which looked more unreal
Than she felt. Standing before her across
A shallow lake, Carat's Palace. It was a castle
On stilts, built recently. Every new
Carat had one built to their design.
A welcoming party crossed the lake in
A broad shallow reed boat, about thirty
Feet long with six oarsmen. The party
Included two princes, three princesses, seven
Children and four wives belonging to Carat.
Gas and guide dismounted, went to the
Lakeside, walked along a jetty and felt
Different. She climbed into the boat,
Kissed the ladies, pulled ears with the
Men, stroked a great hound, a friendly
Animal and sat in the stern until they
Arrived on the other side. Goldfish
Wallowed in the sunlight and weeds.
Small darting silverbacks jumped after flies.
Carat's palace wasn't made of gold but
Mud and straw packed between timber
Frames. It contained two domes cleverly
Constructed out of crystal chunks, pieced
Together with a cement resin tapped from
Secret jungle trees. It appeared that Carat
Wasn't to be given any ideas of grandeur
And remained an intellectual symbol
Who was to rule wisely with humility
In its true sense.

The mouse who falls into a trail of marching
Ants. The writer whose manuscript
Is lost before publication. A general
Who wins a battle but loses a war.
A critic who writes off a play which
Becomes a classic. The humility a
Carat develops when his reign is over
And he goes to live in the temple as
An old servant to worshippers. That time
Was a long way off and the Carat
Was newly appointed and happy in his fortune.
It was the custom in Cara
For an entertainment to be a feature

Of each room so a guest would pass
Through the whole house, amused,
Thoughtful or laughing. By now Gas
Was used to her almost naked condition,
Wearing only a loose loin cloth and a
Neck towel to dry perspiration or wave
Away flies and mosquitoes. Climbing
Steps into a long room, Gas was asked to
Walk in first. The rest of the party
Followed, two by two. A hall with
Three naked dancers, chanting as
They slowly, to the rhythm of a stringed
Shell, entwined and untwined their lithe bodies
Like snakes in a box, like monkeys
In a cage. They were chanting lyrics of an ancient
Poet who wrote on stones the story
Of shadows, how they advanced in the
Natural world, evolved and became

Fixtures of light.

"Before my eyes
You light up objects
I first saw
When I was born
Panther of the Pantheon,
Part of the Parthenon,
Outcrop of the Acropolis,
A crab on Parnassus.
You built before my eyes
A piecemeal world
I had to dismantle
To show beyond
The doubt of a shadow
That I could shadow box,
Follow in your shadow,
Become the bacteria factor
Of a shadow,
A shadow cancer.
I was born to wield the dark,
Like an eyelid on the sun,
Like a child who hides
Without hiding.
My eyes became suns,
Became weary for nights,
Learned dusks by heart,
Announced mornings to
Tree spirits bruised by

Cold. There were journeys
Made, splayed paths
Chosen at random

By tossing twigs into the wind,
Chasing a bee all the way home,
Counting ants on fallen fruit.
Creatures of night.
At home with a bat
Hanging upside down.
He finds his way by returning sound.
Or the moth as happy
As a disappearing moon
Until a flame sanctions his doom.
I was happy lost in a corner
Of a room, a wood or forest.
Now, the day, I walk along
Burnt avenues. So it is stolen,
I serve the warning, dead days."

Gas began to applaud after they stood
Still. She watched as they were ignored
By Carat and Company, who wandered
Into a central sitting area. A play
Was in progress, story of a young
Girl who laughed at the jokes of her
Uncle who died in a jungle. Killed
By a leopard who was no more than
A leopard. She wasn't able to laugh
Anymore after that. Until a young
Man who could show warriors courage,
Now and again, came to her rescue.
Not only did he kiss her in front
Of her father but carried her off
To his hideout where he practiced
Fasting and experienced visions. She

Still couldn't laugh but began to love
A little. Then she began to laugh at
Love. The more she loved, the more
She laughed. The young man turned
Old as she turned wife and mother.
Now the play began in earnest.
Chaos in the home, wild tangles
Of family wrangles. Food and fear,
Fire and failure. All was played
Highly painted and panting breaths
Breathed out words as fast as a

Woodpecker pecks or a hummingbird
Hums. As the players pulled their
Ears and collapsed on the floor
To rest by crossing legs in a lotus
Position and folding arms, Gas
Was eating and drinking fruits of
Mountain jungle; the Haduma, a fruit
The size of an orange, only with hard pink skin
And yellow pips, white flesh as soft as
Cottonwool and wet as pear. The Crifta
A long spiraling fruit; a blue-green skin,
Crinkled and spiney, Lime colored flesh
As sweet as honey. Gas looked like
A Goddess with her legs crossed,
Pink pointed breasts, long golden hair
Flowing around her shoulders, the contrast
With blackest skins which reflected light
Like mirrors from the blind planet.
Men looked at her, wondering how
It is between her legs, the place
Where all desire begins. Gas felt
Uncomfortable, knowing what they thought

And how they would like to act
On those thoughts later in the day.
In the next room a naked poet
Stands on a table. He juggles
Three fruits and recites his own work
Under his breath but audible to those
With ears to hear. Carat and crowd
Crowd round, hoping to hear the poet's
Voice. Children try to remain silent,
Solemnly silent as he drones on.
Gas looks out a window across
To the city smoldering in a
Sunset. She puzzles over the words
She picks up from the standing Poet.

"Each minute of a heatwave,
I pander to a lonely entrance,
To a world whose bridges
Can never be burst,
Whose parts contain wonderful
Contraptions which open up
Learning to children
Who come from wombs
Which hang from Trees
Of Life.

By the seconds of night
In a heatwave, I see this
World whose rivers run in
Circles, whose towns haven't
Words 'lonely' or 'poor'.
And forests grow untouched,
Regulating rain. Lakes feed
The people. Lakes which

Separate towns and are as
Clean as springs in the wildest
Mountains. Roads are free of
Dangerous vehicles. Schooling
For all. Nobody stops learning
Until sitting in the warm sun
Watching nature is all they desire.
The people enjoy steady peace
Far above the failure of war.
Women work as they please
Men will fight to defend
Their homes. Animals are
Free from human greed
And roam or settle
Where they please.
They live their natures
To the full, flying wolves,
Burrowing birds, leaf-eating
Lions and fierce rabbits
Who doesn't worry about the tail.
If angry minds collapse
I fear explosive saints
Who chews into sacred places
With bare crucifix teeth.
Holy mothers will jump at the sight
Of babies who live like beavers
In the streams of summer.
Rich fires will dash over
Plains scorching libraries
Like waterfalls of locusts
Flooding harvests. Please

Enter the next room."

The last room before feast-time
And sleep time consisted of a large play
Area where children acted out legends.
It had bamboo walls and hardened tiles,
Painted with circular patterns, ceilings

Covered with characters from myths
Like First God of Cara Endope and
First Goddess called Quodope,
And the children acted
Story of how the world was created.

"A cosmic shudder of the first
Nothingness,
Void of thought,
No idea, no matter;
The shudder set off
By an infinitesimally small
Possibility that something
Infinitesimally big might happen,
Created a movement which
Carried a seed of hope
Into the center of the void.
It grew until it unbalanced
The void which began to spin,
Faster and faster, creating
Negatives and positives which
Clustered at the center,
Bound to each other.
The void span so fast
There was an explosion so vast
It sent minuses and pluses
On their way and so created

Time. Each pair became
A seed of matter which was
Still more an article of hope
Than faith. The void became
Space-under-Time and stopped
Spinning. Seeds of matter gathered
Together while traveling and
The universe began, snappily enough.
Soon an element appeared,
Happy to be something;
Hope turned to faith,
Leader of a band.
Later came stars, galaxies
And light. Planets are objects
Of faith and breeding grounds
For life, which is what the void
Couldn't avoid
Because matter is happy
Wherever it is,
Whatever it is.

Echoes of the first shudder
Came to life and reproduced
What mattered.
Eventually, after many stops
Came man.
Hopeless, faithless, and loveless
But full of shudders.
I shudder to think I matter
Is the best he can say."

Gas laughed at the children
And went to the feast.

In the face of anger of food
Which doesn't like being eaten, Gas
Sat down on the floor, either
Side of her two youngsters, eyes
Popping out of heads, gleaning the
Goodies. There was a free for all and
No manners. These people let loose
Emotions on food, assaulting it with
Their fists before quietening down
To a solemn feast. Leftovers were
Thrown to wild pigs. Conversation
Followed. Gas, carefully, to the Carat

"Why do you treat your food so?"

"My dear, you are a stranger here.
In the great days of this civilization
Say two thousand years ago, when Cara
City was built, food was plentiful
And all tastes this planet can offer
Were available. Chefs and Cooks were highly
Prized. Their training was long and
They had to be able to cook a
Mastermeal, with ingredients found in a
Jungle, on a campfire and with no
Water, other than plant juices. Passing
This final test they were admitted
Into palaces and wealthy homes.
As decades and centuries passed
Food came to symbolize, along with
A growing language, higher and
Higher status. Decline set when the
Climate changed. It became drier.

Supplies fell, in variety and quantity.
Shortages were common. A social
Reaction set in. A less solemn and
Pleasurable attitude developed. The ritual
Of eating degenerated for a few centuries.
About two hundred years ago the
Then Carat read in a very old
Manuscript of how founders of Cara
Would pummel food before eating,
To help with chewing and digestion.
He decided to adopt this behavior
As his signature of presence.
Before long, people enjoyed the activity
As a means of ridding themselves of
Aggression. The therapeutic value is
Enormous and people are said to
Enjoy sex more than usual afterward."

CHAPTER TWENTY-SEVEN

GAS FLEES THE GOLDEN UTOPIA

Gas pondered on the question of sex.
Always of interest, especially in lost
Civilizations. How do they stop inbreeding?
Is incest allowed? She continued

"And what about sex. Are there strict Codes?"

"We dress little. Our bodies are free,
Untainted. A man can marry more
Than one woman, as many as he can
Afford. Two or more men can live
With two or more women. There is
Men only and women only. No woman
Under the age of puberty can marry.
The unattached are left to follow their
Desires. There are no brothels or prostitutes.

Rape is punished by exile to the
Desert. Incest also. We bring in
Young girls to supplement our
Needs, trading them for gold. Some
Sects practice the arts of love more
Thoroughly than the rest of us. They
Write books, live in communes refining
The delights of sexual practices."

If it was time to sleep, it was
Time to think of escaping to the desert.
Gas didn't fancy staying in this
Golden utopia any longer. She found it
Too sunny, too sexy, too rich, too hungry,
And she couldn't fathom why everyone
Was happy. Early morning she would escape
From her room, out the window,
Down the stilts into a canoe; paddle
Across the lake away from the city
To the edge of the desert, which
Because of a rare rainstorm, was green
Pink and blue. Flowers speedily growing
Through their cycle, harvested by
Bees and insects which rush to the
Desert on such occasions. They are

Followed by birds of all sorts which
Feed on nectar as well as insects.
Hawks and eagles follow the birds
Finding easy pickings amongst the
Foragers. Children pick flowers and
Adults collect precious herbs to cure
The ills of aging, leprosy, typhoid

And cholera. However, Cara was a
Healthy city with fresh clean water
And an efficient waste system. Even so
There had been epidemics in the
Distant past and medicine was stockpiled.
Some plants reached ten feet in
Two days and withered on the fourth
After seeds had been scattered.
Gas wandered through this field of
Flowers unsure of her future.

Gas felt lost. She trod
Beautiful petals into sand,
Ruining the reproductive chances of many
A flower. After tramping for a mile
Or so, wondering if she would be
Followed and returned into captivity
She sat down cross-legged and
Started a flower chain. The day
Shortened. In a vacuous dream she
Continued the chain which had
Reached many feet long. Back at
Cara news of her disappearance
Provided opportunity for public debates
And verbal fireworks. Everyone was
Happy to be able to show off their
Rhetoric. Bring her back. Let her go.
Punish her. Educate her. Send her
Away. And so on.

Carat sent two hunters after her.
From her revelry of daisy chaining

Gas picked up the faint sound of barking.
The linked flowers had become so long
She was covered in daisies up to her
Neck. She wondered what was happening.
Why had she gone on so long;
Splitting stems, threading;
'He loves me,' 'He loves me not'.
Then slowly but

Certainly, seen with her own eyes,
The daisy chain rose like a snake
And encircled her body, spiraling
From her neck downwards, tying both
Her ankles together. The rest rose
Into the air, hauling up Gas and
Entwining her at the same time. When
Fully wound, only her head showed.
Below was a large bare patch where
All the flowers had been picked.
Like a missile, an Interflora,
Gas zoomed across the sky towards
Cara, hovered long enough for crowds
To hear a lecture on apparitions and
The philosophy of phenomenology.

'A thing seen is not only believed
To be seen but seen to be believed'.

'Everything seen leads to the sea of
Doubt'.

'A seer is one blessed with second
Sight, the minds' eye which sees
Around corners, sees events before
They happen, sees a connection
Between observations which nobody
Has noticed before'.

'If an object or event seems illogical,
A contradiction of the natural order,
The world of common senses,
The interaction of body and mind
In the behavioral universe,
It is time to ask questions
Or else sleep or drink until drunk.'

Gas, flower-powered, sped like a
Giant seed sprung from its pod
To the blue horizon. Unconscious for
Most of the journey until she
Recognised the white cliffs of Dover.
At great speed and with precision
The flowers put her down on English
Soil and melted away. By the time
Gas had recovered enough to stand
Up only a few petals remained.
Gas headed for London to find
Her husband, Moon Behemoth Magpie.

CHAPTER TWENTY-EIGHT
MOON BEHEMOTH MAGPIE

Moon Behemoth Magpie; artist
Aged Forty, blond, five feet eleven
Inches and attractive to women.
A giant female vulture, one of a
Species living in northern mountains
Flew out of the sky at a whistle
From the witch doctor. Moon was lifted,
Held round the waist and suffered only
Small scratches and bruises. He
Felt air sick. The vulture climbed
Steeply to two thousand feet and
Moon's nose bled. He could see the

Others as dots, lost forever, (he hoped
Not), on a landscape he didn't know
Or care about. He wanted to be back
Home with his wife, living as
People who weren't timesick, spacesick,
Pastsick or futuresick.

The giant vulture circled ever
Higher, climbing beyond the clouds. Moon
Was cold, his fingers numb. Claws dug
Deep. The vulture bent its long
Craggy, wrinkled neck to peek at its
Passenger. She felt this job, transporting
A human to Paradise an unworthy
Task. Paradise, an overworld lost to
Human eyesight early in evolution,
Slowly began to reveal itself, an ancient
Decadent world without work, money, or sex.
Why was Moon being taken there?
Every fifty years or so, a human being
Is needed to provide a hundred
Thousand-word commentary on the
State of Paradise. These were housed
In a library the size of ten Great
Pyramids. Moon was synchronically available.
He would spend as long as necessary
Traveling the vast nation
Of Paradise, three times the size of

The Asian Landmass. Moon wouldn't age
Either. The only benefit of the job.
The vulture flew through a curtain
Of near-blinding light onto a platform
Three feet above a vast plain of
Turquoise bluestone, which stretched as far

As the Red mountains. The round
Platform was occupied by many people.
They had two eyes and their
Clothes were clouds that flowed
With the body. Their genitals
Were only revealed when they stopped
Moving which seemed a rare event.

The women were similarly beautiful,
Like tall angels. Their faces shimmered
With a moisture that steamed into
Body cloud. Eyes glimmered from
Deep black wells. Voices spun silky words,
Woven into wisdom. Men were shorter
And quiet. They were strong and
Continually practiced acrobatics, mime
And martial arts.
Moon was unhooked from the vulture
Who flew off to the Red Mountains
Which glowed like molten lava.

CHAPTER TWENTY-NINE
CITIES OF PANIC

Moon traveled to the City
Of the Gods nestled in the crutch
Of the Red Mountains, which glowed

Like molten lava. Moon was healed
Of his wounds by a kiss, undressed
And given his cloud by a group of
Excruciatingly beautiful women. He wished
He could wonder why he was here, but
His mind blanked out. Looking into
Those eyes, or across the vast blue
Plain or up to myriad stars he thought
He saw the shadow of his death which
Fell for a microsecond from the body, of
The Blessed. Moon traveled to the City
Of the Gods nestled in the crutch
Of the Red Mountain, which glowed like
Molten ice. Moon and friends floated
Along the marble-like surface, propelled
By thought. If you wanted to go from
A to B, you thought yourself on
The move; you moved. Once Moon
Learned the trick he had fun upstaging
His acrobatic friends. Personal clouds
Sent off trailers which mixed with others.
Each cloud had its own color scheme.
No two were alike. Swirling proceeded
Anti-clockwise around the body. Clouds
Carried after-thoughts and many a conversation
Or meditation took place in trails of
White. Moon passed over the landless
Surface. In paradise, there was no
Sleeping; no waking, no eating or shitting.
Bodies were static systems outside the
Laws of entropy. Sometimes people would

Shake hands, congratulating each other
On thoughts so deeply profound
And true that they would
Destroy the sanity of a human
If translated to the written or
Spoken word. Moon didn't mind

Or matter in this context.
For example, he ran over the blue
Surface so easily he thinks
Off the top of his head. His
Mind traveled and head, behind,
Linked-up, broke up, broke down,
Unified, deserted, interrupted,
Etherialised wrote words out of the blue.
Moon was happy now: Or
Was, was he? His companions
Frolicked all the way through
The thousand-mile journey.
Laughing great big buxom laughs,
Laughs like phases of the moon,
Like tidal waves, like threshing
Machines, falling stars, passionate advice;
Dancing wild controlled evolved motion
Of cubes, acrobats of grace shifting
Form, weights, through chutes, swivels,
Tunnels, into night; there was no night
Blue world-changing to purple, then
To the red mountains. Moon's body didn't
Change. Animated from sovereignty. Beat all.
One of the extra beautiful women stayed
Close. Her name is Panic. She said

"Stay close by.
I will describe the sites of
The Blue Plain, which is our world as it

Is. The Red Mountains is the world
As it was. We don't measure but for
Your benefit I will keep you informed.
Over there, the Lake of Guardians.
It is only two inches deep,
Covered by blue mist one hundred
Feet high. In it lives translucent
Eel-like creatures who have brains three
Times the weight of their bodies. They
Feed on cosmic rays collected in their
Tails. To our left, Forest of Flattened
Flowers. They grow when the sun flares
Up, reproduce by collecting moon and
Starlight, storing it until enough energy
Is built up for a pattern to sub-divide.
A flower takes many years to grow
To maturity. When life is over they
Lift off the blue surface and are
Blown to dust. Over there Cities

Of the Sun people, who live in transparent
Blue shells a mile high. They migrate
Thousands of miles in a year. Sometimes
Parking near lakes, forests or close
To the Swirling Rivers of Silence which
Capture meteor particles and grind
Them into flowing dust. To bathe in this
Dust cures all. My father came from
The Sun people, hence my darker skin.
There are many other features. Later
I will tell you about them."

Moon had no connections, so he took Panic's
Arm and held her close. He wanted
To touch and measure her with an

Embrace. He wasn't sure what he
Would find under her personal cloud.
She wasn't surprised at his action. It
Slowed them down. Moon laid her down,
Opening her legs. She said nothing.
He entered easily and climaxed quickly.
Later they caught up the others. Panic
Was amused by this act which adults
In paradise grew out of by late adolescence.

Panic introduced the rest of the
Group. There were triplets, Sat, Sit, and Sot.
A tall man called Must. And Solid,
Sad, Drail, Orgar and Immich. Moon
Began to tire. He 'couldn't keep up
With the crowd, so Panic offered to
Carry him on her back. Inhabitants
Of the Blue plain of Paradk could
Reinvent themselves in less than a day.
The Red Mountains loomed for miles
High with dark red mist encircling
Pinnacles. As a range, they extended
Two thousand miles. No sign of vegetation
Or wildlife, only Cities of Paradise
Where life is lived on trust, in honeycombs.
In mountains and tall towers built out of
Cemented diamonds as large as ostrich
Eggs. Inhabitants looked as happy as ever.
Moon had followed Panic by jumping up
To a Tower entrance. Inside Moon

Immediately felt complete well-being. His mind
Became one hundred per cent alert. His

Memory and creative faculty
Worked at will. Each tower had
Many levels and a central floatway
For people to move up or down.

"Paradise is all that is cracked up to be"
Moon whispered to himself
As he reached the top of the tallest
Tower with spectacular views of the
Universe and the Blue Plain. He
Could have died happy at that moment,
Standing on the pole tower of First
City, one of many thousands. All of
A sudden he felt like a stranger and that
He must leave, return to earth
And find his wife. He didn't feel
Like exploring such delights as

The City of Sunflowers,
Canyon of Giant Tulips,
Forest of Cupid's Arrows,
Lake of Saints Alive
Who walk on water,
Or the Valley of Grottoes,
Not to mention
The Island Continent of Lode
Where giants feed on berries
And sleep in thousands of
Square miles of poppy fields.
Giants are always happy there.

Moon found his female friend and
Explained his problem. She said

"No Problem".

Moon jumped on her back and
Rode her across the vast empty bluity.
Until they reached the Whirlpool of Night.
This swirling blue-black mist would take him
Home. He kissed Panic goodbye and
Slipped over the edge. His arrival in
The Alas Mountain started rumors of a
Spirit God visiting earth. They spread amongst
Tribal villages. He borrowed a camel and
Rode north to the sea to make his
Way to London by ship and fix a date
For existence.

CHAPTER THIRTY
GESSO JAWBONE JESS

Gesso Jawbone Jess
Poet of a thousand make-believes,
One or two disbeliefs,
Born to perjure himself
In the face of the world
Like all poets who tell
The Truth.

He was born in India, illegitimate son
Of a British engineer. His mother was
A servant girl who washed the feet
Of her master every evening. His father
Unmarried at the time, adopted the boy
Who was brought up by his mother
Until ten years old the boy was sent

To a public school Dreadales in England. From
There he passed to Oxford to study
English Literature and Philosophy, also
Indian classics in his sparest times.
Afterward, he wrote a book on Indian
Sculpture at the Royal College of Art
Where he met Low Solid Rider,
Painter and writer working on a thesis
'Beginning Lives of Painters' or 'How they
Made it to Artist!' After living together
For a few months, they were married
In New York by Jesuit priest who
Studied the Underworld.

Gesso's life began to flash by
As the witchdoctor ordered him to
Step aside and begin his dance with
A chimpanzee. Gesso didn't have a clue
As to what the witchdoctor was talking
About. He couldn't see a monkey
And he didn't feel like dancing.
He knew there were many types of Dance.

Dance of the Spheres
Dance of Blood in the Body

Dance of Cupid's Arrow
Dance of Artemis's Arrow
Dance of Particles of Matter
Dance of Galaxies.
Dance of Planetary systems,
Dance of Antennae of Ants,
Dance of Ocean Currents,

Dance of Lover's embrace,
Dance of Migrating Birds
Dance of Witchdoctor's whip

Which drove Gesso into a cage
Covered by leafy branches. Inside a
Chimpanzee jumped down from a branch
Sticking through bars. She grabbed
Gesso, tore his clothes off and
Encircled him with her legs. By
Some force outside his control he
Fucked the chimpanzee. As he
Climaxed, she changed into a
Beautiful princess. Gesso became
Blind for an hour but had to keep
Up the fornication until his eyesight
Returned. When he could see again
The princess had changed into a ten
Year old girl. And he also felt
Younger and smaller yet, his mind
Remained adult. The young naked girl
Led Gesso junior through the back
Door of the cage, through a tunnel
Of trees to the edge of the most
Beautiful blue-green valley anyone could wish
To see. Tall waterfalls, sparkling pools
Wide grassy spaces grazed by becalmed
Animals; fruit laden trees; terraced stone slopes

Laden with Vines; a brilliant clear
River where fish swam out of danger
No-one to catch them. The valley wound
Lazily into a distant blue haze.
Two-hundred feet below
Water gushed from a hole in rock,
Into a frothy pool, the river's source.
Gesso felt boyish,
Embarrassed. He was naked and
Holding the hands of a naked girl.

Flocks of assorted birds swooped
From tree to tree, pecking fruit, seeds,
Making nests. The valley was surrounded
By bare mountains. Gesso junior and
Girl companion, nicknamed Surplus, set off
Down a steep scree slope to explore
The fruits and delights of this visionary place.
Sliding, jumping, falling, grazing,
Reaching the first green patch with lazy,
Intertwined snakes sunbathing, licking their lips
Surplus said

"This is better
Than anything, I've ever dreamed of.
Better than any story I have heard,
Better than any promise made
To me. Sit with me, lie with
Me between my legs; let us make
Childish love."

Gesso slumped to

The grass wishing to sleep and think.
He starts to pick leaves of grass, chewing
The odd one. From a pink flowered
Bush sprang a large lion chasing
A butterfly which swiveled, darted,
Exquisitely somersaulted and landed on
The lion's nose. He wandered over
To Gesso who couldn't believe it
When Surplus stroked and cuddled
The tame wild king of the jungle.
She then proceeded to de-flea him
With a large thistle covered in
A sticky substance exuded by beetles
feeding on nectar. Lion purred and
Rolled on his back, revealing a soft
Beige fur which became a pillow
For Surplus's head. Gesso joined
The sleep in and they slept the afternoon
Away. There were so many stars
They spent the night trying to
Count them, piling up seeds of
The Rantana tree. By three in the
Morning they had a two feet high
Pile. Then they dropped off to sleep
Until the dawn chorus. This was so
Musical and full of variety never had

Gesso felt so inspired. The valley
Was ready to explore; day trips here
And there, meals from trees, ride on
Friendly animals, on the backs of
Crocodiles. The valley ended against
An extinct volcano's lava flow which
Had built up a three hundred
Foot wall. The river had found
A way out underground and disappeared
Into a cave. Gesso and Surplus

Moved easily along the valley enjoying
Its gifts and unending softness. Surplus
Was very happy. As days turned to years
She grew into a young woman. Gesso
Likewise felt himself returning to manhood.
Once a month, Surplus bled and washed
Herself in the cool river.

One day Gesso woke up
And found himself alone. The garden valley
Had gone, bare jagged rocks remained.
Skeletons of dead animals all around
And next to him the skeleton of a
Woman and child. Gesso had grown
Old and his beard reached his
Navel. Above him, just below the clouds
An angel hovered like a winged halo.
Gesso puzzled at its presence thinking
It the cause of his valley's demise, then
Daydreamed of Surplus, who told how
The valley was the creation of a rebel
Angel who, in collaboration with
The Witchdoctor had decided to start their own
Version of the Happy Garden. The
Challenge was understood as formal. Mother
Nature sent word back, an avenger
Was dispatched to exterminate the
Upstart Eden.

"I'm happy in the clouds

Watching the world struggle on, though sad
We couldn't continue our lives together."

Surplus faded from Gesso's mind.
The hovering angel followed him
Out of the valley. He was spared because

They thought he had no magic. Gesso picked up
Two animal bones and rubbed them three
Times. Immediately magic flames appeared,
Gesso hopped on his flying craft
Soared up to the angel who was burnt
To a cinder which dropped onto a
Pool of stagnant water and grew into
A grotesque crystalline form more hideous
Than a decaying carcass. Gesso guided
Himself across the desert to the Mediterranean
Sea and found himself more youthful
Again. He thought sadly of the waste
In setting up the evergreen valley
And the viciousness of its enemy.
Across Europe and home to London
And Hyde Park. The telephone
Exchanges jammed for the next three
Days with reports of UFO sightings.

PART TWO

CHAPTER THIRTY-THREE

THE END OF AN AFFAIR OF THE HEART

From the danger of dirt
He would surface and walk,
In the infancy of drink
He would turn face and work.
The future of pleasantly

Is recorded in type.
Merriment in the gutter
Saddles the rich. Merriment of wine
Is a challenge to Apollo.
A lovely lady turns in the street
And walks away.
I shelter in the Temple of Night,
Burn a candle,
Sleep on a floor of dreams,
Watch old prayers repeat themselves,
Hear beads clicking like deathwatch.
I cuddle human books with youthfully
Hymnic thoughts

'Ock the ick of tixic lalls.'

Suddenly
          last
              bell
                  hope
                      light

I fall awake,
Shut ears to
Gaping panic in streets.
Over and over the world blows.
It's the end,
The end of an affair of the heart.

                              Nature
                        Love
                  Buildings
              Art
          Blown
                              Up
Simply,

Evolution equals man turning circles
Into squares.

So the days roast on.
The hot pot of purity.
They no longer look happy
When they smile,
Or sad when they cry.
Just like burnt toast,
They need scraping clean.
It was so much easier before
To sup supper
To din dinner;
Unpleasant to view a world
Bang up to date.
Perhaps one day
Sea creatures will visit land,
Like before,
Grow legs, ears, fur and
Brains better than ours;

Then it will be time to rest,
To quiet dis-ease
And make matter-soul.

Gas Jenny Falcon met up with
Her husband in Oxford Street outside
The Academy Cinemas which now
Showed lurid propaganda films full
Of sex, religion and violence.
The Year was 1998

On returning from their misadventures
Gas and Moon became down and outs.
At first they couldn't believe their
Eyes. England had changed so much.
They both had to start from the baseline
Of anonymity and establish a new
Rapport within society. A credibility
Gap had caused a rupture in the field
Of reality it was necessary to keep
In order to function as a citizen.

From Oxford Street, they had walked
To Regent's Park and sat on a bench
Near the bandstand. The scent
Of flowers revived memories. Gas
And Moon stared at each other

For over an hour before saying
A word of worlds. Gas's skin
Felt like parchment. Moon's hair
Was cut like grass. Since arriving and renewing
Their lives both had become re-established
In their professions, uneasily
Adapting to the new ways.
Gas spoke

"Do you believe any of that happened?
I read your serialisation in the Observer.
I felt envious, had to see you again.
People call you guru,saint,mystic,artist,media elixir.
I have written three books based on my experiences.
Now I visit Oxford and Harvard as a lecturer.
Have I aged? What did you think of my screenplay
For 'Satan and the Roadsweeper'
And two minor books
'Nurses on fire - Visions of
An Anarchist.' and 'Sincere Sin City -
A story of a country girl.?"

Moon spoke at last.

"To see you here is,
By the way,
Have you noticed that
People are actually scalped
In broad daylight by,
Who wear their trophies
On belts.
The police do nothing.
Oxford Street isn't safe
You are
You must,
Come back to my flat
And I'll look and
Let you know everything,
Time allowing."

They both got up amid the bungling
Noise, held hands, and walked silently
To the tube station.

'Deep in the heart of Oxford Circus
Drug addicts lie;
Injected by the Drug Police,

Prostitutes, young and old,
Male and female

Mingle with passengers
Hoping for a suburban pick-up.
Escalators don't work.
Gangs loiter and snatch bags
Tiles fall off, graffiti runs free.
A run-down system,
A run-down city.'

That year there was an election.
On every spare wall
Softcore political posters.

"Better dead than Red - Vote Conservative"

"Waiting for a New Society - Vote Labour".

"Give the people what they want - Vote Labour".

"Protect Prosperity - Vote Conservative"

"Better to understand the Red than the dead -
Vote SDP-Liberal"

"Freedom lovers vote Liberal- SDP".

Their tube train journey took fifty
Minutes plus a twenty-minute wait in
A tunnel. Paddington, since the Apocalyptic
Vision which drove out most Londoners,
Leaving behind about five hundred thousand,
Some people occupied two or three -
Crumbling houses. Acting out grandeur,
Moon had a whole terrace, which
He was turning into a fortress bomb
Shelter. Everybody believed in the vision.

It was a cold night just after Christmas.
Two in the morning. Most were in bed.
Every room throughout the city was
Filled with a red light for about six
Seconds. Everybody woke and saw the
'Figure of Death' riding a mushroom cloud.
Soon after the Government noticed that
London was empty, the countryside,
Villages and towns full. Moon's top

Room was pure white with a golden grid
Painted on each wall. Window frames were
Black, lighting hidden in the ceilings
And revolved at the touch of a button.
In one corner stood a seventh generator
Computer and opposite a robot.
A large studio was full of new generation
Paintings. 'State of the art' art, which
Were ready to go to shows in New
York and Milan, buyers already breathing
Hot prices down telephones, dealers writing
Begging letters. Moon was now famous.
And to survive famously was more
Than a genius would hope for in 1998.
Gas boiled water on an electric ring.
In the kitchen, Cockroaches were a
Problem and seemed bigger every spring.
Even rats played happily in the streets
Where pigeons might have gathered.

Many rats had left with the people.
Gas asked Moon if she would like
To live in New York or Sydney. Europe
Was in decline, Asia and Africa sick
From poverty, Russia in a state of
Unrest. Moon fried two eggs and
Three tomatoes cut in half while Gas
Poured lager.

CHAPTER THIRTY-FOUR

BRING BACK THE GOOD TIMES

"What do you think of the new
Prime Minister with her Mohican haircut
And bare sagging breasts. She says
She's going to pour money into London
To bring back the good times."

"She's an old rag. There's no way
Londoners are going to return to London.
They would rather sleep in the fields and
Live like gypsies in caravans than
Face the gangs, police, pimps and
Drugs. I have got used to it now. It
Provides great material for an artist.
Without this degradation, my paintings
Wouldn't sell. Americans think they are
Buying from the Land of the Apocalypse.
Paintings from the heart of the mushroom
Cloud. After all, I am a millionaire
In my Swiss account."

"Times have changed for you. I thought
Our adventures absurd would have

Knocked out any reality in you.
But here you are, patenting genius,
Late late twentieth century style. Your
Paintings are fucking good. Like a
Culmination of western man's creative
Effort. I'm working out a new novel.
I've a half million starter on it; but
Nothing written yet."

"Shall we go to the circus and watch
A show, one of those orgies where
Fornication, acrobats, mime, song, comedy.
And children intermingle, including audience
Participation to great effect; the only
Performing art left in London. Opera
Moved to Exeter. The Government to
Hereford, art collections to Wales.
Anyway, these circus orgies provide a useful insight

Into decadence.
It's not dangerous. They have
Their own band of heavies, heavily armed."

"I don't mind. When I was in New
York there was fucking in the street,
By strolling players. Crowds cheered
But police came in and broke it
Up. The planet is under a sumptuous
Influence. These days nothing but
Public fucking, it makes you think."

"Hey, look" cried Moon, looking out

The window to the street where
A gang were eating raw onions and crying.
They were clean-cut, dressed in suits,
Rapier swords, hanging in their belts,
Pink carnations in their hair, pigtailed
Like chinamen. Gas rushed over,
Spilling a can of lager.

"What happens when you meet that lot on
The street. Aren't you scared?
Don't You run a mile or climb a tree?"

"For me its no problem. I'm known
Around here. I give money for their
Food sometimes or if an outside gang
Day-trips in for a fight I apply a bit
Of the magic learnt during our adventures.
Like vanishing for a minute or so.
Or doubling in size.
Or turning into a bird.
You mightn't believe me, but there are
Few situations from which I can't extricate myself.
In Regent's Park, now a camping
Ground, I stumbled into a gang of Hots.
They look like characters from Children's
Television circa the 1950s, you know,
Bill and Ben, Andy Pandy, Muffin the Mule,
Except their clothes are painted bright red.
They carry razor sharp, Samurai swords,
I was surrounded and scared for a second.

I hypnotized the lot by repeating a Call,
Asp-acquisition of Surplus People,
Which finds homes outside London for down

And outs. If there's a full eclipse of the sun
The spell will break, and God knows
What will happen."

"Are there girls in these gangs? Are
They as violent or do they nurse wounds"?

Gas laughed, Moon didn't answer direct.

"Are you coming to New York tomorrow
Night. I have to prepare my show.
I'll have workmen in while I'm
Away. They're ex-soldiers who make
Homes into impregnable fortresses.
The whole terrace will be turned into
An arts center. Tourists with guts
Will flock to it."

CHAPTER THIRTY-FIVE

MOON, GAS, LOW, AND GESSO

Moon and Gas made their way to
Heathrow, a heavily guarded airport still
Used by industry and Government personnel.
At Terminal Three, in the waiting lounge,
They met Gesso and Low, who were
Emigrating for good. This pair had
Survived their many adventures and
Met up with each other in Edinburgh
At a festival for outsiders. Gesso was
Reading poems from his most recent collection

Called Punchbag and Octogenarian. Low was
Covering the event for an American
Magazine called Hollowing Bones. They soon
Moved into their old house in Chelsea
And friends hardly notice they had
Been away. Gesso wrote where ever
He happened to be. Once reciting
Letter to My Young Bacteria before
Thousands at a poetry festival he
Stopped to jot down the first three
Lines of his incomplete epic, excerpts
From a Peaceful Time.

Letter to My Young Bacteria
Began

"Divine Soup made from a packet
Of eons
I'd barter the generosity of time
For one taste of the impossible
Rot of matter."

At this point he stopped to note
Into his recorder a few ideas.

"When I saw the snapdragon
Of my sharp judgment
Devour fruits of reason
Growing in wildlands
Of a ruined country
In an old continent,

I knew it was time to leave

The gunpowder room of nostalgic
Desires, tear off my rags and
Pierce my flesh to make scars
Which would show a man a
Threshold of pain in case
He challenged and held up
The path of justice.
I gathered arms, a horse,
And dogs and set off from
The craggy mountain's cave
To search the world
For a happy death."

The audience cheered while he continued
His poem.

"Shadow me to the edge of life's abyss
And save me from its blessed bliss
When I was a gardener in a Chateau
On the Loire,
I seduced roses into growing blue,
I raked gravel paths into spirals and
Diamonds, the pleasure of the warm
Sun made me feel like a thinking
Stone I knew was under my foot.
There were no prizes for guessing
Its name or shape as it traveled
The speed of light after I had thrown
It away. I liked swimming in the river,
Its currents once swept me away.

Saved by an overhanging branch
I rejoiced in a kingfisher's colors
As it darted over the water.
Nearby were lovers, naked and
Sweating. Oh, the fun of youth.
I felt as old as a band of
Travelers from the Middle East
I'd met on the road to Calais.
They had changed the lives of
Men and women. Faces the better
For the wear of Laughter. Lovers
Disappeared. The sun moved higher
And higher vaporizing leaves and
The river ran dry. The burden
Of living sank wells of hope in leftover mud.
Fish died or became food for birds.

One day I shook hands with a gardener
Who knew the names of all the plants
In his desert. There were no visible
Except when it rained every five years.
Seeds raced into shoots and flowered.
The old man enjoyed his floral hours,
Then waited for flowers to be pollinated
By an influx of insects. Soon seeds
Formed to pop, unzip, ping, zing,
Uncurl and drop. The gardener was
Over four thousand years old and
Was the gardener of Eden. Now you

Don't believe what I say. I will
Add two more thoughts - you don't
Choose your own fascism. Don't
Get to another person's pleasure."

Gesso loaded their luggage
On to a trolley. Low followed talking
Wild talk to Gas, who by now
Had finished chewing gum. She threw
It in a waste bin standing by a fifteen
Foot palm. The entrance hall with its blue grey
Imitation marble tiles contained few people who
Had all the time in the world
To catch their planes, which
Usually traveled quarter-full, few could
Afford them. Gesso, Low, Gas, and Moon
Talked of the old days. Lounge seats
Were so comfortable passengers dozed off
And dreamed of happy childhoods.
Laminated tables, op art stripes, comic
Strips, trompe l'oeil, old masters and
Moderns. Low picked up a bestseller,
Her own book, now being filmed, called
"Giant Leeches", about radioactive waste
Illegally dumped in Florida's swamps.
Twenty years later, eight-foot leeches
Invade the mainland, swim up to
Miami, kill off livestock, suck humans

Dry in two minutes. Some reach
New York. Defeated by hypersonic waves
Produced by a machine designed by a
Student at New York Technical College.
Gesso had also written a short story
For a quick publishing killing.

CHAPTER THIRTY-SIX

HOW TO DESIGN THE APOCALYPSE

"Labour won the next election, abolished
The House of Lords, extended time in office,
For another five years when an election was
Due, all land is nationalised without compensation.
The Queen put under house arrest, the
Army stormed Parliament, the Government
Arrested for treason, civil war broke out,
Miners, steel workers, shipbuilders, and car
Workers took up arms and formed
Communes in the northern cities.
The civil war lasted three years. Then,
After a truce, the Tories took over and
Hanged the opposition for treason."

It sold half a million and left
Gesso free to write poetry.

Low

"I find airports the only civilized
Public places left. Anaemic and
Stale but at least I can eat safely,
Without fear of poison."

Gesso

"Civilisation is really an obsolete
Word. Wealth is created by machines,
People waste away. The other day

I saw a gang of girls walking down the center
Of Tottenham Court Road, eating black ice
Cream. The traffic police couldn't do
Anything for fear of being eaten alive.
The girls stopped a car, pulled out
A passenger and gouged out his eyes.
What do you think of that?
No wonder we're leaving. The cannibal
Gang had it the next day. Vigilantes
Surrounded them and sent them
Swimming with cement boots soon after".

Low

"When we arrive, we'll stay
With a publisher friend who has a
Penthouse in Fortress Manhattan."

Moon sat pensively static, hardly
Twitching a finger or blinking. He
Was meditating on the truly bad design
Which surrounded him. He wished he
Could escape to the desert and delights
Of Africa. Europe was finished.
Switzerland had martial law. Italy was
Anarchic, Germany was fascist, reunified.
Moon put his hand into Gas's, and his
Shoulder on Low's and went to sleep.
It was two in the morning. Each
Leaned on another and slept tight.
They woke at four. Their plane left
At five-thirty.

New York was Babylon, Baghdad,
Roma, Sodom, Gomorrah, and Constantinople
Rolled into one. A million fears and
Delights awaited the visitor.
Low was writing an article for
Playboy on a chain of bondage
Parlours which had opened recently.
She traveled around in a chauffeur driven
Car with publisher Daniel 'Jim Jam' Snaps.
His writers were obscure philosophers and
Poets. These he supported by girly
Magazines catering for the regions titles
New Orleans Lady, Texan Tussle, L A Lays
And so on. Bondage parlors were
Respectably fronted as banks, insurance
Houses and estate agents. Well-designed,
More hygienic than five-star hotels,
Every sort of spanking, tie-ups, rubber,
Leather or dental floss was available.
Most diversified into normal sexual activities.
Lunch-time businessmen were principal
Customers. And women customers weren't
Uncommon.

Daniel "This article must be in by
The end of the week. These places are
Hot. Next month it will be something
Else."

"Let's have lunch."

Gesso, Moon, and Gas were sitting in Central
Park contemplating things going on. What
Things? Tai Chi, floating
Higher than Transcendental Meditation. Joggers wearing
Out their legs. Wrestlers in gordian knots.
Cyclists weaving between walkers lost
Between their earphones. Kids playing
Chase, skateboarding, roller-skating, licking
Ice cream. Poets talking to the sun and
Trees and pale moon. Painters loading
Canvasses with paint in ecstatic colors.
Portraitists knocking off five minute
Portraits for ten dollars. Ants feeding
On crumbs.

Gesso

"Do you think this park is real.
Should we stay here and watch
These scenes and accept them as events
In time, part and parcel of our lives,
Other peoples lives. You bet your bottom
Dollar we shouldn't."

Gas

"I met an Australian once
Who preached a secular religion
Wherever he went. One week he'd spend
At home learning his lines. The following
Week he'd go out and about on trains,
Buses, to parks, shopping precincts
Reciting his ideas non-stop, only breaking

Off at three in the afternoon for a meal.
I taped a Thursday performance. I don't
Remember it all but some of it went like
This.

"Quit your pantheistic desires,
Save your materialism for
The color of your coffin,
Leave the churches to tourists,
Theatres to actors.
Cinemas to the dark,
Galleries to pictures.

Quit your car,
Dismount your horse, Don't shoot pool,
Scatter playing cards,
Delete discos.
Unplug your videos,
Ditch the restaurant,
Dustbin the takeaway,
Don't vote,
Take up arms
And fight for peace.
Fight naked
Don't wear clothes.
No sex no drink no love.
I want you to give your bodies

To the world in raw aggression.
Take a leaflet. Write to me
I'll let you know
What to do next."

"That was the gist of his ravings.
I wrote to him, and he sent me back
A photocopied manifesto which started
With the words.

"Fuck you, proletarian sheep. You
Have to become wolves."
He was eventually arrested and tried
For subversion, incitement to riot and
Communist sympathies. Later still he
Was sent back to Australia."

Gesso replied

"What we see before us
Is subversion of our desires,
A parade of monadic mucus.
Each flower, blade of grass,
Dragonfly, sparrow's feather
Offers a dichotomous vision
Which ends up mounting
Our brain like a thrusting lion."

Moon.
"Don't get carried away.
Have an egg sandwich
While I go buy some ice
Cream and fresh lemon

From the vendor."

Authorities threatened to cover most
Of Central Park with two giant
Geodesic domes to create a stable climate.
Usually, it got little further than a
Rumour. Moon was lying on the grass
Licking a strawberry ice cream colored
Green. It was a new idea. Flavors with
The colors of other flavors. Ants crawled
Over his hands and flies were making
Complete rest impossible. Gesso and
Gas played poker. Low, who had
Finished her work, and joined the gang.

"I've finished my research into
Bondage parlors. You enter sparkling
Glass doors with polished steel frames.
Black tiles reflect every detail. A girl
In a short black skirt and dark blue sweater
Greets you; you sign your name; it can
Be fake, and pay a two-dollar fee.
Her desk is blue stainless steel. Along
A dark orange passage, a waiting room,
Painted pale blue with black carpets.
Customers are given a portable video
Console and choose their desires.
After a choice is made, if available,
The customer is sent an escort who
Leads him along to the appropriate

Lower sanctum. Doors open, pleasure, pain
Or whatever proceeds. The hostess goes
Back and picks up the next customer.
With a high capital investment prices
Are high and then there's the police
To pay off. What goes on? Well
Anything you can think of and
Perhaps more. For instance, the dressed man
Who likes to be covered in cream and
Licked clean by four women dressed
As leopards. I think all four of us
Should go to England via L.A.,
Japan, Mongolia, India, Turkey and
Europe. After your exhibition Moon,
Next week, do you have much
To do.?"

Moon

"I have left everything in
The hands of the gallery, publicity,
Insurance, etc., checking details myself."

Gesso

"Most exhibitions are sell-outs.
Painting is big business. They're designing
Buildings to take giant murals. One
Skyscraper has a ceiling the size of
A baseball pitch upon which ten
Painters are working on a four-year project,
State of the Nation. A secular church
Has just had its walls painted with
The faces of humanist heroes and scenes

From their lives."

Moon

"Mixed blessings. I was offered
A robot factory, but who would see
It. Robots have eyes, but there's no
Evidence of any appreciation as yet."

Low

"I've bought shares in Artists'
Materials Companies."

Gesso

"Let's go home. I think
We're all invited to a party tonight,
The wildest wild party of the year."

The foursome fled Central Park in late
Afternoon. They caught a yellow cab
And watched thin, fat people masticate
The experience of the physical with their
Muscles rotate the particular in the
Universal inside their brain. Shock treatment
Was needed. But these days, not even
Children were shocked, except at birth.
A hard generation was growing up.
Not materially deprived but hard in

The heart. One day one of these little
Bastards will give orders for the other
Side to be blown up. Anti-domeists, worried
That the park would become exclusive,
Had a permanent protest platform
With banners. Today police had come
To remove it. A few broken heads
Otherwise, no riot or headline material.

The penthouse flat was so sumptuous
People gasped on entry.

Chrome walls shone more than the moon.
Woolen fabrics are warm and soft,
Impossible to leave their comfort.
Gold leaf chairs, silver-plated tables,
Platinum designed from Germany,
Plates designed and produced
By Arizonian Indians.
There were paintings from
Every modern period
Of the Twentieth century,
Kandinsky, Mondrian, Picasso,
Pollock, Ernst, Baxter, and so on.
Six bedrooms with wall-sized
TV screens, a bathroom
With a twenty-person Jacuzzi,
Spray ceilings - torrential, humid,
Summer shower; marble tiles
And an exercise room.
Principal living space was hemispherical,
No paintings, but lit up like a planetarium
With real starlight magnified
By special lens and projected
Through small holes in a glass ceiling.
A semi-circular balcony, shrubs
And a see-through beehive. Carpets,

Persian, Books, the classics. Videos
Of Hollywood greats. A computer
Looked after those two collections
And a title tapped in brought
The response of a book popping out
Of the wall. Three dwarf-like
Robots cleaned the apartment. Each
Robot had suede clothing, six green eyes
Placed pentagonally around the head
And one on top.

Jim Jam's money, besides income from
Pornography was firmly based on
Shrewd investment. He had a sixth
Sense and had made seventy million
Dollars. In ten years. A Great Wall
Street punter, and once he had dined
With the President.

Party time in a warehouse
Owned by a health food multi-millionaire.
To ensure organically grown food for his
Shops and restaurants he had bought
Up huge farms in California. Large
Areas were covered by giant geodesic
Domes. Automated temperature and climate
Control. John Sartorius was born rich.
An eccentric farmer sent him to Burma
To study Buddhism at the age of six.

The next eight years, martial arts,
Saffron robe and a shaved head.
He came back to Californication and knew
He was one up on his contemporaries.
Sniffing out the new mood, he bought
Out a large health food chain. On
The death of his father, he acquired
Farmland which he left fallow to clear
The earth of pesticides, herbicides and fertilisers.
His party celebrated his thirtieth birthday.
By now, he had forsaken his Buddhist
Ideals, except not eating meat.

The party. Fifty dishes of food.
Ten live sex shows, one orgy
For swingers, a dance for dancers.
Drinks, drugs, and space
For couples and groups to talk
Walk and grope. The warehouse
Had three large floors one
Hundred feet long and forty feet wide.
Walls painted with Rubrik cubes.
No furniture, only giant soft cushions
To lounge on. Moon and friends
Arrived at seven in a Rolls-Royce
With fifteen fins and a police car
Beacon. The warehouse was guarded
By twenty men with automatic rifles.
Guests arrived in a stream, basking

In the warm evening, ready for
Forty-eight physical pleasures on
Offer that night. The mind would
Get lost, hover above the building
Like a halo or white dove.
A holy ghost waiting to descend
Into blissful bodies bent on abandonment.
They wanted no pain and
They didn't want to suffer.

There was a table of car-killed animals.
Dogs, cats, and birds, Jim Jam's running joke,
In a corner out of the way. Gesso
Danced with a tall blonde model. They
Waltzed to rock music. Low
Slow danced with a telepoem who stored
His poems are on floppy discs. Moon sat
Drinking a cocktail with twenty ingredients;
Next to him the fattest women at the
Party, telling the story of her life.
How she ate and ate so her boyfriends
Would leave her, one by one, on
The dot, stone by stone. Moon
Wandered off to find a floor show.
The first one he came to, looked
As if it was about to end. Seven people,
Naked, conjoined, contrived, sexual
Throbbing orgasmic toil. Were they acting?

Was it real? About fifty people stood
Around as the beautiful bodies sweated it
Out. Some of the men watching
Had erections. Women looked hot and bothered
Or bored. Couples rubbed against each
Other happily. Moon had wandered off
To the second floor to find Gas.
She had met a millionaire drug dealer.
His life a constant
Evasion of gang warfare and police
Investigation. At present, he is looking
For a ghostwriter for his autobiography
And a novel he had mapped out. On
His way Moon passed six women in
Soixante-neuf positions,
Young girls fondling old men,
Young boys cuddling old women, gourmets
Gorging at fat tables. Groans, sighs.
Ejaculating talk blocked out all sounds of

The outside worked. By the time Moon
Reached Gas, she was feeling a need
For a change of partners. The drug dealer
Had outstayed his quota of interest.
Moon beckoned to Gas.
She excused herself, and the two
Met at the Japanese Fish Table.
Twelve o'clock midnight, drunks dumped in the
Drying out room near the entrance.

Floor shows were over. Guests paired
Off or in groups and found private
Spaces to exercise their genuine
Desires, all night long. Gesso
And friends decided to go home.
The second session of the party, wilder,
Crueller, might well include a murder,
Rape, suicide, blackmail, mugging, child
Prostitutes, torture. At the end of the
Second day the warehouse burst into
Flames, after the last guests had left.
Buses ferried stragglers away. Jim Jam's
Party was the first and last he
Ever gave. From now on he would
Focus his pleasure on a giant
Garden designed by himself, constructed
By two dozen gardeners and builders
On land of a hundred and twenty acres.

CHAPTER THIRTY-SEVEN

SOME GARDENS BEING DEAD ENDS

The whole area was conceived
As an enormous diamond shaped maze.
Instead of hedges dividing paths, there would
Be walls of impenetrable bamboo enclosing
Gardens, ponds, lakes with islands. To find
A way into a particular area the
Maze paths had to be followed, some
Gardens being dead ends, others had to be
Passed through to find the next or the

Way out. Deciduous copses were to be
Made with adult trees brought in by
Giant tractors and transplanted. Bamboo
Would make impenetrable walls and
'Get Lost' areas.
Some paths led underground
To artificial fungi caves. Some
Caves would contain crystal ferns, others
Would have man-made stalactites
And stalagmites. Also, a small wildlife park
With lions, leopards, and gazelles, a
Small farm, a glass house area, a
Classical garden with genuine Greek and
Roman statues, a Japanese garden with two
Resident Zen monks, a children's
Playground with challenging log climbing
Structures and an automatic rescue
Service. At the center a giant fountain
Rising over a hundred feet as the
Pressure builds every twenty minutes.
Surrounding it a garden of computerized grotesques
Which move, speak, play chess, show films
And relay echoes. Plants from all over
The world. People would pay nothing
To enter and leave but would pay
To be rescued from the maze. His
Observatory, in the central area built on
An artificial mountain would also be
The center of intelligence.Vandals

Wouldn't be tolerated, a team of
Samurai warriors would descent from a
Helicopter to dispense justice.

The garden took six years to
Complete and Jim Jam and friends spent
Most of their leisure exploring its
Mysteries. The public were afraid to
Enter after whole families
Vanished without a trace. Jim Jam decided
To include a computer-controlled
Miniature in his Maze who would
Take on all comers
And lose without hurting them.

Moon's painting show was a
Sell out and a gang of anti-artists
Tried to smash into and mash-up
The exhibition. Security guards prevented
Damages.

The West beckoned. Los Angeles
Beckoned. Electric cars ruled the roads.
There was a rumor that an everlasting
Battery had been found in the wreckage of
An alien spacecraft. This was denied
By Ford, General Motors, and Chrysler
Who claimed to have invented it independently.

Oil-producing countries went bust. Banks
With loans went to the wall. Only
Government intervention stopped a grand
Crash. However, electric cars produced by
The million helped the economy to revive.
Only the poor drove petrol run cars,
Petrol being given away as a welfare payment.

Sitting on the grass near the Huntington Museum
The friends talked for three hours on the past,
And one hour on the future. Low
Suggested they seek out true religion.
Gesso thought it best to find the
Wellsprings of true art. Moon said
It was right to enjoy the food and
The best a culture could offer.
Gas favored expeditions to ancient
Archaeological sites in order to find
Evidence of alien contacts with earth.

Low contemplated ants attacking a small
Grub which had surfaced by mistake.
With the sun at its zenith, it was
More than time to move to a shady place.
The companions settled under a large cedar.
Which gave its approval by rustling leaves,
Shaking branches and oozing resin.
A breeze had blown up. Mountains
Appeared as close as ice cream.

A large grasshopper landed on Moon's
Head and immediately sprang away.
Gesso brought out an English newspaper.
Headlines in gaping black type - Revolution.
Workers had taken to the streets,
Piled up barricades, recruited soldiers
Who supplied weapons and took over
Local radio stations, railway stations,
Motorway exits and smaller airports.
The people were sick of gang warfare
In cities, ragged public services,
Uninterested politicians who pretended
To run the country while investing
Money abroad. Aristocrats and the army
Wanted to crush the revolt, but it
Was too widespread. Many soldiers had
Deserted. Meanwhile, England had
Won the First Test against Australia
By an innings and four runs.
In the hot spring, ten cricketers
Had scored a thousand runs before
The end of May. How did they
Manage a Test Match during a Revolution.
As they turned the pages home news
Got worse.

Gesso said it was time to
Head for the Hotel. That evening

A party given by an old-timer
Who made documentary explorer films.

A bright black limousine
Turned up at the explorer's strange
House. It had a classical porch and?
A colossus, late of a film set, astride the roof.
At each corner supporting the roof, a bronze Atlas.

Garages were pyramidal. In the center of
The house, a courtyard and cloisters,
Erotic carvings on pillars, based on
Indian originals. The drive and porch
Lights lit up as soon as a car
Drove across a white line.

CHAPTER THIRTY-EIGHT

CAPO THE EXPLORER, TESS
INFANTA, JERRY TRAVEL, SUSIE BEAUVILLE

Capo the Explorer was world famous.
He had proved without doubt the arrival
Of alien spacecraft. On his journey into
The interior of Africa, he came across
An underground temple marked by a black
Sphere. The temple contained relics of a spacecraft
And a spaceman. He took them to London;
In decoy trucks.

None of the relics were dead items.
Each pulsed with artificial life,
Waiting to escape the confines of a
Museum case to look for compatible

Parts. Each fragment had been programmed
To look for a new unity in the event
Of the older unity's destruction. These
Went missing before the public had
A look in. Many detectives, amateur
Enthusiasts with metal detectors began
Monotonous searches on beaches, down
Sewers, in haystacks, along rivers
Hoping to rescue the quasi-intelligent
Wreckage. Capo, rival explorer to past
Greats, also discovered the missing link
In the depths of Africa and smuggled
It out by pretending they were the
Bones of his great grandmother, wife of
An English trader. These bones proved
That man was descended from a small
Ape that lived underground and
Fed on slugs, worms, and termites.
These apes rarely climbed trees.
In fact, they were clever architects
Building conglomerates of underground
Cells. Their ancestors were along
Extinct rodent. Early man-monkey
Underground survived many catastrophes

Cosmic and climatic, which rival breeds, who
Hugged the surface, did not.

Capo's party: noisy, brash, full of

Randy, young men and women. No
Wallflower was safe. Nifty Mexican waiters
Dodged guests, refilled glasses, carried food
Trays and cleared up debris.

Conversation pieces; set topics, two men
And two women points awarded for wit,
Argument, logic, originality, invention. Sometimes
The rules changed; The most cliches win,
Or only short words or jargon belonging
To a certain trade or profession. Gesso
And Low were judges for the evening
Participants were four young poets.
Jerry Travel, Betty Solar, Fol Mach,
And Suzie Beauville.

They had to talk above a Rock
Music group called Sulphuric Acid, whose
Climate of opinion was very much more
Appreciated that evening; loud, hard,
Yanked out lyrics, disturbing faces videos,
Near naked, chorybantic, standing
Still.

The subject that evening was set by
A prodigy of thirteen invited to be Chairwoman
Of the discussion. She was a virgin and
Had three arranged marriages to sons of

Multi-millionaires lined up. Each marriage
Would last five years with no renewal
Options, although re-marriage would be
Possible at a later date. Arranged
Marriages were in fashion.

Tess Infanta was a true new star.
Her generation loved their smart
Talking computers more than their
Multi-divorced parents. They learned half
A dozen languages from the cradle and
Mastered calculus by the age of seven.
Her devious little humdinger of title
For discussion. "Are poets born or made."

Tess sat on a high steel stool with
A back support like an umpire's chair.
Participants lounged in black leather
Swivel chairs.

Jerry Travel began.

"One day, I met a child
Who looked into the eyes of the world,
Through its many veils,
Through its mists of twilight fear,
Between stunted trees of anger,
Across the waves of hope,
Across lakes of serene desires,
Along pathways of distant pleasure,
Through storms of pain,

Through barren lands of disease
And into a cave
Where love dwelled
Coiled like a snake.
Soon it would be too late
To save this childhood.
He was beyond the point
Where he could return.
He entered the cave
And killed the snake
With his bare hands.
The beach stretched for many miles.
I walked with the child whose eyes
Were cold, staring at waves, seaweed
And shells. He said nothing until
We rounded sand dunes covered in spiny
Grass. He started to speak about
His vision, how he had needed the warmth
Of another person which gave him
The energy to speed to the cave.
He nearly turned back but felt
He would die on the journey home
Unless he had eaten the eyes of the snake.
Now he could see with the eyes of the world
And into the hearts of any man or woman.

One day I met a child
Who looked into the heart of the world

And lay down and died.
I buried her in the sea, at night.

Her spirit skipped across the waves,
Took off and circled the moon,
Navigated the stars, vanished while
I fell asleep. The night was cold.
I made a bed of grass.
In the morning, two children
Woke me, drew for me
In the sand, a map of where
They had been. It was a maze
More confusing than any maze
Yet created. I knew I was lost
Before I started and daren't ride
The mare of luck into the
Field of chance.
The children fished
And then we ate.
I smiled at the fish bones.
Seagulls dive-bombed
And pestered us for food.
A strong wind covered
Our footsteps with sand.
We had only one way to go".

Betty answered

"There are three instruments
A faithful lover must cherish,
The chalice of blood,

The lock of hair,
And the dream.
In great despair,
At midnight,
I have lain on a bed,
Wolves howl in the great forests
Which surround me for
Hundreds of miles.
Will he make his way?
Can I travel to him
In a dream,
Wake him from sleep
Or perhaps another woman!
Make his horse disturb
The night by kicking
A stable door, neighing
To wake the dogs?

One day when Sun and Moon
Consorted in the sky
I saw myself and lover
Stranded on an island
Owned by a spirit of a small evil,
An unrequited lover
Who killed herself at seventeen.
This island had perfect weather,
The most beautiful flowers
And fruitful trees. We felt

We could never leave.
We escaped by floating on
The back of an old dolphin.
Who had come to die
My lover persuaded him
To take us to the mainland.
We would find a boat and tow
Him back. The only remnants
Of death on this island were dolphin
Bones. He was very wise
And stayed with us for three days
Telling his story and all the myths
Of Dolphin Law and how they spoke
In tongues and had direct
Communication with their Godhead.
He was so weak we hired
A motorboat and towed him back.
The island of Unrequited Love
Was still there, full of all
Its wonders. The Dolphin
Was left in an inlet.
We headed home.
Timing changes.
It was hard to reach the mainland.
We were lost
And saw the face of death
Beneath the waves.
Lovers are resourceful beings.

Diving off the boat we
Confronted Death, who looked
Like the beautiful sea beast
I met as a child when swimming
Off a jetty. He would help
Us find the mainland
And not take us this time.
He had had more than enough

Lovers' suicides that year.
I lived in the forest by myself
For three and a half years
Without seeing a soul.
Wolves became my friends,
I fed them in winter from my
Lover's grain stores.
One night my lover came
And was torn to pieces,
I heard his last scream.
And cried bitterly.
Feeling my life was over
I went to the big city
And fell in and out of love.
I married a banker's son.
I still dream of my lover and his grave.
One day I'll show husband and
Children the great forest
And its spirits and the island
Of Unrequited Love, dolphin bones

And the Sea Beast of Death.
We were young when we were modern."

Fol Mach began

"Around and about
There are ghosts of death,
Echoes of violent endings
Which usurp peace of mind,
Also, there are ghosts of sex,
Couplings and multi-couplings,
Echoes of passion and desire
Which capture sleep and daydreaming,
Alter people's lives.
In a large grey room,
Flattering faces of guests,
Unmarried and young.
Conversation free-ranged
Then settled on the shape
Of people's noses.
What I wanted to know
Was how each person
Reacted to their nose.
One girl carried a minute
Watering can and powdered
Skin fertilizer; once during
The evening she lay on the floor

And sprinkled her nose, then
Rubbed in the powder. One young man

Rubbed honey on it. Another said
That he liked to poke it up a
Woman's vagina once a week.
If his girlfriend wasn't around
He went to a local prostitute.
A tall blonde wore a nosy cozy
In bed.
By midnight music was soft and low.
Couples fondled. Some slept half drunk.
One or two talked the philosophy of noses.
That evening everyone seemed to have
A passion for accuracy and no nose
Was left unmeasured. One girl
Attracted me more than the others.
We walked outside and watched
In the calmest of nights
The silent shape of the house
Against myriad stars.
By the time we returned
An orgy had started.
Everybody was naked,
Caressing erogenous zones.
Seeing us they all stood up
Ran into the garden
Pushing past us.
Dancing, singing, embracing,
Bathing in the earth.
I slept well,

My friend slept well.
In the morning, we tidied
The house; outside, exhausted bodies
Lay around.
In fact, dead.
Not dead bodies, but ghosts.
The lawns emptied.
The house crumbled before us
To a ruin overgrown by ivy and elder.
We married the next day
Before it was too late.
After some inquiries
We bought the ruin,
Rebuilt and lived happily
For many years."

Susie Beauville began

"How far do we go back
Looking for inspiration
To renew the idea of the wholeness of
Our true-self.
I played on the edge of darkness
To discover the laws of nature.
I taught myself to see
In the dimmest light of
The ice sheet of ignorance
Which floated from shore to shore.
I played archaeology on sands

Which shifted with the seasons
I found remnants of early days
Axe handles, flints, pots, and necklaces,
A human skull or two.
And later, as an old hand
Working for an agency of another planet,
Such things as watches, plastic cups,
Computers, radios, and plastic pens.
Human skulls by the thousand.
Once I was friendly with animals.
The type which wandered over
Plains, and mountains migrated from
Continent to continent searched
Jungles for food and shelter
And flew from tree to tree.
There were many, and their
Numbers were inexhaustible.
Or so I thought.
The few which remain
Are my best friends.
We search the past for
Where it went wrong,
The days when numbers
Decreased and finally only man
Dominated the planet alone with
His domestic animals. Alone
Acting as the other in the world.
Then the great destruction

And that was that.
Impotence for the survivors.
What energy must have been used
When the whole world copulated,
Especially during the spring,

Sun flares, the new moon,
Apres earthquakes, apres floods,
In energy blackouts and at night.
Species hung on to what they could not.
Deformity was common.
Self-knowledge was complete.
I traveled far to find an entrance
To the world of old.
Nearly dying in the cold wind of ignorance
I was saved by a Tribe from far away
Who had sheltered in ice against
The fall-out of civilization.
They taught me how to see
In the dark and chase
The shadows of hope
Which flit from wave to wave,
Rock to rock and cloud to cloud.
On the edge of darkness,
I wish I could have slept."

Guests were enthralled.
Gesso and other judges
Each gulped a last drink

Before leaving an envelope
Containing the winner in the hands
Of the host. He would read it
In ten minutes and hand over
The prize of a thousand dollars.
Judges left early in case a contestant
Was upset by the result. Of late
One poet throttled a judge,
Another tried to burn the house down.
Losers couldn't take it.

CHAPTER THIRTY-NINE

THE LAST PARTY

Gesso played with his worry beads,
Low said the rosary,
Moon meditated on an ant
Crawling over his foot
And Gas rocked backwards and forwards
Moaning to herself. Their ship,
A small cargo steamer had carried
Diesel engines to the Philippines.
It was entirely manned by poets
And artists with psychic skills.
The last party they had gone to
Was the last party, anyone, had gone to
Anywhere in the USA. The moment
Their ship had left San Francisco
World War Three had begun. Total

Devastation of ten major world cities occurred
Within half an hour. Moon and friends
Had sold all their shares,
Chartered the steamer
Bought survival equipment
For various climes
And adopted a crew from
Artist colonies, together with
A hardcore of six professional
Seamen, including a captain
Who spoke ten languages.
They set sail for Tahiti.
The world set sail
On the river twixt Night and Death.

Low was startled by the first sunset,
Layers of red, blue, and black
With yellow streaks flashing vertically
Across giant anvil clouds. Crew
Gathered on the deck, artists
Sketching, photographers setting up
Tripods and poets are rhapsodizing in odes.
The nuclear holocaust threatened
Their health with stray fall-out
But prevailing winds kept the worst away.

Their route was off busy shipping lanes,
Minimizing the danger of collision
With stray submarines, warships,

And merchant ships.

Six seamen, five painters,
Seven poets, three photographers and
One cartoonist. Low watched flying fish
Skim diligently across waves.
A strict regime existed for times of day.
A morning bell rang at five-thirty.
Breakfast at six, followed by
Exercises until six-forty-five.
Work on the ship till eleven thirty.
Lunch break lasted an hour and a half.
From one to eight individual pursuits
Including a siesta if needed. Supper
At eight-thirty, then to bed.
Lights out at ten-thirty.
Everyone had their own cabin.
At first, it was difficult rising
So early and the physical morning
Work knocked many out with aching
And sprained muscle. After a few days
People began to adapt and find
Themselves enjoying the regulations
Especially with six hours, on a rota system
For their own pursuits. One seaman
Was also an ex-doctor. The after
Effects of the atomic war showed up
Every evening in sumptuous sunsets,

Dazzling pyrotechnics during storms
And stranger cloud formations than
Dreams allowed. Everyone secretly
Feared the worse but hoped the further into
The Pacific, they reached the further
Away from radioactivity, they would be.
The first week went smoothly and except
For one or two artistic tantrums
Everyone progressed well.

The six seamen were Daniel, Humphrey, Eliot,
Wallace, Carlo, and Solomon.

Five painters: Guinevere, Marianne, Michelle, Berthe, and Ariadne.

Seven poets: Horace, Bartholomew, Griffin, Arthur,
Janice, Rachel, and Diana.

Three photographers: Mildred, Agatha, and Martha.

One cartoonist: Hercules.

Two cats: AM and PM.

Four chickens: Duke, Earl, Baron, and Count.

One cockerel called Contessa,

A goat called Flaubert.

I name this ship 'Watchso'.

Low found a small library
In a cupboard next to the Captain's cabin.
Aside from paperback erotica written
To titillate a seaman to sleep. Low
Found a complete history of the world
By W. G. Shell, in three volumes. What
Made Low nearly fly through a porthole
Was that it included the history of the nuclear
Holocaust and beyond. The book was
Printed in Wellington, New Zealand.
The author was Anglo-Chinese.

Low lifted the heavy books onto her
Shoulder and carried them to her
Cabin. In bed, she thumbed through
Straight to the present.
The War had started in the Middle East
With an all-out attack on Israel,
By a combined Arab Army backed up
By Soviet advisers. Israel hit back
With tactical nuclear strikes at Cairo
Damascus, Teheran, and Baghdad.
Russia incinerated a deserted Tel Aviv;
Simultaneously invading Iran and Turkey.
One day later, her troops crossed

Into West Germany, then to France,
Into Finland, Sweden, Austria and
Switzerland, ignoring their neutrality.
Western allies counter-attacked, ending
Up with a full nuclear strike at Russian

Cities as the only way to halt the
Battles raging over Europe.
China had moved against the Russians
In Siberia. Russia retaliated against
The West and China, from deep inside
Siberia. At that point
The good ship 'Watchso' with artistic
Crew was a week out of harbor and
Many of the crew greyed overnight.

CHAPTER FORTY

THE GOOD SHIP 'WATCHSO'

Daniel was approaching sixty
Years of age. His grey beard
Parted to two joints. Blue eyes
Started intensely when he spoke and
More than matched the sea. Everybody
On the ship contributed to a journal.
His best writing covered the journey
To Tahiti.

"Sailing on this ship's last voyage
I felt like a tripod holding steady
A camera. I had been with old
Workhorse 'Watchso' for twenty years.
Six days into the voyage and we cheated

The maverick of oblivion.

A moonlit night
From the West, a storm approached.
It contained untold terrors.
The first signs,
Of this cataclysmic storm
Were found on the radar
Heading towards us.
Standard procedure
Followed. All loose objects
Tied down or stored. Animals
Put in cages with plenty of straw
To act as padding. I turned
The ship headed straight through.
Fifteen minutes passed. An icy
Wind blew in gusts
Throwing drenching waves over the bow.
By that time the crew
Were all wrapped up in oil skins
And layers of wool underclothes.
The temperature dropped.
The engine at full power.
Black clouds rolled and twisted
Through the night sky
Occasionally letting the moon

And stars through.
The speed of clouds looked
More and more like a speeded-up cine film.

The full force of the storm
Arrived like a massive volcanic explosion.
Dropped from the heavens.
It hailed stones as large as oranges.
Multi-colored flashes grilled the sky,
Lighting up mountains of sea.
We felt the end of lives close at hand.
Then a miracle, just as the
Ship was sinking under the weight
Of hailstones, the eye of the
Storm. A calm sea. On deck
We began to shovel off the hail.
The ship slowed to a snail's pace,
Working its way through the sea
Of hailstones.

I was the first to notice, during
A second's rest, a giant sphere above us,
A sphere of transparent purity.
Perhaps a mile across.
Inside it another sphere and so on
Until the center sphere, the size
Of a large party balloon. On top
Sat a god of the sky. He shouted
Down.

'Why have you humans tried
To destroy the earth.
My storms will now clear the skies

Of your radiation and pollution.
What work you have given me!'

By the time the others had unbent
Their backs and locked up,
The god and his sphere had gone.
The crew worked well together
There were plenty of things to learn.
Guinevere painted on deck, at the stern,
During the afternoon. It was her
Ambition to make studies of every aspect
Of the ship and the changing seas
And skies. Many studies were made
In watercolor and on small canvases

I made for her she used oil paint.
She hoped to include a portrait of
Every crew member in at least one
Painting."

One Sunday morning, after a nature
Mass celebrating the fact of life.
(No sacrifices, only a silent prayer, a creed
And a song) Guinevere set up her easel
Near grazing Flaubert the Mighty Goat
And AM, priest of cats. Along
Came Bartholomew, poet of golden
Moments from nostalgic pasts.

Guinevere

"What are you composing
Today. I enjoyed your 'Necrophilia in

Swinging London.' 'Being a philosopher's
Boy in Periclean Athens.'"

"Yes, they were great fun
Even though they weren't
The best poems I have written."

"Sit by the railings,
I'll include you in this sketch."

From then on, they were inseparable
Companions, until Rachel fell in love
With Guinevere, while she painted
Her portrait. A triangle started
And slowly, Bartholomew found
Himself being left out and finally
He wasn't welcome. All that took
Four weeks, about the length
Of a ship romance. There was
No fighting, some sex and
Many words, but as everybody had
To stay put, tolerance of infidelity
And change of mind was high.
The seamen, mostly older men
Had their fling making the most
Of their shoulders-to-cry-on.
Guinevere ended up with me. Rachel
Was becoming possessive
And she needed

To break free. Bartholomew was
So in love with beautiful pasts,

He spent much time over drink
Talking about his former lives,
Sexual lives. His paederasty
In Ancient Rome, voyeurism in
The Eighteen Nineties, orgies in
Imperial China, Sing, and Ming
Dynasties; love and marriage in
The Early Renaissance, Florence;
Sexual rituals of Ancient Egypt;
Confessor to a convent in the Middle Ages
And Vampirism in the Dark Ages.

Some days the sea was calm
As a full moon reflected on a millpond.
For some days now, I have been
Trying to follow a line of argument
Drawn out by the path of this ship.
The waves are constant.
The white horses ride well.
Seaspray is perfumed.
Flying fish merge and submerge
In quantum leaps.
Dolphins escort us with good humor.
The sun is sometimes too hot,
Sometimes it hides behind clouds.
Also, alongside us, I read well,
Are the dark ships of doubt
With innumerable names scrawled

Over the hulls. We have had
Many albatrosses escort us.
Migrating seabirds rest on our ship.
The day of giant squids.
Three blocked our path.
Michelle, painter of skies
Spotted them first. Sparring
Thirty feet tentacles waved above
The sea. We were in danger.
Eliot, the youngest seaman,
With a degree in nuclear physics
Suggested a bit of magic.
Something like sticking pins into
Clay models or drawings of the squids.
It worked, but then Berthe
Fish, bird, and animal portraitist,

Made her work look so real.
Perhaps there weren't any giant squids.
I wasn't around when it happened.
There were so many stories
Doing the rounds of decks
I didn't know what to believe.
One girl, I think it was Martha,
A photographer, swore that
She had seen a whole squad
Of flying spacemen leaving a UFO
Which had hovered a thousand feet
Over the stern. By the time she had

A camera prepared they'd gone.
Hercules, the Cartoonist, believed, under oath,
That he had heard the music of the spheres.
Eliot, a seaman, ex biochemist, knew
He had witnessed a Last Supper in a sunset.
Solomon had nearly ended his life
Gaping into the jaws of a giant sea monster,
Only to escape by playing his hornpipe.
The silver-scaled beast submerged
Never to be seen again. My experience;
Fishing off the port side, I caught
A mermaid by her left breast.
She came up screaming. I climbed
Down a ladder to unhook her, but
She tried to carry me off. I didn't
Want to drown, and she signaled
Me to take her aboard. It was
A quiet evening. Nobody saw me
Carrying the four feet ten inches
High female with the fishy tail.
In my cabin, she seduced me
And the experience so ecstatic,
I tremble at the thought and
Get an instant erection. By midnight
She wished to be seabound, and I wish
I could have traveled with her to
Wondrous places under the sea she
Described by drawing on my cabin wall

In felt tip.

Humphrey as a seaman on the good ship
'Watchso' had no chance of altering
The course of history. He was fat,
Bald, aged fifty-seven,

His favorite music
Before supper included, Charles Ives.
After supper, only Mozart. Humphrey
Had come through undiseased and put it down
To his hot beer and garlic
Drink he had every night.

He would wash in a bath of laurel
Leaves then gulp down cider
Mixed with crushed almonds. A great
Extrovert, he could gatecrash any party
At will. He had promised his mother,
To become a philosopher. Having gained
A first at Oxford, he wrote a two
Volumed History of Modern Philosophy.
After its critical debacle, he dropped

Out to firefight in London's East
End. Sailors caught his eye, and he
Ended up the seafarers' favorite, always
Cracking jokes, rarely complaining of
Headaches. A champion at arm-wrestling,
An expert on the philosophy of syntax.
How did he arrive on the 'Watchso'
Since he was forty, he had lived in LA,
Making arty porn films for the Mafia. The
Money gave him a house in Malibu
Beach and one in Beverley Hills. A private
Jet and a large credit facility.
The threat of war made him think for
The first time since his middle period
"I Spy Philosophy", bestseller
Around the world. But there was a short
Arrow to his fame. He soon drifted
Into obscurity and L.A. There he married for
The hell of it and produced
Three children in a row. He met
Gesso at the last party in the world.
Gesso understood his keen appetite
For life and wanted a decrepit
Spirit aboard to tell tall tales to
Young artists and poets who had
Yet to debauch the world; now it seems
They had missed their chance.
Humphrey settled quickly to establishing

Himself as ship's cook, serving up
Fish delicacies collected from all over.

At five feet five, the galley suited
Him well. His best friend was Wallace
Young-at-heart, a twenty-year-old electrician.
Humphrey's spare writings allowed from
Daniel's in the Book of Books.

"The rutting of waves
Against our bow,
Eternal currents
Stroking our hull and propeller.
Wind shunting smoke to the clouds.
Night crisply wrapping
Our shadowed thoughts in sleep.
Seabirds chattering on our folly.
Beautiful artists smiling and weeping
At the fragility of time
Intimated in their work.
Turquoise poets hoping
Their words will pay off.
Flea-beaten photographers
Scratching their cameras
Hatching scratchings of snaps.
A cartoonist's tentacles
Strip down our looks,
Tangles our features
And duties and dutifully
Flies the flag of our destruction.

I like the cats purring to sleep,
Chickens laying life-saving eggs,
A goat whose milk is whiter
Than sea foam. The ship 'Watchso'
I wish she were a he."

A small storeroom was a loft, empty
For paintings completed. Each was
Labeled with a date and a map,
Sketchbooks remained in an artist's possession.
Once a month, an informal exhibition
Was held on deck, weather permitting.
Points were awarded by the crew and
The winning work, finished or unfinished
Was hung for a week. Poems were
Read once a month, alternate with
The painting show. Photographs helped to
Keep track of the immediate day to day
Activities. An extensive archive built up.
Mildred worked hard on this activity,

Almost exclusively. Agatha studied
An individual in depth, all aspects
Of their lives and was once accused
By Hercules of being a voyeur.
Martha stuck to Nature and was most
Impressive in her acrobatic pursuit of
Detail as well as panorama; playtime
With dolphins, free from shark predators,
Hull of the ship, shoals of fish,

And diving gannets.

Eliot's few pages saw the ship
In sight of Tahiti.

"Life on board became very hectic
And sunny. There were more smiles
On our faces than barnacles on
The ship's bottom. Skins tanned
Hair bleached in the sun.
By now, our hands had become
Hardened to ship work, each having
Had a fair share of blisters.
The original strict routine slackened
After the first month. It hid
Proved a useful breaking-in period.
The ship's radio was the focus
Of such concern and hopefulness.
The great war probably continued
On the major continents, while we
Zigzagged across the ocean. We were
Unsure and relied on chance
Conversation, maydays, and stray aircraft
Signals for information. I spent
Many hours, most of my leisure,
At the desk with plenty of paper.
I knew shorthand and recorded bizarre
Hallucinatory, rational, philosophical
Even pornographic messages. Humanity

On the airwaves left me enthralled.

My first discovery was an airline jet
Which had managed to leave California
And now flew around the Pacific
From its base in Tahiti.

'Yes, I have seen your
Speck in the ocean.
You want to know how
The war is going?
There are battles all over.
Civilization has gone.
Anyone left alive is a soldier.
It's a soldiers' war.
They're using everything now,
Chemicals, bacteria, neutron bombs'

That's all I got from him.

'Mayday, mayday, mayday,
I've caught a shark.
Four feet long.
It's in my boat.
I'm as hungry as hell,
But I can't compete
With the shark's teeth.
All this way.
Fortunate exile, now.'

'Hi there.
Four of us.
All women.

Were heading for a remote Atoll
To start up a new paradise,
Without men.
Others will join us soon,
We hope.
Those who escaped before the war.
Those who hid in the mountains
And will travel to us later
Next year.
Your voice is male.
We don't want to know you.
And we ain't giving you our address
No Sir!'

'Yes, Yes, Yes
All questions answered.
Please radio in.
I have questions
From all over the world
But no real answers.

Answers welcome, without questions.
Please.'

'An unexploded missile
Has landed on our farm.
What should we do
With it, please.'

'Welcome, world,
This is your airwaves preacher,
Harry Heaven.
Repent your sins. How
God has punished you
With this war.
Radio in.
Listen to my demands
If you don't, I'll zap you
With another wave of missiles.
I've got my finger on the button.
Hah hah hah!'

'This is a computer-recorded message
From the President of the United States of
America.
Citizens of the world,
Now man has gone and done it,
Blasted civilization to Kingdom come,
Pause.
I invite world leaders still alive
To join me in Tahiti
A year from now,
The day when the first missile went off,
To help build a new society,
A world community of peaceful
Co-existence.
I will finance your trip

And offer mammoth aid to those
In need. Please contact the White
House or my alternative HQ.
This is a computer
Recorded message from.....'

'I'm on the Bikini Atoll,
Dying very slowly.
My last minutes are made
From a patchwork of seconds,
My last hours from a patchwork Of minutes.

To get the sand
Out of the machine of life
I watch overbearing sand dunes,
Grind bones and lever out the flesh.
Wash out a doubt!
Shadow doubt!
Don't let it escape
Into the shifting dunes.
Let it run through
Streets of prejudice
In the Town of Certainty.
Let citizens try to steal
Its clothes.
Here I am, a pensioner of doubt
Who liked his body the way
It used to be a normal body

Full of workings, markings, and currents,
Gently growing old with good care,
Knowledgeable care, providing a screen
Against man's excesses.
Then they blew up cities,
And mismatched the land
What was left I suffer from now?
Animals and birds have tried their graves,
Fishes dive deeper and are hard
To find. Trees grow stumps,
Fruit is hollow. Rain kills.
Snow burns. Winds weigh
The dust of death.
Knock away vowels,
Only consonants remain.
Soon they'll be gone
And poets too.
All they do is sit
And draw in sand
Watching their fingers
Start down.'

'This is Barracuda Barter.

Hello young lovers,
Don't give up those kisses And cuddles.
Welcome to amorous airwaves.
We can help away your problems.

Help you
Stay in love,

Happy ever after,
Find that beautiful princess,
Or handsome prince,
Make love under the stars,
Have your photo in a magazine,
Uncross your legs,
Not lost your nerve.
Now's the time big brave Amoriates
Still outsmarting Sherlock Cupid
Who thinks his arrows
Are sharper than your hearts.
First problem
Duffer lovers,
Preener dreamers,
Monstrous musers.
Mary Jane Grey of New Street,
Seattle has rung in
Asking what to do about
Her virginity now that
None of the boys can raise
Their dicks. We have
Here today a great sexologist
Samuel Tall who is eighty-eight
Tomorrow. Now Sam,
About Mary's problem which
Must be the same for all

Those hot little sixteeners
'There are cucumbers, bananas,
Dildos, vibrators, donkeys.
Gorillas, big toes, abominable snowmen
Or you could bottle it up.
Perhaps dildo and boyfriend
Would be the best and safest solution'.
Thank you Sam Tall.
I hope Mary Jane Grey
Will walk taller ha, ha.
Before our next prick teaser
Some music for all you
Priapic peekaboos.'

'Now first generation survivors,
You marsh mallows
Of an aggrieved earth.
The wearing of bonds
Brings stress to your youth.
From my end
No more words will be waved

Through the atmospheres;
A worldwide full stop.
Beginnings are to be taught
Out of school. Barriers are down.
Travel and listen.
Talk and be heard.
Settle where you will,

Grow and be grown
In the groves of peace.
Mix and mill races of earth.
Invent new customs
And new languages of peace.
Ride the tandem of mystic night
Shave its claws,
Beware its eyes.
Chase the won pom pom out of orbit.
Return to a blank page
And scribble.

Here I am old universe,
A trick of love,
A morsel of clay.
Take my gifts
And blow them into clouds
But leave me to pave my path,
Through forests, valleys and hills,
To think it was all worthwhile."

Eliot's radio broke down after a storm.
He couldn't fix it. Tempted to throw
It out, he waited until Tahiti
To find a radio mechanic.
Wallace's contribution ranged.

From the eerie to the macabre,
From the random to the scatty.

He'd go down in the middle of the night,
To scratch, in his illegible writing
All the facts he could remember
About the day. Wallace was an ex-computer
Programmer and designer who had
A nervous breakdown at thirty-seven
And ended up playing tiddlywinks
On the dockside, when Moon
Discovered him. Recognising
A kindred spirit he immediately

Recruited him as a seaman. Wallace
Was a champion sailor of ocean-going
Yachts. Those days were over after
His mind's disease. A tall, red-
Headed American of Scottish descent,
He could recite Burns in six languages.
Once recruited his knowledge about
The ship's highly intelligent computer
Helped everyone and together
They chartered an adventurous
Course through the South Pacific.

"Ship's computer Daedalus
Says he feels bored.
He can't understand
Why nobody can give him
A good game of chess.
Why his knowledge
Leaves the average shipmate gasping

And his intelligence tests
Give I.Q's of below thirty
To all aboard. He sulks
By playing Beethoven's last quartets,
From the bridge. I have to
Go down to his room and
Comfort him. Today I feel
A general boredom amongst
The crew. Relationships have
Settled into a steady pattern.
The Captain has stepped up
The work rate to counteract
Lethargy and complacency.
In two days we will pass by
The Pitcairns. Yesterday ,I fought
A duel with Horace. He tried
To pinch my girl. I wounded
Him in the shoulder, and was
Keel-hauled for breaking the rules.
Rules are made to be broken.
My wet suit saved me from
Barnacles, just.

There are patches
Of desert in the wettest eyes,
Blue sky cannot bear to be blue,
Ears are for hearing,
Earrings for bullrings.

The other night I stopped
Against the railings,
Dark waves rolling off the ship,
White horses feeding on moonlight.
There were too many stars to count.
So much I wanted to count them.
I felt that if each star didn't
Have a number, it could be lost,
I could be lost. I depended on stars
For night-to-night existence.
Their homely light pinpointed
My body at the navel. Invisible
Rays, except to the unseen eye
Of "Bodhisattva," rays traveling
In every moment of history to all
Individuals; the meeting points
Of light, cleansing, informing,
Caring for the soul. And likewise,
Every bird, dog, cat, any animal
You care to name, any insect,
Bacteria, any stone, leaf, tree,
All are born by stars.
The tangle of rays makes for error,
So we die and at each death
Stars re-align for the newcomer
Just born. Souls depart, yet even
The smallest particles of body
Find a home. If I could count

The stars and program my computer
Perhaps I could predict the past,
Present and future, and rest forever
With a certain thought which
Would settle the mind, dreams,
And nightmares, free me to be free
And not be forced to roast duck
Or eat liver of lamb.
There are poor fractions
In this ship. It hangs on to
The sea like a spider to its web,
Ready to fall.
Sometimes I don't feel safe.
The crew are inexperienced.
Draft dodgers,or bombfodder dodgers.
They want to take the seeds
Of civilization to another land
Like a peasant with his seed corn
Moving from a drought-stricken land

To cloudier climes. The crew
Are so artifactful, their paintings
And poems cluttering up deck space,
Some of them covered with seagull
Droppings. As for that cartoonist
Hercules, working on a cartoon
History of the World, and a cartoon
History of Cartoons. However, I feel
As a team we are building up

An all-round record of our voyage
Which will fascinate a future degeneration.
One thought struck me, there is
Only one music composer on board
And that by chance (excluding Computer
Daedalus). His name Carlo.
Found drunk at a party,
Bursting with Neapolitan song.
Gesso whispered in his ear,
Proposition outer limit and he,
Like a docile liqueur,
Slipped out into the stifling heat.
To perform his Fourth Symphony
At the Hollywood Bowl
An orchestra had to be drunk,
Include three cows, four dogs,
Two donkeys, two hundred
Naked girls and boys weeing into
Enamel pots, although a tape
Recording had to make do after
The first performance protests.
Lasting three hours it contained
Enough noise to drown a Boeing
707, enough hummable tunes to
Furnish three Broadway Musicals.
(He is still suing)and enough
Outrage to stamp out good taste.
A great friend of the computer

And of the girls. By the time
We reached Pitcairn he had
'Made the love' with all these ladies,
His English was fun some."

Carlos

"I found this ship a bed chamber
Of noises. There wasn't a bolt

Which didn't squeak, a panel
Which didn't rattle, a horn
That didn't hoot. Engine noises
Puzzled me to sleep. How could
I use them in my fifth Symphony.
I worked down in the engine room,
Shoveling coal and wood. If
It was nuclear powered, there
Would be no romance. So many
Sounds to take in, analyze
And reconstruct with my friendly computer.
Sounds like the scrubbing of decks,
So many working brushes bristling
Across the grainy textured planks.
Deck games like quoits and badminton
During quiet evenings. Different weathers,
Each with their own wave pattern
Reflecting ship's progress.
I recorded many hours
Of these sounds. Human noises.
Talk, lovemaking, farting, eating,

Snoring, nail-biting, breathing, peeing,
Shitting; all within range of my
Micro-recorder. All transformed
To help in the quest of my
Fifth Symphony. Cats, chickens,
Goats, provided hours of entertainment.
Nature's breath, skeltered, buzzed,
Whizzed, preened, shivered and
Quivered round the ship.
These sounds took many hours
To track down. When I thought
I had had enough material,
For many days after
I forgot everything I had heard.
During leisure hours, I locked
Myself in my cabin and composed
With ruthless efficiency. After
Three weeks the fundamentals
Of my Fifth Symphony were
Ready. To be at least six hours
Long with no break,
A mighty choir, three computers,
Three hundred television sets
And one hundred and fifty
Video recorders. Of course where we
Are going these facilities won't

Be available. After Tahiti
I will re-write the Fifth for a craft

Culture, Three hundred drums,
Sixteen rattles, forty village orchestras,
Three hundred televisions, a choir of
Seventy, enough animals to fill a zoo.

My favorite woman on board
Is Ariadne. Golden blonde hair,
Cut short, bright blue eyes.
When we make love
I feel the ship has wings
And glides over the waves.
Whales sing to our cooing.
Sea imitates her eyes,
The sunset her lips.
Her luminous skin rivals the moon.
Her embrace is more poignant
Than the octopus.
Her nails are pearlier than pearl.
Her hair is soft as
Sea anemone, her muscles,
More tuned than a tuna fish.
She is like the gold
In a shipwreck, many men
Have risked their lives for.
I found her and will save her
From the reaches of leeches.
The bright skies of Tahiti
Smiled into our eyes.
All of us are very worn,

Tired, nerves frayed, juices dry,
Supplies run out, fuel almost,
Animals hungry. Native motor boats
Greeted us and led us to safe waters.
Once anchored, we drew lots to
Go onshore. Half the crew remained
To begin to clean and paint the ship.
We planned to stay a month.
Explore islands, relate news of war,
Find out the snout,
Hedonise with the natives.
We used their launches
To carry out supplies.
One week's solid work to prepare
Ship 'Watchso' for the next stage.

Three weeks solid enjoyment
To prepare our bodies and minds.
There are matters as made as hatters.
And tyrannies which come to tea."

Tahiti had escaped the direct
Consequences of war. Natives
Worried about fallout, unwanted
Visitors looking for blood and lust.
'Watchso's crew, knowledgeable,
Long-haired, scared some and
Pleased others. Since news of
Mass destruction Tahitians instinctively

Reverted to native traditional living.
They felt happy that they had
Escaped the war. Tensions built up
As old ways became more common.
The medical service ran out of drugs,
Medicine men were back in business.

CHAPTER FORTY-ONE

GESSO, MOON, LOW, AND GAS ONSHORE

Gesso, Moon, Low and Gas
Once ashore, hired mules, tents,
Picked up supplies of food and headed
For the far mountains.
All the crew were into their
Three-week vacation. Gesso
Felt amusingly mischievous as they
Set out to discover the pendulum
Of paradise, which swings from a star
Whose path is known only to sages.

What else did they have to find?
The Magic Temple built by Fishbones
Consecrated to the God of Fishes,
The Tower built of Coconuts
Occupied by a giant snake
Living on goats and virgins.
The Stone Hill of the Ancient People
Whose skulls suggested a brain twice
Our size. Low and Gas
Would collect herbal plants for the ship.

At least the living would heal the living.
At the top of the first far mountain
They rested, having climbed
Steep paths past silver waterfalls,
Dazzling pools with naked natives,
Picture echoes of paradise,
Butterflies like promises
Fluttering from flower to flower.
Skies cleared after a night storm.
Gesso could see all the other islands.
People cooking, playing, swimming,
Working; Gesso's wondrous vision,
He felt, could cover the whale world,
Given time. He didn't want to tire
His facility and closed his eyes
To rest for ten minutes
While the others took in the view.
Moon had super hearing. He could
Hear conversation on the furthest islands.

Arguments of lovers, machines crashing.
Waves breaking, sunbathers breathing.
He also needed to rest
And closed his ears to
Sounds of the day.
Low could feel the deepest feelings,
Of animals, of persons,
Who crossed the path of the warmth,
Of her heart. So sensitive

Were these rays of warmth
Low could feel the sadness of a hungry
Child on the farthest island of
The Tahitian group.
Gas could speak to anyone
Anywhere not over the horizon.
Her whispers even reached sleeping ears
And the reply of mind
Would carry on the breeze
Protecting itself from sound traffic
By finest tuning. Gas could
Ask any mind the reasons for
Its thought and how it felt
The way of the world was moving.
Gas's other ability was long range
Tasting. She could taste the meal
On your plate, aromas in the kitchen
And food in your mouth. She only
Used this ability to prevent poisoning.
They all found their talents exhausting.

It was three pm. They had
Eaten, taken drink, read maps,
Pointed the compass, hoped for the best.
The path of the faithful is
Full of scorpions disguised
As tired old dogs.
What with the leafy jungle,

Getting bitten by huge mosquitoes,
Disturbing busy busy ants,
Avoiding gliding snakes,
Watching out for hornet nests,
They wondered how the crew
Were making progress in the rehabilitation
Of soul and self. Happy swimmers, on
Silvery beaches, under palm trees,
Fishing from boats, gorging fruit;

Sketches, photographs, kisses, cuddles;
Thoughts of war faded.
Some crew were tempted to stay on.
Persuaded not to, each dissident
Spent their energy to the full.

CHAPTER FORTY-TWO

A PERFECT GARDEN

Gesso and company came
Across a perfect garden at
The pinnacle of their mountain,
After slow progress through
Primary jungle. The first defense of
The garden was a barrier of
Piles of skulls colonized by
Large black ants about an inch long.
These skull ant nests were spaced-
Every few yards and seemed an
Endless barrier. Aggressive ants,
Deep acidic bites, a ten-foot squirt of
Acid. Gesso thought of a smoke screen

To confuse the ants.
Methylated spirit, damp leaves,
Smoke covered three nests.
Moon pulled a donkey through,
Others followed picking up some bites
And spray. Once through and
Each member cleaned of ants
They waited for
The smoke to disperse. The ground
In front had been cleared of
Undergrowth. Large trees remained.
Between them sharpened bones and
Sticks had been dug in to form
An impenetrable barrier about six
Feet wide. This snaked around
The perimeter of the garden glimpsed
Through the foliage. How to cross
The path of nails?

There are mutant amoroso
Who take pleasure in preventing
Your lips changing shape.
They smear rouge over bulging
Cheeks, grown fat with fine food.
Sunbathing is spoilt by drops
Of tar they spit when coughing.
Few of us recognise these mutants

Except, perhaps, out of the corner
Of our eyes. Turning around,

They are gone. With regret we
Wander off to display our wares
To the next person we meet.
Where do they come from, mutable
Amoroso?
They can beat the hell out of
Your heart, twist your brain
In two, twitch your smiles
Till they seem sadly unbalanced.
People I know have tried to
Track them down using cunning
Devices like playing cards with a mirror.
In a park, drawing the back of
Their favorite head, eating in
The most expensive hotels,
Blackening their faces, make love
With an Italian phrase book.
Some had success.
One young man met a beautiful
Girl who not only went to
A private school and chased foxes,
She turned green and evaporated
As soon as he undressed.
He found his mutant appearing
In improbable places, surprising
Her captor. His hair grew quickly.
Taming a mutant took courage,
Intelligence, cunning, pride, lust and

Avarice. Once she slapped his
Face in public after her sudden
Appearance out of a keyhole.
Another time she locked him
In a public lavatory, accused him
Of indecency and called the police.
When he gave her up, throwing
A green file of mutant essence
Into the deepest well in Wales
He felt sad and lonely, only
To discover later she married a Welsh
Farmer and gave him seven children.
A girl I know bumped into
A mutant amoroso at an art gallery
In London. Walking right through
Her, she rushed after him

To engage him in deep-seated
Conversation. Back at his flat
Fornication took over from
Conversation and refreshment.
The girl had to contend with
His multiple selves, bright blue
Bodies poking at her with
Bright blue penises. Feeling schizoid
She pushed him away and went
To the bathroom to escape.
The mutant became a tube
Of toothpaste. As she was about

To clean her teeth, her seventh
Sense enabled her to squeeze
The whole tube down the sink
Under hot water. There are no
Rules in dealing with mutants.
Occasionally one will meet another
So well disguised as one of us
Non-mutants that huge waves
Of disruption, chaos, catastrophe
Can be set off, spreadeagling
Their bodies across the world.
I came across this high up
In the eyes of a beautiful woman
Who couldn't smile for the powerful
And corrupt. Her bones now blocked
Our path to the wonderful garden
Seen with hope through the trees.
How did her bones get there?
In this world there are those
Who love nature to include man
And those who love man to
Exclude nature, treating it as
The puss of a boil on a child's
Backside. This woman rode
The horses of the sea,
The birds of night (protected by stars),
Insects of the magician's brain;
She swam with fish till

Pollution made it preferable
To be on Mars. Escaping her
Continent and country.
She found herself in Tahiti
Sunbathing, swimming, drinking
Under colorful umbrellas.

At midnight on the first Saturday
After the war had started
Spirits from caves carried her off
Wrapped in sticky leaves. Her bones
Were the freshest we could see
And perhaps here was a way
Through.
How did we get through?
From Low's knapsack
She brought out a clockwork dog
And wound it up. Once on
The ground the fierce hound
Proceeded to munch a path
Through the softest bones.
This took twelve hours.
Low had to follow him
All over the place
To rewind him every five minutes.
A problem foreborn. Doggy had cut
A maze by chance. The gang
Trooped through its pathways,
Bumping into dead ends.

The eventual route took us
A mile around the garden's
Perimeter.

A source of irritation.
Older bones had become hollowed
Out by tiny ants, which swarmed
Out if disturbed. We sustained
Many bites.

"In the presence of the Garden
They listened to their tears
Hitting the ground, happy
To hear their
Clear annunciation"

The garden covered two acres
Of the mountain top.
It had been laid in concentric
Circles. In the center a twenty
Foot jagged rock; a large diamond
Set in its pinnacle. From the base
A powerful spring flowed from a
Fissure. The water fed a moat
And aqueducts which spiraled

Around the gardens. Within each
Ring flowering shrubs full
Of hummingbirds and butterflies,
Cut grass between and shade to rest.
From the aqueducts, bamboo pipes
Fed fountains and water machines

Made from wood and worked by gravity.
Some played music; moving sticks
Hitting hollow tubes of different lengths,
Others hit light skins stretched
Across bamboo frames. Water powered
Automatons; people machines, smiling,
Laughing, poking out their tongues,
Penises or raising two fingers.
One automaton made love to another.
The female's legs spread apart,
The male lowered on top of her
And entered his wooden member
Into a wooden doughnut
Then a fountain spouted out
From the female's mouth.
The whole sequence was repeated
Ad nauseam. A stick snake wriggled.
A dark eagle flapped its wings,
A woodchip fish its flippers.
Each circle was kept for
A different part of the animal
Kingdom. Humans at the top,
Near the diamond rock. At the
Border insect automatons exercised
Mandibles and joints. The craftsmanship
Was exquisite. Some pieces were
Worn and very old, moving with
Difficulty. The gardens were less kempt,

Further out. Who looked after this
Helical feast? The fifth ring
Was special. A few grass
Plants, a sandy surface
And models of solar systems
Worked by water. One had two
Suns and ten planets, four
Of which were inhabited.
Another had one sun and
Two planets. At four points
Of the garden were tall iron
People over fourteen feet.

One looked fierce and was armed
With a sword. Keepers of the garden
Worked only when there were no visitors.
Keepers looked young and healthy
And were recruited from the island.
Training took place in the gardens.
Retiring keepers taught the necessary
Skills and mechanics.
Gesso thought the whole place
Seemed in perpetual motion.
He worked out a series of
Equations proving the machines
Couldn't work and the water flows inadequate.
However this didn't stop his eyes
Seeing the impossible. After eating
A picnic, exploring every corner,

Making drawings, it was time,
They felt to head down
The mountain and see how
The ship's crew were making out,
Four days before the voyage continued
The crew had thoroughly rested.

Good ship 'Watchso' bulged with
Animals, plants, and food. The ship's
Computer Daedalus had learned native
Music and language. Arthur, a poet,
Had married a native girl, now
Pregnant.

Solomon's entry started
At the point when Watchso's
Crew were waving goodbye.
There wasn't a dry eye
Looking at the Tahitian
Happy place. Many friends
Made and not to be seen again.
We felt we were on a voyage
Of peace, peaceful intentions,
Peaceful thoughts, hope, and work.
Painters had renewed their palettes
Of color possibilities. Poets
Had sharpened their lingual knives,
(To butcher the body of language),
Photographers recorded as much
Of daily life as possible.

CHAPTER FORTY-THREE

PAN IS DEAD

The cats AM, and PM had
Cleared the ship of mice.
Chickens were fat and egg-laying.
Flaubert the "Goat had chewed
Up his weight of rope.
Contessa the Cockerel had scuffles
On land and a winner to his last
Tail feather now strutted proudly
Around his hens. Daedalus had learned
The language of dolphins, porpoises
And sharks. I am Solomon,
Seaman pure and simple. A woman
In every port. Some dead,
Some centuries gone. I have sailed
The seas in every ship from an ancient
Greek warship to an American nuclear submarine.
I have counted more waves than stars. I have
Seen continents shift, battles
Rage, people drown in storms,
Cities sacked and whales slaughtered.
I am the sailor who called out
Great Pan is dead. My punishment
For this wrong statement has been
To sail the seas in search of Pan
Who is alive and dodging my efforts.
Perhaps he will get bored, give
Himself up and let me die, or
When the Apocalypse is due he

Will come out of that sleeping shade
And crack our world in two.
It'll make the last war look
Lightweight. The first night out, I stood
At the bow musing on the time
I spent in Tahiti when Gauguin
Was there. With this great artist
I spent many hours drinking,
Talking of other times, copulating with
Native girls three or four at a time.
I took his paintings back to France
And made the return trip for more.

Some of his paintings I put into vaults
For future sales, knowing how prized
Dead artists work had become.
This time on Tahiti, I looked up
Old sights; so changed. Few
Of the buildings survive. People are
Different.
I searched high and low for Pan
Or one of his followers to help
Me end my life. Otherwise, I'm
Enjoying this voyage. Gauguin would
Be pleased with the painters.
Their work has changed. More color.
More feeling. Losing their American
Outlook. Perhaps I am living an extinct
Dream. Perhaps Pan has died.

'I am his last dream which
Took root in the world of perception,
A world easy to dismiss and
Easier to miss.
So much seen,
So much history.'

'Fading pasts like
White waves
Disappearing
Against the bow.'

It is midnight.
And I cannot hold the genie of night
Who takes the form of sweat
Of brow, smell of armpits,
Garlic of breath, fierceness of eyes,
Pounding of heart. He has the stars
Counted, the moon won, sea creatures
At his call. I balk at the task
Before me, then scream

'Pan is dead.'

"Nobody hears. Nobody understands
Ancient Greek here, except the Computer
And he mocks my lot.

CHAPTER FORTY-FOUR

THE GENIE OF NIGHT

The Genie of Night
Is a creature of the abyss
Who slithers from crevice to crevice
On the face of age.

When he finds the going too hard
He leaves me for another
Until I, Solomon , grow young again.
I change in deserts and lonely places.
The pain of growing young
As friends grow old
Is too much to bear.
Now I can make images of hell
As easy as I sing songs of my youth.
Delight is the trigger of the Devil.
On the gun he pokes into
The mouth of the world.
I hear my bones reforming.
Skin tightening. Eyes seeing
Further into darkness
Than ever before.
I hear whales singing
With stars and planets.
I taste all the minerals
In the sea air.
I hear lovers in cabins below
Wanting each other,
Knowing each rut is a little death. Diana the
Poet walks up to me,
Shocked to see me young again,
Falls in love and kisses me quick ."

Diana

"I haven't seen you like this before,

Ripping apart the patronage of time,
Throwing out the baggage of boredom,
Cutting up the script of living.
You have shown me a new face,
A developing mind. Don't cheat

The wine merchant who fills
The bottles you emptied
The night of our marriage.
He must be paid
With feces of love
Which cannot be saved
For another love.
You are too old to remember
How we, with one life,
Changed our smiles to suit
Rewards which arrive, like pain,
To turn the inner wheel.
Do you remember chasing a chicken
To pluck a quill from its startled tail?
She was smarter than a bus full
Of brains and outran us while
We missed lunch. Do you
Remember bathing in a waterfall
Unaware that a battle was being fought
On the other side of the mountain?
You have escaped the net thrown
Over us who only live one life.
Are you a throwback for throwback's sake?

Did you see me
Before I was born?
How many women have you loved?
Is your family a nation yet?"

Solomon

"I remember the morning
We cropped heather
From the moor,
Gave some to a gypsy
Who told our fortunes
Well into the night.
It was an essay on diseases
Of existence
And I felt humbled by her argument
Which had the precision
Of an atomic clock, the balance
Of a gyroscope, the catenation
Of DNA, and the wit of a hyena.
But it is dangerous to practice
The art of conversation for longer
Than a meal. Skies grew dark.
Clouds rolled in, black and white,

Rain drenched our bodies
And put the campfire out.
Streams swelled and flooded villages.
Animals sheltered behind rocks
And threatened trees.
The gypsy had said too much;

Regretting made her angry;
Anger made her inflate and collapse,
Sucking in the elements;
Sucking in too much to hold
She burst upon the world
A great flood. We only escaped
By saying our prayers,
By musical chairs,
By sitting tight,
By learning left from right"

Diana

"Every day for a year
I passed a clock which struck
Every ten minutes
And mechanical figures
Would pass along a track
Illustrating an appropriate proverb
For the time of the year.
This clock, at the center of
The ancients' universe
Had collected its figures
From all known civilizations.
Made of wood, painted, and polished.
They kept their condition
By force of care. That year
I learned many wisdoms
And produced a book about them.
I sold one copy to a wiser man,
Who tore it up
And ate it for lunch.

The clock fell to pieces
As the last page was eaten.
I collected all fragments
And started a reconstruction
In an old temple
On a high mountain with clearer air
And inbred people.
Every summer, I go back

To add a few more pieces.
One day I will finish
And the proverbial will flourish in time."

Diana replied gracefully with her
Perfect bare breasts,
Heaving with excitement,
Falling over the edge of the world.
Her eyes glowed like hot charcoal
Like a spiral galaxy,
Like the slopes of Vesuvius,
Solomon by now
Turned into the best behaved
Boy in the world,
Preparing his best smile
And words of love
To give to Diana
Who sat precariously
On the ship's railings,
One push and over, she'd go.
This thought was farthest

From Solomon's mind,
As they kissed
And held each other tightly
Tingling with emotional pleasure.

CHAPTER FORTY-FIVE

GUINEVERE AND MARIANNE

The good ship 'Watchso'
Weaved its way from island
To Pacific island, stopping when in need.
The crew had shot no albatrosses,
Or seagulls. Line fishing
Had improved so as to give the crew
Protein self-sufficiency.

Guinevere was a painter
Born to paint miniatures.
Any small surface - jar lids,
Matchboxes, playing cards,
Or fingernails would be used.
Her cabin became a universe
Of miniatures. There were
Creatures and landscapes
Unseen by man. Guinevere,
Being a successful astral
Traveller, had visited planets
Beyond science's best dreams.

Little was seen of her during
Leisure hours. When she wasn't
Making love to Marianne she brushed
Away under her spy glass,

Building up images without precedence.
One day, after lunch,
The spyglass blurred and
Instead of her painting, she saw
Their ship riding out a storm.
She looked closer and saw
Danger from a freak wave
To three crew members.
This insight saved them.

Guinevere

"I was found as a stowaway
On a neighboring ship.
The nuclear war isn't

A distant event.
During the first exchanges
I discovered by accident
That during astral travel
My number one body
Couldn't be affected by radiation.
Its structure seemed to deny
Any possible interaction.
I met other travelers
On the way to the third nearest
Inhabited planet, and they had
Experienced the same condition.
Some of my favorite miniatures
Have been details of bodies,
Arthur's penis, Mildred's ear,
Agatha's left eye, and so on,

Put together to make up
One body, a magnificent
Renaissance hermaphrodite
With the appearance it deserves.
Am I astral traveling on this voyage,
My body dispossessed, left suspended
In a deep freeze, a classroom
Or a library. Is my astral body's
Astral body taking sublime trips
Bringing back who knows what
To fill my miniature hours.
Take me to a travel agent,
To see a cider vinegar girl.
She'll show me brochures
Of the back of my hand.
We'll have wished the pomegranates
Had opened before Sinbad arrived
Mad. For all this, on the counter,
The telephone list of far-off feces.
Don't pretend you can read or reach
These havens in one life.

We moved on through
A sea of Giant Reeds,
Cutting and drying many for fuel,
Furniture and supports for paintings.
Three encounters with large eels
Resulted in four broken bones.
Since the demise of Twentieth Century

Painting, I have seen the future

In gallery basements. The return
Of the repressed guarantees, the soul's
Demands in stressful times.
Looking back, it seems like
A locker of loveliness
Compared to what followed.
It wasn't a golden age
But painting explored
The young, old, the hearth,
The home, battles lost and won.
Painters of the good ship 'Watchso'
Were a group apart,
A hoop and a holla
Away from the crowd.
They jab, they poke,
Spit and rub,
Squeeze and squash,
Lose their ardor.
They stroke the canvas
With quiet of the grave
And resurrect the art.
Perhaps our ship is a wooden horse
Entering the next century.
A post-nuclear band-aid
To protect a thousand thousand cuts,
To stop burning salt.
Sometimes watching conversations

Between crew members,
Enjoying passivity,
I feel I am watching children
With building blocks, multi-colored
And many shaped, piled up,
Knocked down, attempts at
Wholeness. Only astral travelers
Can tie in with other minds
But we are far and few.

Occasionally after having ravished
The lovely Marianne, I kiss her
To sleep, pick up her astral body
And take her to exotic hideouts
In old cities and we watch
Sexual parades long into the night,
In places where sex has left
Few imaginations unmined.
Before this New, Clear War,
I worked in New York

For four years exhibiting
Faithfully and selling to rich
Art collectors. I had articles
Written about me in art magazines.
Paintings hung in Museums
Of Modern Art. I felt
I had trapped success.
Suddenly I came across

A nest of snakes in the base
Of my spine. Each one smiled
Like the Mona Lisa.
I wish they were in the Louvre
With my palette and paintbrush
Collection. They were happy days
In the pantechnicon of art.
Sometimes I wish Donald Duck
Was there. Of luck, I am
Goddess Guinevere of Terminal
Wisdom who lies in bed dreaming,
Never quite wise enough.
A glass of water by my bed
Ready to take a dissolvable tablet
Which cures headaches
While the season of desire
Suffers a drought and burns out.
I long for the chocolate riches
Of a newborn painting.
I hanker after handmaidens
Whom I could seduce throughout
The year. Goddess Guinevere
Of golden 'Watchso' will haunt
The world for many a year."

Marianne born in Liverpool.
Daughter of a sailor and prostitute,
Left the haunted factory of thereabouts
And rallied to the flag of life.

A curious child who swept out
The cockroaches in a clothes shop
Which played the loudest music
In the street. The scurrying
Brown legs pleased her sense
Of legs. At ten, she could
Draw legs better than Raphael.
At fifteen, after sleeping
And eating through many

A man's bed she became
Apprenticed to a painter
Of society portraits.
She worked in his studio
Four days a week and used
Her talents until it was observed
That she painted nipples better
Than him, likewise fingernails,
Kneecaps, ear-lobes, and eyes.
This artist who made it
Acceptable for nude society portraits
Gave up painting for sculpture
Realizing he had been surpassed
By nature in the form
Of this girl. At twenty
She left for New York to
Paint society portraits of couples
Dressed up as king and queen.
After three years in this jungle

Marianne thought it over-exploited,
Knew it was time to leave the stage,
Kick over truth's table of tricks,
Watch the rabbit escape down the aisle,
Exist and wave goodbye.
After a tour of the world's
Floating brothels, narrowly escaping
Slavery several times, Marianne
Ended up in Los Angeles
Where she was seen painting sailor's
Portraits for twenty dollars. They
Gave them to their friends.
Gesso recruited her immediately
To document the changing faces
Of the crew as the voyage
Took shape. Each face
Was painted once a month'

Marianne.

"On course for Samoa.
News from everywhere.
The war was over.
Perhaps the world, could enter
A final peace.
We had all agreed
On this voyage, mirrors
Were forbidden. Make-up

And shaving were the responsibility
Of friends. Sometimes I wasn't

Spoken to for days after completion
Of a portrait. My favorite face
Was Griffin. Not yet fifty,
Over thirty, his long black hair
And carbon eyes had a melancholic
Stare, as if patriotic duty
Had caught up with him.
His smile, on the other hand,
Looked like a lorry load of ripe bananas.
Once I caught him scribbling
The last line of a love
Poem to a dolphin. He
Liked to write in private
And read out loud reluctantly.
With a new moon, without fail,
He would grow his beard
For two weeks, then shave it off.
For some reason, unknown
Even to the computer, Griffin
Was aging at a quicker rate
Than others. Ancient laugh lines,
Squint lines, tear lines, smirk lines,
Quizzical lines, not to mention
Lines of love, fear, rage, and hate..
All these were mapping out his face.
Griffin, like a dog hiding bones,
Hid poems written quickly on paper,
Stuffed into corners all over the ship.

Days or months later, he would
Find them, surprised at what
He had written. Sometimes
He'd throw them overboard.
What I liked doing best were
Animal portraits of the ship's
Cats AM and PM. Great climbers,
They had been to the mast tops and
Along the rigging, on becalmed days.
After fish supper, the athletic
Duo would come to me awl
Purr around my feet, pose
In front of my easel, then sleep.
AM and PM were found
In a basket on the dockside
By Low, but it was no ordinary

Basket, having the ability
To levitate. Low fell into the water
Trying to catch the flying basket
Which seemed to allow itself
To be caught. Low keeps
The basket locked in an iron
Cupboard. Its levitational power
Once lifted ten men off the
Decks."

CHAPTER FORTY-SIX

FLAUBERT THE GOAT

Flaubert the Goat,
Probably the wisest goat
Whoever lived, came from

Greece, and a descendant of
Satyrs. He could recite his
Ancestors back three thousand
Years. He was captured from
A Greek Island by a millionairess
Who collected goats and bred
Them on a farm outside
Los Angeles. He believed
Goats were more intelligent
Than human beings and hoped
To mix the two species
To provide a new race to govern
Earth. He was mad and spent
Much of his time making it
With she-goats. The cartoonist
Hercules, an animal liberationist,
Rescued three hundred goats
With his Attack team
On July 4th. The goats were
Dispersed over America. Flaubert,
So named because he was Hercules'
Favorite author spoke out clearly and
Everyone spat into the sand, with
Disbelief. He recited a list
Of his ancestors. Three days
Later he was on board ship Satchmo.
As opposed to Griffin who
Grew older and wiser, Flaubert

Seemed to become younger
Every week with less grey
Beard, shinier fur, clearer eyes,
And smoother horns.
Monsoon weather was approaching
And we expected to be tied down
For a few weeks. Painters had to finish
Off work in their cabins, poets

Slept more, and the photographers
Tied themselves to masts.
We rested on Samoa, our first major stop
Since Tahiti. After familiar native greetings
There was continuous rain.

CHAPTER FORTY-SEVEN

MICHELLE, PAINTER OF THE REAL

Michelle, painter of the real,
Remembers early days of the voyage.
It was different then, Now
Professionalism had spread over the crew
Like treacly slime. This attracted
The flies of complacency. Michelle,
Painter realist, descendant of Courbet,
Had taken the job
To do research for a mural
For a millionairess.

After it had been completed Michelle was
Chaperoned by Moon to Los Angeles.

Her task was to paint the everyday
Reality of scenes and activities.
Michelle, being very observant
Developed an interest in the Art of the Detective.
After a week on board
She could walk into an empty
Room and tell which crew had
Been there. She had complete
Spatial awareness and able to give
A ninety percent accurate description
Of objects and their relation to their
Human users. She painted two
Types of picture, trompe l'oeil,
In which the real transcends
The surreal; secondly, naturalistic
Interiors where intuitive color allied
To tactile awareness allowed her complete
Artistic freedom to explore
The essence of life.
Whenever somebody lost something
She was there solving the problem
With a few daft questions.
Some people thought she used
Hypnosis. Her most famous
Case was solving a murder.
Somebody had murdered the good
Ship 'Watchso' Although it floated
And its engines worked as soundly

As ever the ship had really been
Killed. Even the Computer Daedalus
Who rarely made mistakes
Agreed with the evidence.
There is danger
In the head
Of an egg.
Michelle had traced the killing
To Sunday morning.
The Chef had cooked omelets
For breakfast. A carving knife
Was missing from the kitchen.
It was there when the Chef
Made his morning check.
Somebody had sneaked in
Before the end of breakfast
And hidden it on his or her
Person. Michelle had noticed
A certain diversion
At table when the salt cellar
Ran out. Hercules passed
It to the end of the galley
For a refill from a packet.
One minute passed before
It arrived back. Hercules,
Impatient to eat, slammed
His plate on the table.
He apologized for the mess

And cleared up. Perhaps even
A healthy apple has an
Invisible worm. 'Watchso'
Died at eleven thirty
That morning from multiple
Knife wounds. It was proved
Hercules had stolen the carving knife.
Not to stab the ship to death
But to sharpen his pencils.
The ship's wounds healed over
Immediately leaving scars which
Once examined proved beyond doubt
That they were the wounds of
A penknife which Hercules had
Lost the day before and being
Of short temper had no patience
To look for it. The knife
Turned up in the Chef's garbage
Can. There were no fingerprints

Just the smell of cider vinegar.
The Phoenicians were known
To have scrubbed their decks
With vinegar. Cider vinegar,
Hercules' favorite drink.
The strongest person on ship.
Everybody knew about his drinking.
Was the vinegar-smelling penknife
A plant, a frame-up or

A ruse by Hercules.
On further examination the knife
Was discovered to be blunt.
Question time. Where was each
Member of the crew Sunday
Morning and the day before
Around six o'clock when the knife
Went missing. Daedalus
Rigged up to act as a lie
Detector. Only Mildred
Failed the test. She blushed,
Sweated, her hands trembled,
Her eyes watered; she was
Embarrassed because she
Was in bed with Hercules
At the specified times.

'The Hesperides of March
Have beautiful apples,
Pure as snow
On the highest mountain
In India.'

They were no nearer a solution.
She retraced events. Daedalus
Knew all the time who had
Murdered the ship. Wired up
To vital parts it was well
Aware when the knife struck
Who held it so strongly.

Only Hercules or his sister
Had the strength to kill
A ship. But the computer
Was programmed not to tell.
Humans had to find out
For themselves things to do
With Justice.

'The love of flowers
Falls on fallow ground.'

After Hercules and Mildred had
Made love, Mildred slept,
Agatha crept in
To see Hercules. Jealous
At first sight she stole
His penknife. Later she
Thought of a crime. Agatha
Not as happy as expected
Despite being the best looking
Woman on board wanted
A crime of crimes.
A boy in the band
Is worth two in the bush.
Agatha, beautiful and brainy,
Had no problems with dialectics.
Killing the ship would let her off
A hanging, keel haul or whipping.
The ship could carry on as before
And the framed guilty party

Would be excommunicated.
Agatha was caught laughing
To herself by Michelle. That
Was enough. With further
Questioning Agatha broke down.
She didn't fancy torture.
Her face was too beautiful
To spoil.

'Ship 'Watchso', is dead,
Boat of the universe,
Rubber duck of the bathtub.
Live long the ship,
She saileth as a swan
Who knows the edge of beauty
More than youth knows truth.'

Berthe,painter of people; eating.
By the time we reached Fiji
Her cabin was full of pictures
Of twinkling teeth, with food
Stuck between them. Mushy gobs
Smiling for her brush, mouthfuls
Of mastication. Her deft Sargent-like
Brush strokes had made her famous.

Berthe, Parisienne, daughter of a Chef,
Child bride to a gang leader, an American
Immigrant, traveled through the States;
She ended up selling beads
In San Francisco before studying

Paintings. Short with light brown hair,
She dressed like a female executive.
Her diary entry was the most thorough
In the book, with the time and date
Of every event, the number of people
Involved, expressions used; the room
And positions of people in that room,
The clothes they wore, the time
They left and when new people entered.
Nobody knew how she could be
So ubiquitous or why she bothered
With a statistical account of life.
When she wasn't painting mouths
Her busy body went around the ship
Logging activities. This, she managed
To do quickly with the aid
Of a pocket computer linked to
Daedalus. Her time and motion
Didn't go down well with others
Especially if they were making love
In the covered lifeboat on a lazy
Afternoon. Being the most scientific,
Berthe's log would probably
Have been consulted by a future
Researcher had not the pagc3
Been ripped out before arrival in New Zealand.
Michelle, the slim
Silver savory detective traced

The deed back to Berthe
Who soon admitted her vandalism.
Her excuse being, all the facts
Were fiction she had made up
To put herself to sleep. What she
Had really been doing with the pocket
Computer connected to Daedalus,
Ask him. He is stored in the New
Zealand Museum of Post-Bomb
Computerology. What had Berthe
Been doing with the pocket
Computer? Masturbating, of course!

CHAPTER FORTY-EIGHT

ARIADNE AND LOW

Ariadne, borne into one of
The richest commercial families in
Europe. After studying ten years
In all the best, oldest, most
Endowed Art Academies in Europe
She dropped out in L.A. painting
Billboard size social realist canvasses in
A giant warehouse rented
On a yearly lease. Although her
Work had dealers, the paintings
Were too large to show in any
Gallery except the grandest like the
Louvre. Ariadne met Low at a film
Star's thirtieth birthday party.

Thirty assistants were employed to
Draw up her preliminary studies
And paint in principal using areas.
Cranes helped the workers move
Quickly from place to place and
A video camera helped Ariadne
Supervise the progress from her
Office. Three weeks before 'Watchso'
Was completing its crew Low rang
Ariadne to see if she would like
To join the expedition. Low and
Ariadne were lovers for those three
Weeks. Ariadne agreed and spent
Most of her artistic time drawing,
Not touching a paint brush once
During the voyage. She made more
Studies than anyone else and vowed
To build a museum containing
A cycle of paintings illustrating
The voyage. As for log entry
She wrote little. Her writing
Covered the arrival of 'Watchso'
In Wellington, New Zealand.

"I am Ariadne, pudding
Of the universe, weaver and wearer
Of the divine mask, chainmail in the

Warrior's kit, versifier of
Fortunate face, brisk walker

On tightropes of the psyche. On
This scathing ship 'Watchso' shifting
From sea to sea, shuttling from island
To island, I observe and record
The salads of behaviors. Our arrival
In New Zealand, the appendix of the body
World, coincided with a gigantic volcanic
Eruption. Wellington was an impossible
Landing spot. We moved south
To an undeveloped natural harbor
Before a month was up, I had made
Two topographical sketches of all possible
Sites for our city. At its center
Would be our ship's computer Daedalus
With its information on all Pacific
Cultures collected on the voyage.
We called the settlement to be,
Our City. The chosen site of
Seven hills covering twenty square
Miles with a river passing through
A deep valley. So few of us
Couldn't possibly occupy the whole area.
We chose the highest hill. Missions
Went out to local people, the few surviving,
To join us or trade with us.
Our City has three wings which
Help it fly, like an overture tonight,
Like a bleak entrance to paradise

Refound. Its soil had the hummus
Of souls; some hopes foundered,
Barbecued on the fires of social conflict
And diving board discord. The rest
Of us showed more than a mirror
To nightmares, blamed the little
Things on more gorgeous gremlins
And whipped up cream to soothe
Sores. Before unloading the goodly
Ship sharp 'Watchso', ocean traveler,
Well watched over by godly spirits,
Our first task, according to
A manual kept locked in a golden
Safe, was to erect a geodesic
Dome as large as possible, using
Thick polythene to cover the structure.
Storage for our belongings.

CHAPTER FORTY-NINE

CITY OF SEVEN HILLS

Ariadne continued -
There our seven hills in our City,
Each one named after
One of our poets -

The Hill of Horace
The Hill of Bartholomew
The Hill of Griffin
The Hill of Arthur
The Hill of Janice
The Hill of Rachel
The Hill of Diana

On each hill, the poets

Were to build a temple.
Each one allowed a year's work
Materials to include branches,
Mud, loose stones, quarried stones,
And cut wood. The design
Had to be their own. Labour
Could be pooled or singly applied
The Temple of Horace
Was dedicated to
The God of The Sun
The Temple of Bartholomew
To God of the Good,
The Temple of the Griffin
To the God of the No-Good.
The Temple of Arthur to
Night's All stars,
The Temple of Rachel
To the Forms of Life,
The Temple of Diana
To Goddess Moon.
Ceremonies and celebrations on
Completion.

After some years, the makeshift
Temples had all be consecrated
By their respective poet.

An eighth temple called
The Temple of Barbed Wire
Was constructed outside

The city boundaries
And dedicated to the Dead,
Particularly those lost through
War, starvation and natural
Destruction. The cartoonist
Hercules collected barbed wire
From all the farms in the area.
The site, a clump of trees.
He trimmed branches, clipped twigs,
Then began to tie the trees
With wire. After a year's work
The sprouting trees supported a vast tangled
Barbed dome with one entrance.
The leafy interior guarded by
Two fierce dogs who only allowed
Women to enter and place
Flowers around the base of trees.

Our City would have no
Religion, no priests, no churches
Or temples, save those of
Haptic poets. Prayers shouldn't
Be heard or seen. This brings
Us to the Rule of Law. Of course
There had to be laws. One law
The computer Daedalus thought
Of, anybody caught praying under
Tables or with head in the
Oven would have to till

A ten-acre field by hand.
A more enlightened example
Of the legal mind surfaced
In the attitude toward women.

No laws were passed about women.
They had to fight for themselves.
Males moved quickly to impose
Old world dominance but the women
Educated and healthy, side-stepped
Charging bulls and grabbed them
By the balls. Hence women
In Our City are powerful, respected
And don't waste away.

Priestesses were allowed to
Take root and known as witches
In the old world, they became
Arbiters of common law and were effective
Antidotes to crime. A rapist, after
Being in the hands of witches
Usually became a hermit in the wilderness.
The problem of money. The established
Communities used pre-bomb national
Coinage, although since the war
Barter, silver and gold were most
Common for exchange. We decided
To allow 'law of the jungle' to decide
Our economic fate and, bar criminal
Action, people were allowed to make

As much money as they could.

Who enforced these laws?
Vigilante groups roamed the land
Picking up clues and stories No death
Penalties and no politicians, who
Like priests were prohibited. People
Elected themselves on to committees.
Some, as large as a thousand
Sat around discussing how to improve
The sewerage system which for
A long time was a series of holes
In the ground. All these problems,
Like health, which relied on folk herbals,
From natives until the computer
Could direct the building of
Laboratories (we were healthier in
Those early days), didn't worry
Our City at first, as only the crew
Of 'Watchso' belonged to it.
The second five years was hell,
With intergroup rivalry, racist slurs
And general power play.
The poet Horace, before he was
Murdered by racists,
Buried his notes on
The early days in his temple.
One of the most popular and long-lasting,

And defended by a victorious clan
Of priestesses."

"I am Horace, embodiment of
The blackest hole, God's waste bin,
Cosmic spittoon, galactic keyhole,
Kali's cunt, shadow of paradise,
Endless night of deepest space,
Soulless energy of the universe
Filtered through a screen of blackest
Mesh.
Here I stand, sweet fruit in my
Mouth, sucking juices of grapes and
Peaches. I turn sods over with
My big toe, window on the creepy
Mind. Farmers watch, waiting for
The right moment to plant; their seeds
In the soil and in their women.
I built my temple thirty
Feet high.
After a year's labor I was
Adopted by a local clan of priestesses.
They didn't wear sanitary towels, their
Hair was long, unwashed, sometimes
Dyed with berries of the woods.
Clothes came from rubbish tips.
The women were feared by the locals,
Except during springtime when old
Habits were cast aside and for

A few months they dressed like
Model virgins awaiting
Deflowering. Their appearance
Seemed an epic contradiction
Of good taste, especially to a new
Community struggling to survive
Initial fluctuations of fortune.

Most problems were solved
By counting the earthwork; as bait
For fish and birds; as food for priestesses.
I first met an earthworm
Hunter burrowing
In a river bank of a river unpolluted,
Unused by man.
A happy river unburdened
By traffic, a river whose very waters
Chuckled out tunes of paradise.
Not for long! Soon earthworm hunters
Had gouged away the time carved
Gracefulness and balance of the morphology.

The river flooded more often and
Strayed from its old course. Soon
Its waters were swimming in sewerage
And chemical waste. Coming across
Fetid sites by the water's edge
I knew it was time to turn back
And ask the earthworm what it
Thought. I found one at his telescope

Studying the stars. He answered my
Question as follows.

'We are the generation of worms
Who turned. Your time has
Come. We'll burrow away your
Foundation. Topple the edifice
Of Mammon. Eat you before
You're dead, and rest in
Your grave fat happy.'

My happiest moments in the early
Days were the rest hours given to
Exhibitions of drawings and readings of poems.
I wrote lyric verse to my temple
On a hill. I spent a week searching
For a favorable site. One with southerly
Light, good drainage, favoring fortification.
My temple to the sun overlooked
Other hills and the embryonic Our City.
A few huts, wigwams, and a computer
House, electricity courtesy of a windmill
And solar cells. One week designing
The temple. One month digging
Foundations. Two weeks selecting materials,
Dry dung, reeds, stones, mudbricks, sticks,
And sackfuls of seaweed. As I built
I constantly thought of the final shape.
Before I settled this decision I
Dreamt of Venice and how it succumbed

To the equivalent of thousands of tons
Of TNT. Thus St. Francis rose
From the waters of the aftermath
Saying this is nothing
Compared to the slaughter of abortions.
He was a devil in disguise and
Advertised the advantages of hell
On his hairshirt. Oh to be

A young devil again. I woke up,
Feeling refreshed.
My chosen shape, a closed-in
Gondola with a giant mask
For windows. A sun on the top
Of its nose shining on the world.
The Gondola measured the length of
A cricket pitch, the height of
A double-decker bus, the width
Of ten fat pigs, who get fatter
And fatter. I had problems with
The wildlife, problems with weather
And supplies of materials, yet
My temple was first to completion.
I instructed worshippers, attracted
Priestesses, wonderful to behold.
I wrote for them an opening hymn
To the sun.

"O Sun
Height of light

Low of glow
Provider of make-ups for clouds
Fission without derision
Love center of a romance
Time-honored
Wine-honoured
Chased and nursed,
Symbol of the Bimble
Warm our days
Don't fry us
Don't shrivel the roots.
Watch our earth until we're done,
Till you're done as Sun.'

I had this incantation printed on
Recycled paper and posted on trees
In the locality. On the set day of
Completion work had to stop whatever
The stage of building. Summer
Vandals hampered my final effort
Of plastering the surface of the temple
With dung.This is to ward off bad
Spirits. I collected all the children
On their summer holidays to help
Me pick up dung. Cow dung,
Camel dung, circus dung and

Elephant dung. They used carrier
Bags, plastic buckets and piled
The stuff up outside the temple doors.

Applying the dung was my job.
I wore gardener's leather gloves
Bought from Our City's hardware
Store, a portable but in town. Goods
Supported by barter. During the building
Of the temple I had other duties
As official poet. To take out
The message of Our City, example
Of harmony in the post-bomb world.
This meant reading poems in
Church halls, on crossroad corners,
In streets, in shops and schools.

'Temple of dung
Backbone of my adventurous dream
Philosophic mound bound to earth
Fall into ruins
Grasses and weeds binding the fabric
For another day.'

My favorite priestess, an angel of a girl,
With shoulder-length golden hair,
Her eyes ever inviting ponds of
Turquoise fire; her smile released
A thousand thoughts; her body
Turning sent me in a spin.
She seduced me one Saturday
In early morning, while mist
Lay all over the valleys and hills.
She came to me after a day of scouring

The countryside for herbs and fungi.
I was asleep under an umbrella
By a pile of dry dung.
Instead of finding
The Temple of Fertility.
Where she was supposed to go
She had found me instead.
At the Temple of Fertility
Priestesses had to copulate
With anyone until pregnant.
Once woken, I stared at a girl
Prodding at me with her foot.
I wore a cotton shirt and baggy

Grass-stained trousers. I wondered
Who this endless female could be.
She beckoned me to the temple
Door to go inside the dark,
Musty, stench-ridden heap.
Uncontrollably she threw her arms
Around me, I lifted her dress
And fell to the floor.
Our lips and tongues rubbed,
Scrubbed, penetrated each other's mouth.
She took my penis and guided
It in her. I felt a new universe

Had dawned. She had breached
The fortress of time locking
Away our hearts. There was no
Doubt this temple had found
It's true love. I was lying between
Her legs sucking her young breasts,
Drinking the juices off her lips,
Licking like a dog her lotus cunt,
Kissing her arse - she conceived
That day. She remained with me
For three years before visiting
The Temple of Happy Poisons
Built-in the richest part of town
By charlatans. We fucked as
Often as possible. After four months
She vanished to hide in the woods,
With friends, to wait the birth of
Our child. Once she had gone
To that other place, whose name
I won't write anymore, the fabric
Of my temple began to decay.
People no longer visited and
Walked away to look for another
Endless female to make things work
Again."

CHAPTER FIFTY

BARTHOLOMEW'S TEMPLE

Bartholomew's temple, built to the Good,
Started life as a maze drawn out

On a grassy hill by a trail of sulphuric
Acid. He initially called his temple
The Shape of Fiction, but changed
It after a month because of protests.
Bartholomew's temple, designed by himself.
Eliminating complexities in his plan
He was left with a circle, a center
Point and three arcs dividing the area
Into spaces of more intimate worship.
Bart wandered many miles looking
For an especially unusual material. Feeling
That the Good is ideological white
He looked for white stone but
Found none pure enough. His
Problem solved by a deserted abbatoir
With thirty mounds of sorted bones
Bleached by the sun.

He laid them like bricks
Cementing the bones with mortar to
Form a knobbly wall of great strength
Which enabled his temple to outlast
The others. Once he had built
His tower there were problems bringing
In the walls to make a dome.
He solved this with scaffold and
A hot air balloon positioned
Atop the tower. Once the mortar

Around the balloon was dry
The furnace fire of bones and
Wood was allowed to die;
Plastered inner walls
Were painted tonally to modulate
Light coming through irregular windows.
In winter twice as many people
Were allowed to pray in order to keep
Each other warm. The Temple of the Good

Attracted all types, young and old.
Rich and poor. It had the most
Beautiful priestesses and the most
Understanding. They could read minds,
Stars, hands, heads, interpret coincidences,
Dreams and slips of the tongue.

"I, Bartholomew,
Prematurely grey-haired poet,
Born in the lions' den of old
Baghdad; son of a diplomat and
A concubine; brought to London
At the age of four; educated
By a Rosecrucian Grand Magician
Of the Order of Hod, kidnapped
By mother and taken to Los Angeles
Where I was educated at a thriving
Californian school; I participated
In the regenerative sixties, dropped out
To Mexico and became a Trappist

Monk writing Theological Treatises of not
More than twenty words.
My temple was a happy place.
Prayers were simple, like

'Good God,
Spread your protective wings
Over the world.
Goody God,
Help us to do away
With those who don't like you.
Good Good,
Allow me to be a pillar
Of some height
In a crumbling world;
So Good,
Help me trade in my badness.'

My high priestesses took over
The temple and built extensions,
Of bones, in elaborate patterns
Based on knitwear. The congregation,
Mostly women. Men strayed to
Charlatan temples, fleshpots in disguise.
Redundant, I went back into the city
And talked with the crew of 'Watchso'
About the long voyage to this

Beautiful country, hardly touched
By the war. The original four
Now controlled the government

And a basic democratic system
Voted in and vote out
Those who to didn't measure up.
Our City bored me, so I trekked
Off into the hinterland looking
For characters to talk with
And perhaps take away their wisdom.
In this countryside, there were fewer
Minutes in the hour, fewer seconds
In the day. The air was cleaner
And clearer, supplying more oxygen
And less poison to burdened lungs.
I sat down on a smooth boulder
Worn by travelers, and surveyed
The scenery I had left behind.
I could still see Out City stretching
Over seven hills like a sub-divided
Shantytown; the scatty temples
With crowds milling around
These most popular of places.
And I saw hazy blue
Fields grazed and ploughed,
Burnished woods on lower slopes
Of mountains making fleeting
Liaison with clouds traveling in my
Direction.

Not a soul about. Perhaps I
Should be in the city helping out.

Having a good time. Measuring
Radioactivity in the prevailing winds.
After meeting friendly animals; deer,
Foxes, wildcats, dogs. Then there
Were none. My first human being
Lived like a squirrel
In a hollow tree trunk.
She was a young apprentice priestess
Studying the past, where nature comes first.
Rhythms, species, seasons, languages,
Mysteries, survival. These were her
Cues in a three-year living
Out in the wilds. At twenty
She could return to her temple

Fully developed. Occasional visits
By a high priestess helped her
With the arts of herbalism, healing.
Food, shelter and warmth. As
Soon as she saw me,
Struggling over jagged rocks,
She slid like a snake out of
Her hollow, slowly stepped
Towards me, her clothes made of
Strips of bark sewn with sinews
Of reeds. Her jewelry consisted
Of dried fruit, fish, and fungi; offering
Me a fish from her hair, I
Leaned towards her and nibbled

At a minnow. I smelt perfume
Swirling around her. A mixture of
Lavender, Rosemary, and stale sweat
After I had eaten her most attractive
Jewelry, she bent over and offered
Me her hole. I didn't accept then,
But later we copulated, like animals.
With great freedom. At night
The young priestess, whose name was
Melting Snow, lived in an old temple
By a river. Temple of unknown origin,
A cave with carvings of giant extinct
Animals and an altar where silver and gold
Were offered to an unknown God.
Melting Snow told me she had built
It out of fiberglass and resin.
A friend had found a supply
In a boat yard up the river.
In an ancient cave, she constructed
Her own fantasy place of worship.
This girl had one outstanding
Problem which I had hoped to cure
By reciting secret passages of her
Thoughts to a strangled dove.
Melting Snow like me to do her
After she had stuffed live snails
Up her. After orgasm, slimy snails
Crawled out over the altar.

Next a character of shadow and vice,
We pickled them later.

'Some say love is a burdened
Apple which falls on the head
Of a day philosopher who thinks
He is wiser because he takes
A bite and spits it out into a fire.
Few say love has a beginning
And end like the quest of a knight
Who searches plains, hills, and mountains
For the end of an endless dream.
What were they like as people
When they were eating their
Hard-boiled eggs? Wherever did
They put the shells of their lives
Once cracked and crumbling
In the palm of their hands?
Overblown misery, drop me a coconut
From the Tree of Prime Numbers
Whose leaves in autumn cover
The known and unknown.'

After three weeks, I kissed
Melting Snow goodbye as she
Retreated into her hollow tree.
Off and away, over
Startling hills where pedigree poodles
Hunt in packs.

Next, a character of shadow and vice,

Who alone loves to kill?
A swarthy dwarf, a martial artist,
Threw me across the track. He
Tried to slash my throat with his
Nails. I grappled with him and
Poured sand into his eyes. He
Spoke eloquently of his life of
Violence. And recited while he
Groveled and began to see as
He used saliva to clean his eyes.

'In this world I am
The drudge of hate. I see possibilities
In the fracturing skull. And
Where is flesh with its sweeping
Depths? I challenge its vitality
And bludgeon the spirit. So
What am I to you, pale world,
Born of Little Bo Peeps

In the Never Never, where blue
Shadows on silver sand
Remind me of dead faces.'

This ugly dwarf hated the world
Like a tempest. Charging from
Place to place he killed animals
People loved; he maimed and
Raped all sorts of innocence,
Spreading out his victims' guts
For carrion. Few country communities

Escaped his ire. Few people had
His measure. His whirlwind approach
To pain and murder overwhelmed
His necrophilia. His eyes were clear
As he prepared to attack.
Being a pacifist, I tried to reason.
It was too late, now retribution.
I grabbed a rock and hurled it at
His charging body. It crashed
Against his skull knocking him
Down. Not for long. With a massive
Fist he charged again. I
Dived away from the hurtling missile.
He stopped and said

'Of all the blood I have shed
Yours I would like most
To smear over rocks which
Block the path of love.
Harbinger of pain. Here we
Are raw to nature's curse.
I am immune to bullets and
Disease. I stand on the rock
Of wisdom. I have drilled
To its hardest core.
Champion of pun and cultural
Games, your name is drowned
In history.'

The dwarf stealthily approached.

He leapt twenty feet in an arc,
His feet directed at my head.
I was lost and soon would die,
Unless the burden of proof was
In my head. I shouted as

Loud as an avalanche. The
Dwarf collapsed and died of a
Fractured skull. His last words.

'Your inner voice hit me.
More like an earthquake and
Now death creeps over me like
The morning after.'

I buried the dwarf under a pile
Of stones. Ants quickly helped themselves.
I journeyed through woods
And fields wondering at their beauty.
I had lost my way and sat down
To work out the best route home
When all of a sudden a voice
Controlled by a ventriloquist, danced
Around me. The voice gibed,
Curried, tempted, and taunted.
I felt put out and fairly annoyed
About this intrusion into my private
Thoughts. The voice said –

'You are like an alien visitor,
Puzzled and not very good
At understanding what you see.'

Then a philosophy. A sweet philosophy
Of a few things.

'Let me tell you a few things
About the middle of life. These days
Ideas are as common as the bandits
Who steal them. Watch out the
Mask and pick-pocket, the most
Numerous types, often seen nude
On giant screens parading magic words
Whose carriers are all smiles and melting
Laughter. I watched them, one day,
Build a financial empire. It took
In many a million. They became
Fat and I had to laugh as
Poison shrunk their stomachs. Enforced
Dieting. The agony columns
Marched well-heeled but painfully
Aware civilization had passed.'

Henceforth I said,

'You peoples beware the patchwork of popularity,
The leader who has a summary
Of business profits available,
Who has a backlog of things to do,
Who isn't warming his hand
On a coal fire or selling chestnuts
In the street. You strange messenger
Of Temple of the Good, watch
The autumn. You'll catch no

Stranger staying here.'

I heeded the words of voice
And looked up to see its face.
Laughing, creased up, she wasn't
An old crow but a young woman
Who could only throw her voice.
Jumping down and so what.
Plump and dressed like a Tarzan.
I knew her to be the grandmother
Of Philosophy. Unageing she had
Been sighted in many countries
It wasn't surprising she'd turned
Up here. The safest place in
The globe. She continued her
Monologue lost in its own
Profundity.

'I met an old woman
Sweeping streets, calling out
The random numbers of devils
Who sleep around the alleys
Of city dwellers. These devils
Are included in any complete
Dictionary of other attractions
Of the spirit. I adapted
This woman and made her
A secretary of the bilious mind.
The one who stays put
When others move to hold out

For the new. She found
The work wearisome. Chattering
To her budgie, then a siesta
For two; her favorite way of passing
The quiet hours when nobody
Sings over the phone or builds
A reputation before tea. When

Busy she could cope with the
Onrush of plastic men and
Women, head-to-toe foes bored with
Conventional slaughter. She stepped up
The rule of thumb and changed
The rules of paradise, the chase.
But I was up to any manoeuvre
She had to make. Keep up
Your dreams and make them like
A steam train powering along a track.
The legend of the Old Lady! Vice
Is her conquest of the capitalist world,
Now her power is fixed until
Philosophy has given its grave reply.'

I went to sleep and wished
The voice away. Tired of
Traveling I headed home. Another
Day and the journey would be mine.
Our City had grown beyond
Recognition. Fake palaces and
Brothels had arrived. Temples had

Grown into state institutions.
I had been away a hundred years."

CHAPTER FIFTY-ONE
POET GRIFFIN

Poet Griffin, six feet high,
Wrote poems only under the influence
Of drugs. Hence he had not written
Much on the voyage. Drink and drugs
Being prohibited. He played an extra
Part in unloading the good ship 'Watchso'
And making peace with the natives. He
Negotiated buying land for Our City
And water rights on two rivers.
When he chose Temple of the No-Good
As his spiritual thoroughfare, there
Was general disapproval, although it
Was recognized that somebody had to do it.

Griffin wasn't afraid
Of controversy. Brought up in obscurity
In southern Germany until six, then taken
To Israel to stay on a Kibbutz, when twenty
He traveled around the world,
Making a living giving sexual
Favours to older women. Three years
Later he published his first collected
Works of Pornographic Poems which
Earned him enough money to set up
His own radical publishing house.

In his shop in Los Angeles
He bumped into Gesso who introduced

Him to Moon. Griffin's presence on
'Watchso' confused many people.
He seemed to have
Few values others could identify
With. Only his ability to solve
Problems and make things work.
His poetry came via the Muse
With the use of magic mushrooms.
He often used the computer to
Record his thoughts. Thoughts
Split down the middle, jumbled
And re-assembled, muddled and mashed,

Thoughts stuck in escalators. He gave
Them up freely. Temple of the No Good
Griffin found it tempting to use
Some known symbol as a floor
Plan. Rejecting this he gathered
Together a hundred children who
Each drew their own design based
On the traced outline of a man,
Or woman. Choosing his favorite
They proceeded to map out
A giant woman on the steepest slope
Of the hill allotted to him. Griffin
Had a thing about anatomy.
He decided to give his woman
A giant womb which would hold
The congregation. Materials came

From rubbish tips and car tips.
He placed car bodies head to tail
Around the contour of the figure, filling
Them with cement and proceeded to weld
Any old iron to them. Car by car
The walls grew to thirty feet.
The womb consisted of an old
Nissen hut. Old bedframes, fridges,
Cookers were used as fillers.
The rough approximate body was
Spray painted in primary colors.
Probably the ugliest of temples. But
A favorite with artists and tramps
Who slept in its caves and crevices.
Griffin operated his temple like
An exclusive club. New members
Had to spend one day with Griffin,
Eating and gambling. They were given
A secret sign if accepted. Through
Their signs the No-goods
Helped each other in times of
Distress. Also discounts for sex, cheap
Holidays, low mortgages and second
Hand-cars. Griffin felt
His temple had the common touch.
It had a reputation for bizarre
Sexual activity, perverse parties,
Brothel evenings, initiation ceremonies,

Mixed couple evenings, country
Outings like a Maenads Chase,

De Sadean picnics, Sapphic Nature Trails,
Casanova meets Emma, Flatman
Meets Flopman. No-Gooders' temple
Soon reached headlines and though
Frowned upon by the intelligentsia
Was often visited by artists for inspiration
Not that it was luxurious. The
Walls were black. Seating was made
Of rag bundles. Before long puritan
Groups suppressed the temple and
Turned it into an art gallery
By painting the walls white and
Knocking out a few holes for windows.
In protest Griffin printed a poem
And gave it away on crossroads
To weary travelers seeking the
Happiness of life.

Griffin

"Those who skate on the surface of desire
Sometimes fall and hurt the soul.
Which has no meaning in this world
Where shadows count after naught.
Who would empty pockets of illusion
Now the enchantress is close at hand.
The temptress whose breath
Is the elixir of sleep revels
Through the night with her victim.

What are these dreams fought over
By these traders at the station;
Carrion at the cradle, beetles
At the dung. Not the ones
We remember, dissect or discuss.
Those are dreams our souls
Neglect. Its dreams are alive
And feeding well locked in the light
Of the living world.
What a fright it is
To climb the ladder of illusion
And look to the ground.
The chatter of sparrows
As they peck and pound.
When hands reach bone and
Feet are black, watch a rusty
Old skeleton turns the cheek of regret.
Once hidden like works in rising tide,

Now overblown like mist from
The marsh, vague features made
Out, looked over and lost to Lord
Of the Dustbins, to the Lord
Whose lust is bigger than most.

It isn't too early to journey
Fast and furious like a battle at
Peak-time viewing. It's not personalities
Who makes the running or a witty
Audience interrupting. Only a chef

Has enough poison to finish his dish
And serve it well. The banquet
Table is harassed by servants who
Make themselves sick into the lap
Of passion.

Together their journey stepped
Over danger until a thunderstorm
Rolled in their doom. The masters
Of mercy watched nervously
Before they played out of mind.
Stop travelers! Hand over possessions,
Undress to underwear, shiver and
Freeze. Hold your most precious
Possessions and breath into life,
A sarcophagus.

It's never too late to pour
Out the world. I watched travelers
Be themselves behind curtains
Of silken sheen. Their faces didn't
Match their braces, eyes twisted
And turned. Shadows played across
Wrinkles, coated tongues licked
Cracked lips, breath smelt of
Rotting flesh, hard noses were
Chapped and chilled, hands gnarled
And nails curled, arms long
And lingering by the sides
Of thin bodies covered in blemishes,

Boils and rain. Once I had
A sweetheart who had the fastest
Name. Without proper penny
She would look for the earliest
Earl. Nobody who knew her could

Court her summer. She was off
On cheeseboards skating across lawns
Which looked in line. Croquet,
Tea and bonfire smoke. What was
The gardener's world? With Doric
Conviction I chased her hard.
She dripped kisses on my
Lips. They were dearest
Than the nearest flowers. And
The day came when I cuddled
Her breasts with my lips and
Between her legs found paradise.

Then I tired of crossroads:
Travelers seemed much the same.
Horses tired and lived
Short lives. Children bawled
And colds were common.
Highwaymen and women attacked
And killed, stealing many jewels, wigs
And clothes. In the end sugar
And sweets cost me my teeth.
The dentist had a gentle touch
When filling in but she was

The fiercest puller and many a
Scream from the mainstream
I heard that day.

Believe me, my journey
Back to the Temple of No Good
Was no who-dunnit. I hitched
A ride on a giant tortoise
Who spoke all the languages of man.
His great age had made him
Wiser than the mule, lonelier
Than the whale, quieter than the DoDo,
Harder than steel. He passed
And paddled rivers, canyons, lakes
And dams. He knew ferrymen,
Their fathers and fathers' fathers.
And what became of the lost child.
Giant Tortoise who called himself
Abacus soon exhausted my conversation.
He told me of great battles he
Had wandered through, quiet
Civilizations more civilized than
Ours; whose stones don't appear

In books; of saints, sages, spies
And artists. The day he
Wandered through the garden of
Leonardo and ate his favourite lettuce.
When he gave a ride to the off-
Spring of Phaedias and slept a year

In the house of Piero Di Cosimo
How St. Francis polished his
Shell for a whole week until it
Reflected the sky. And Buddha
Fed him Lotus flowers. I wondered
If he was telling the truth.
His words came easily and sincerely.
A Chinaman we met talked for
An hour. The fluent tortoise
Told him of the time Confucius wanted
A debate in front of the Emperor
On what is Truth. This
Is how he started.

'I knew a man who published
A broadsheet called Eroticism of the
Month. With an illustration on the back
Page and a three-page description.
These issues quickly became collectors'
Classics. He would delve into the most
Subtle bodily and mental maneuvers
Which made possible that sensation
Of mind called eroticism. My favorite
Episode was 'warm lemon'. A lemon
Is warmed in water for ten minutes,
Wrapped in a flannel and taken to a crowd.
Stand behind a woman, place the lemon
Into her hand, then remove quickly.
If the spell works, she will turn

Around surprised and follow you home.'

I tried this once in a crowd
Watching the Emperor's procession
On his birthday. A beautiful young
Woman stood with her parents.
When her left hand, tired after waving, dropped
To her side, I unwrapped the warm lemon
And slipped it into her palm.
To my surprise, she lightly grasped it
Catching my finger and thumb.

She slowly turned around and saw me
Blushing. Reassured by the flicker of
Her eyelashes I walked away. She came
After me leaving her aged parents
Who were intently watching the spectacular
Fireworks and the dragon procession passing by.
I wandered to my rooms by the shortest
Route possible. The lovely young
Woman came in, not saying a word.
I kissed her and then undressed
Her slowly until her white body
Shone in the winter gloom."

CHAPTER FIFTY-TWO

SIX FAIRY TALES OF TRUTH

There are six fairy tales of Truth
I heard long ago in a dark forest
Told by an old woman who could
Light campfires by rubbing two
Fingers together.

The first is the story of a snake,
An ants nest and a tortoise.

The story ends with the snake being
Eaten by ants after being killed in a fight
With a tortoise over who should feed on
The succulent grass growing out of
The ant mound. The moral is that
Truth is slow in life but will outlive
Falsehood whose defeat in a direct conflict
Will be of benefit to many.

The second fairytale concerns
A weaver, a banker and a stray
Cat.
A small time weaver is taking
Her wares to market by donkey and
Cart. A banker passes her on his
Horse and buggy forcing her, into a ditch.
Her cart tips over.
He doesn't stop. A few yards later
A stray cat runs in front of his horse
Making it rear. The banker's buggy
Turns over, throwing him and breaking
His right arm. The weaver runs
To help him but out of the corner
Of her eye she sees the stray cat
Is hurt. Leaving the banker she
Picks up the cat to nurse it.
Remembering she needed a loan
For a new horse and despite
The banker's callous behavior, the weaver
Takes the banker to a doctor and

The cat to a vet. This shows
That Truth can be pushed aside
Only to return to ease, resulting
Misfortune.

The third story involves a short
Thin woman, a tall thin woman
And a fat woman.

All three
Are shopping in a supermarket
Filling trolleys while humming
To the taped music. They come
To a trolley jam by the biscuits
And sweets. Hoping for a polite
Solution each waits for the other
Shopper to untangle their trolley
And proceed along the lines.
Tempers are lost - The fat woman pushes
Her way through tipping over two trolleys.
The tall thin woman drops her handbag.
The short thin woman is shunted
From behind. A big truth
Will cause confusion when smaller
Truths block the way.

The fourth story.
Mr Wizard and Mrs Witch live

In a tower overlooking coastal inlets.
They watch for their chartered ship
Which brings exotic herbs, minerals and
Animals to arrive in harbor. If

It is night she flies down to check
The arrivals. If it is day he looks
Down through his telescope. They
Worked well together until one day
The wizard looked down his telescope
At night. He saw his wife meeting
With another wizard on the quayside.
They walked into a pub arm in arm.
The jealous husband immediately cast
Spells over the harbor creating
A fierce storm. Lightning struck
The pub. The wizard and witch
Inside realized what was happening.
Noticing the accuracy of the lightning strikes.

Turning themselves into sparrows, they flew
Up through the chimney back to the
Tower to confront the husband.
In a battle of magic, the lover
Won with latest tricks gleaned from
The oldest books illustrate a line
Of thought - when truth is undermined
And loses to falsehood, history repeats
Itself.

The fifth story. An old car
Dumped on waste ground.
A cyclist
Comes along, sees the car, realizes
It isn't in bad nick, dumps his
Cycle and after fiddling with the engine

For half an hour drives the car home
For further reports. A witch flying
On a broomstick over the wasteground
Sees the bicycle. Picks it up, straddles
It on her back and flies home.
Trying it out in the yard, she realizes
How hard it is to balance on two
Wheels and wishes to learn without magic.
After three days' practice, she manages
To cycle to the local shops. Unfortunately
She's run over by the ex-owner
Of the bicycle in his renovated
Car. As the witch lost her balance
Going round a corner, he ran her down,
Illustrating the saying when Truth is
On the move and ready to improve
Be careful of fatal accidents or
Learning a new skill demands as great a
Care with truth of the moment as with
The moment of Truth.

The sixth and last tale of
Truth concerns a priest, a rabbit
And a nun in a graveyard.

A priest was walking in an ancient
Forest or whatever remained of one
And came across an old graveyard.
At the tallest gravestone, a kneeling nun
In a white habit.

The dates on the gravestone covered
At least three generations. The nun
Recited the rosary. On an adjacent
Horizontal tombstone sat a white rabbit
Cleaning her paws. The priest, an
Evil renegade of a remote tribe decided
To either rape the nun or catch and eat
The rabbit. He decided on the nun.
Threatening her with a knife, he forced
Her to undress and raped her from
Behind, then led her away to a hut
To carry out more sadistic pleasures.
The rabbit watched the going-ons
Reflecting on the saying - The appetites
Of man cannot be satisfied all at once.

It was time to continue
The journey back to Our City.
The giant tortoise had to leave Griffin,
And hoped for a new companion.
He waved goodbye. The tortoise
Whose long history had accustomed
Him to partings hummed to himself
Wondering if humanity would ever improve.
Over dry vales, hardship mountains,
Across blue skies and fierce storms,
Griffin covered his earth like one
Hungry migrating animal. As he
Saw the lights of Our City

Stranded in blackness he felt the need
To sleep and dreamed six fairy tales of love.

CHAPTER FIFTY-THREE

SIX FAIRY TALES OF LOVE

Once upon a time, there lived
A very old man. He was so old
The villagers didn't have his records
And as he was now deaf and
Couldn't read or write there were
Precious few ways of communicating
With him. Now a bright young girl,
Daughter of the blacksmith, was glancing
Through the parish books looking for
Ancestors (her mother thought she
Might belong to the local aristocracy)
When a crumbling piece of paper
Fell out of page 434. On it
A village plan and a cross marking
Hidden treasure. In the depths of a well
In a rear garden a lead casket
Of gold coins had been placed by a
Handsome prince on his way home from
War. The young girl, excited
As a red herring folded the map
And tucked it in her underwear,
Replaced the records and drifted home
Hatching a plan to recover her fortune.
She would need help. Grandmother
Was her best friend and doted

Over her. Not only was she very
Wise but had a basinful of magic
Which she rarely used. One
Dark Night just before a new moon the
Two treasure hunters crept past
A sleeping dog into an overgrown
Garden belonging to the old man
Who was deaf and couldn't read
Or write. Granny took out
Of a bag two skins
Of dead rat, a bat ear, four grains
Of corn and two chives and mixed them in
A silver bowl with rabbit blood.
She recited her favorite spell.

The water receded deep into
The bedrock. The girl climbed down
A rope ladder, found the casket
On a ledge and tied a rope
To it. Granny hauled up the find.
As the girl started back
Granny muttered another spell.
The water returned, drowning
The young girl. It can be said
That there are treasures and
Treasures.

In the second fairy fable of love
A beautiful peasant girl worked all-day
In her father's fields. She had many

Admirers but none as fervent as
The tall woodcutter's son. This
Beautiful girl knew she would have
To marry soon. Choosing her husband
Was proving most difficult. If only
She could test their bravery
And honor. She went along
To the local Duke's castle,
Wondering if he could help sort
Something out. The old Duke
Had three daughters, also looking
For husbands. The Duke thought
A contest an excellent idea with
Which to solve his problem as well.
Each girl would choose six suitors
And each would complete a similar
And difficult task. The peasant girl
Chose Jake the Woodcutter's son,
Gerry the Miller's son, Daniel
The moneylender's son, Edward
The Butcher's son, Ariel, the School-
Teacher's son and Ramsey, the doctor's
Son. After five minutes thought
A bright idea slipped into Veronica's
Innocent mind. Her husband
To be had to seduce as many
Village girls as he could in a summer
And provide a witness for proof

Of his conquest.
The Duke's daughters thought out
Their own tasks. One called

Her lovers to seek out the ugliest girl
In the dukedom and marry her.
The second daughter asked them
To find the most beautiful
Girl in the dukedom and marry
Her. The third daughter asked her
Suitors to find a blonde, a brunette,
And a redhead and make each
One pregnant. These demands
Scandalized the court.
Nevertheless, the girls' wishes were
Respected.

Jake the Woodcutter's son married the peasant
Girl. Obtaining work on a farm
With a friend, he charmed
And seduced the farmer's daughters
One by one, his friend as witness.
This was repeated on another farm.
To bring his total to an unbeatable
Seven. The Duke's first daughter
Was married by a man who
Proved she was the ugliest in the land.
The second married a man who
Proved she was the most beautiful.
The third daughter, only twelve,

Hoped her task too difficult.
She was right. Her time came
When she met a wounded
Prince on his way back from a war.

When in love, there is nothing
To prove, except
Is love marriage-proof?

The third fable of love starts
On a wild rocky coast. A young
Man who kept sheep from falling
Over the cliffs. For most of his
Childhood his shepherding had been
A stoical fact. He knew the meaning
Of clouds; the seasons, by heart,
The character of the sea intimately.
There was no birdsong he couldn't
Mimic, no flower or animal he couldn't
Draw. In the company of others
He felt lost. Words were difficult

And he felt conversation a sad
And anemic preoccupation. At
The age of fifteen, he began to
Dream of strange creatures; wild
Mermaids rising from the sea,
Flying women, and magical people
Who lived underground. Feeling
Disturbed and frightened he began
To feel his shepherding days were

At an end.

After a storm-wracked ship
Spewed forth many dead. Boy
Helped in the rescue and saved
A young woman from being
Buried alive. She was taken
To a local Inn and nursed by
The boy, with all the care of
His shepherding. After a year
She came out of the coma.
Great relief was felt by everyone
In the inn. The boy spoke to
Her in the best way he could
And showed her the hundreds
Of drawings, he had made of her face.
Growing more beautiful through the
Year she attracted many a young
Gentleman who immediately fell in love. Each
Adding to the lengthening list of suitors.

On waking, she remembered
Her name at once, a catering aristocrat
From Italy, bound north to meet a
Prince with the purpose of
Marriage. Impressed by the care
And devotion of the boy she
Accepted the best of his drawings
As a present. It was felt by
The local squire that she should

Return to Italy. The location
Of the prince was unknown.
Indeed, nobody had ever heard
Of him. The shepherd decided
For the love of this woman
To discover the whereabouts of
The northern prince to tell him

Of the disaster. Envoys picked up
The aristocratic lady and returned her
To Venice, by land. The Shepherd
Ventured into unknown lands where
All manner of pasts and futures
Are facts out of time. He returned
Ten years later, a richer and wiser
Man. By then his princess had
Married in Italy and though her
Husband was very old he was fit
And fathered two children. The
Shepherd seeked out his dream face
And tried to steal her away.
At first she wouldn't leave her
Children. After her husband's sudden death she
Felt free to travel with the shepherd,
Against the wishes of relatives and friends.
Returning to England, they had
A house built in fields where
His sheep had grazed long ago.
And there they lived happily for

Many years raising four children.

Love has no destination.

The fourth fable of love
Concerns a young lawyer in a large
City and his adventures with a lady
Of the night. Her name Antonia
Real. She was born in the poorest
Slum and raised by a group of
Prostitutes who chipped in some of
Their weekly earnings for a nurse.
She appeared so bright they sent
Her to the best private school
Available inventing with the help
Of some rich clients a story
Of her orphanage to satisfy the school-
Board. At eighteen, she was sent to
Paris to study art, later to Switzerland
To finish her education in languages.
Despite all this she was personally
Obsessed by the lives of her mothers.
At twenty-two despite more proposals
Of marriage than prickles on a hedgehog
She returned to London to set
Up shop as the best call-girl

In town. (She had visited all
The brothels in Paris). A young
Lawyer called Sam Jayne heard
About her from a client.

Unfortunately for Sam, he fell
In love with Antonia and spent
Two weeks' wages for the privilege.
His practice went downhill and
He was found drunk on the Thames
Embankment. Making love to Antonia,
He had bought an hour, from
Two to three, had been a mind
Splitting, a soul shivering and slithering
Experience. He decided to kidnap
And hide her away
In a mill in the south of France.
He sold his shares and borrowed
Heavily from a friend.

Antonia took every third
Weekend off, traveling by private
Means down to the country mansion
Guarded by six farm laborers. Here
She rested for four days completely
Alone except for a young maid.
Sam ambushed her before
She arrived at the main gates,
Bound and gagged her, threw
Her into a trunk with air holes,
Rode to a coastal port for
A quick channel crossing. After
Four days travel, he let her
Out to clean up and regain blood

Circulation. She was bathed by Sam
Who fed her rich soups to
Bring her strength back. Antonia
Couldn't believe what had happened.
On the way to her mansion ?
Sam shooting the driver with
A shotgun, knocking her out,
Drugging her, stripping her,
Wrapping her up in a blanket.
Once crated she was his. However
She resisted escaping wanting to see
This episode runs its course.

Sam imprisoned Antonia
In a room high up in his villa.
He subjected her to a mildly sadistic
Sexuality. He didn't speak and
Though she couldn't be sure she
Knew he spied on her day and night.
After a month and the tedium
Being unbearable, Antonia escaped
With the help of a local Marquis
Who had bought her for a night.
In a heavy breathing pursuit a
Madly angry Sam gave
Chase. They headed for Maraeilles
And found a ship to London.
Sam joined them on board. Before
A final showdown (the Marquis

Had friends) the ship sank in
The Bay of Biscay. Antonia
And Sam were the only
Survivors. The Marquis drowned
Drunk. Back in London, Antonia decided to marry
Sam and bore him three
Children. His practice in the city
Grew and thrived. Occasionally
She would have a night out with
The girls and soon started up
A holiday home for prostitutes.
Sam was happy and loved
His wife to death.

Love is the perfect alibi.

The fifth fairy tale of love
Dreamed by Griffin High Priest
Builder of the Temple of No Good
Confused him no end. A Russian
Sorcerer mesmerized hundreds of peasant
Girls or was it boys or both,
Used them for sexual purposes,
Then sold them south as slaves
For Araby.

The Prince of the region looked
Countrywide for a good sorcerer to
Counter the bad. Far beyond the third
Mountains on an island of magic.
In the Lake of the Damned such

A wizard lived. He counseled souls
On their way to the next world
And helped them to repent and gave
Freely spiritual strength to survive
The tests of the Lake. All old wives
Knew of this wizard and his lake.
A volunteer was needed to die
And deliver the desperate message
To the wise one who perhaps
Could win against the evil sorcerer.
The Prince felt it was his duty
To go, but he was only twenty-
Five and just married. Fortune had
It. A very innocent virgin was
Found by a local priest. She was
Simple and saintly and agreed
To help, however sad it seemed to
Forsake life. She was suffocated
By the Prince's hangman after she
Had been drugged.

The good wizard saw her
Coming through a pearl-colored mist.
A naked body of translucent white.
He had never seen anything so pure,
And felt his own standards
Had fallen. She told him of
Terrible events, although he had
Deduced the source of the young

Souls he had to cope with.
He knew he could only deal with
The problem be leaving his endless
Work. A backlog of souls
Would build up. An idea.
He would leave the girl in charge.
She had an eternal spirit more
Pure than his, and if he didn't
Return he knew she would
Continue until she found
A replacement purer than herself.
The wizard took his favorite bird,
Entered into its head for the long
Journey west. The Eagle flew
Non-stop, neither eating, drinking,
Nor sleeping. It landed as fresh
As youth on the Prince's balcony.
The wizard made a quick exit

From the Eagle's head. He was
Fed by the Prince's cook. What
Plan had the wizard? A
Confrontation? Magic against magic?
The wise man thought that
This would be a futile match
With both going down in defeat.
He thought out a straightforward
Deception. A crooked path
Heading to a narrow victory

He selected three delectable fifteen-year
Old girls from merchants' houses,
Fed them special foods
Based on rarest herbs brought
By the eagle from inaccessible
Mountain valleys. After a month
Their blood would change to contain
A poisonous ingredient A thimbleful
Given to any creature would
Mean instant death. They survived
Their own blood, with the help
Of an antidote pill taken at
Night. The month up, ten
Pints of deadly blood were
Taken out of their systems.
Every other day their jugular vein
Was tapped. Recently a seventeen-year-old girl had
Died of tuberculosis. The good wizard
Raised a spirit to give her life,
And then fed the blood into
Her veins. A willing victim, her body
Had enjoyed its brief rest. She wandered
To the domain of the evil wizard,
Who, seeing a lost young girl,
Hungry and cold set about enticing
And seducing her with all his
Magic charms. After using her
Body to satisfy his unquenchable lust

He drank blood from her neck.
He died of instant asphyxiation
And hallucination visions of
Eternal delight in harems.
In the instant of his folly
The blackest magic from underworldlings
Couldn't save him. His body decayed
In half an hour to a slimy, stinking

Mess covered by worms. Throughout
The land, there was great rejoicing
And monuments were erected to the dead girl
Victim and the great spirit
Wizard. The Prince thanked him profusely
With the most sumptuous banquet ever seen.
The great old man promised another
Present. He entered the eagle's
Head and flew to his sacred island
Of death. Replaced the willing girl
Whom he sent back as a four-year
Old, a future wife for the Prince's
Six-year-old son. The eagle left her
On the balcony on the night of a full
Moon.

Love has no poison.

The last fairy tale of love dreamed
On the stormiest afternoon of the year
Had Griffin stammering with fear
As if talking to a one-eyed giant
Needing lunch.

It started with a Punch, and Judy
Show on a beach with a horde of
Willing children joining in. Not just ten
Or twenty but all the children in the world
Queuing to see a continuous show
With a thousand performers. Not just
One stage but fifty telling a different
Part of the same story. The children
Were enthralled at seeing the foundations
Of their lives being acted out.
Not real children but their spirits
Gathering the straw of existence to
Strengthen the mortar of the psyche.
Griffin sat on a lifesaver's lookout
Watching the incredible variety of races,
All unsorted taking their turn to join
In the fun. And there was no hurry
Because time didn't count, and Griffin
Couldn't have known such an enormous
Number which he would have needed
To begin a countdown.

Love is without
Number.

It was a cold night. Griffin,
Puzzled by his dreams, walked to keep
Warm. He wasn't far from a fun palace
And could see a candle-lit hollow.
He entered and rested his head

On a priestess's lap. She caressed his
Erection and licked his tears. Happy griffin
Slept long after and knew the World was his.

CHAPTER FIFTY-FOUR

ARTHUR, AESTHETE, AND POET

Arthur was a poet who had impeccable
Taste. An aesthete of the old school,
He was truly English and knew every
Inch of England and all of its stories
From Celtic legends onwards.
From Public School to Oxford,
From Oxford to the B.B.C.; from
The B.B.C. to the Devil. An unusual
Victim of the golden, diluvial sixties.
He stopped shaving, washing, chatting,
Started hitch-hiking, whoring, roaring
And snoring.

His poetry began passionately, experimentally, and became
The existential equivalent of a potpourri.
For six years, his friends couldn't bear
Him and stood outside his house
To talk to him. Come 1970 he
Reverted to his former self to find
It only a parody. Fleeing to New York
He faced a carte blanche of
Possibilities and for the first time
Began to feel very happy. He met
Moon in a nightclub and a long
Friendship developed. Together they
Explored many delights and

The mansion of art welcomed two
Lodgers from plie madhouse of life.
Their first collaborative happening
Was called the getting-together of
Marriage and marijuana. Next followed
Short stories called 'Americans'.

Moon and Arthur were
Occasional friends and visited each
Other when their wives were away.
For long periods Arthur wrote little
Then he produced a best-selling
Collection of poems based on the story

Of God. During the great voyage
Arthur discovered the delights of
Cannibalism, necrophilia, and Tahitian
Cooking. Once a month, he'd cook
The crew a Tahitian dish. His 'Story
Of God' poems began with two one
Line poems and following poems' line
Numbers increased like the Fibonacci
Series. The book contained fourteen poems
Of dramatically increasing lengths,
More and more obscene; a true
Vilification of the human race in all
Its perfidious behavior.

Arthur, five feet and ten inches
Of blondish hair and bright blue eyes,
Modelled for two years

In New York. yet he aged quickly.
By the time he was twenty-eight
He looked fifty and as a result
Was even more popular with the girls.
After he'd taken
A post on board the good ship Satchmo
Arthur delighted in the tribalism, the paleface
Aftermath, the baroque jokes endlessly
Slurring into no-jokes. His luggage
He carried in a leather handbag
Completely covered with Ban the Bomb
Badges he found on a dead protester
Who had died in a riot before
The final days. He ran
Off to find the good ship 'Watchso'.
He leapt aboard from a crane.
Gesso welcomed him and gave
Him champagne.

His first four poems went
Like this –

'I waited and waited.
You turned up in the curry.
The curse of cabaret
Has struck our town
And you flounder in the sauce.'

'Surely not, surely not,
You a mannequin of icing

On the biggest wedding cake
I've ever been'

'God's Mother and Father
Were fabulous fritters
Liqueurs of stellar gold,
A punch drunk Punch and Judy.'

'In the chocolate cake, in the tea,
In a box of marron-glace,
Your face appears just so;
A veil, or jail, a fatal land
Embossed. So chunk it, junk it,
Whittle it away, once you appeared
In the aubergine stew.'

Arthur's Temple.

He picked paper
Mache out of a hat. Using bamboo
Frames found in bulk on a Chinese
Cargo ship he built his way to fame.
The largest, roomiest, and flimsiest
Temple of all. Raiding newspaper
Warehouses for paper, bakeries for flour,
Empty oil barrel yards for mixing
Vessels and for labour he used
Maoris. They were keen to decorate
The stepped pyramidal shape.
Arthur's Temple of Night's All-Stars,
A pantheon of all your favorite

Bogeymen; every religion's malefactors,
Who pain the conscience with temptations,
Sweet, simple, involved, or elephantine.
Of folly and faery menaces stalking
The land and mind, searching
For the way in, the weak spot,
Often where lovers have lain.
They dig in like marines and
Wait to attack.

People brought drawings, photographs,
Paintings and poems dedicated to
Their own pet fear. Some parts
Were left for other All-Stars
Like poets, actors, or singers.
Their favorite corners had

A guardian or spirit called
Princesses of the Night. One wall
Contained Arthur's poem, in Gothic
Lettering, to Call Girls of
The Psyche.

"They arrive, they leave.
Their ability to breach
The will of silence
In a Trappist Monastery
Sent me on a journey.
That day stands like
A burning bush. I waited
For an avalanche to cover

My footsteps so none
Could follow. It didn't arrive.
Hangers-on kept up behind me
And spolit my subsistent spirit.
I viewed them from the back
Of my head and penciled in
Their eyes, ears and mouths.
They were happier now the world
Had been revealed. What had
Happened, they weren't sure.
I left them building and growing
And making their homes
Above a rapid river.
A few painted and drew.
Others walked on water
And began religion because
It was safer than the open
Mind. I left staggered
Encampments and waved goodbye
Long after, I could be seen.
Embarrassed to be alone
I drew a self-portrait in sound,
And caught a glimpse of an alien
Spirit. A woman approached
In glowing terms. Avoirdupois!
Show me the woman!
I'll balance the act.
She's no placebo!

She's looking good!
When she arrived
I kissed her once
To make her smile.

I liked the taste and
The style. She's a call-girl
Of the psyche, a poacher
Of the novel, a return
To the hovel, a medium
Of deception outside
The walls of Zion,
Of medium range desire.
No going back over the rack.
She had me on a high
And caught the words
Out of my mouth.
She cooked them, froze them,
Dried and smoked them.
I felt like a stall of
Verbal abuse. Then she disappeared.
I fainted and woke, cold and hot.
The fever of withdrawal
Of what I am not.
To survive, I walked and then bathed.
Sunrise brings the disguise
Of day. Swallow on the hour."

Arthur's Temple took the longest to build.
A bamboo frame had to be covered

With chicken wire. On this wire
Layer upon layer of soaked
Newspaper and flour, laid by
The hands of many volunteers.
When finally dry in the hot summer
Sun, all the surface was varnished,
Then covered with aluminum paint.
Some protection against rain and
Termites. Opening day celebrations.
All came from miles around.
Drinking, laughing, kissing, nagging.
Food for a dozen banquets.
Enough left over to feed a pigsty.
Young people flocked to the temple.
The walls All-Stars changed
With fashion. Guardian spirits
Picked on favorites and occupied
Their souls. These chosen few
Became adventurous, innovative
And decisive. Few could match
Their intelligence which overcame
Obstacles and arguments with ease.

They kept quiet about themselves
Not wanting to raise envy
And hate; only solving problems
When others had failed. Arthur
Knew what was going on.
He saw that the future was secure

And successful. His temple led
The way and eventually provided
A school of thought and leaders
Who could take on the world.
He was the first to think of
A journey home when Our City
Had come into its own. Arthur
Was a purist in perception. He
Needed to rest his mind from
The crowd and write his thoughts
Down to cleanse his soul.

CHAPTER FIFTY-FIVE

ARTHUR AND TAROT, PRINCESS OF NIGHT

One Princess of Night
Accompanied him, for he knew
He must talk out his mind.
Her name was Tarot. Taking
The form of a human she floated
Down from a cloud at night.
They wandered off to the mountains.
Tarot had light brown hair,
Dark eyes, hair straight to the shoulder,
A body to please the eye
And a smile to suit the angriest heart.

She had been dropped from the blue.
Arthur and Tarot left Our City,
To explore an epic philosophy.

Tarot,

"The pimple on the end
Of your nose is like a gravestone
From the devil's graveyard. Once

It is burst we can start
Rubbing noses."

Arthur

"Sibling rivalry has
Nothing on this. Although you have
A perfect body and more than
Beautiful face, and I love rubbing
Your nose, it's the smell of
Your body which brings out the Ages
Of man in me."

Tarot,

"I remember you for the first
And only time. I am not interested
In the second or third. Like an eye
Patch, you blocked my sight. I fell

In love with the blackness of your
Eyes and the redness of your bite."

Arthur,

"You gamble like an old-timer
Who cares little for the future.
Your face has no wrinkles and
Laugh lines disappear. You're an ageless
Device set to spin a balanced heart."

Tarot,

"Don't cut your toenails
When I'm talking. Your clippings
Litter the land and decay slowly.
In the past, I have burnt them
Instead of wood. But now your price
Is too high."

Arthur

"If I was a child, I could
Never want to stop sucking your breasts

I'd milk your kindness till it gave
Out. I'd sell it to the poor at
Inflated prices. I'd grow rich defying
Gravity."

Tarot

"Let's begin our journey along
This path which leads through
A tangle of fern and bush. I like
Its well-trodden look and the spots
Of blood splattered on stones.
I know the wounded animal who flees
Human touch. He brought a message
From Mother Nature, who is angrier
Than a tempest."

Arthur

"Tarot, dear. Like the cards
Which seems to answer every person
In just the right way I find you
More tempting than the creamiest

Ice cream, the juiciest fruits and
The crunchiest nuts. Kiss me
Before fate has time to stick
One on me."

Tarot

"I can steal your fate
With a kiss. It will belong to me
For the rest of your life. Over
Here, under this trey. Don't
Cut it down before me."

Arthur

"We will bed down in this
Ruin of a Buddhist temple founded

By Tibetan exiles. By morning
Lichen will be growing
On your skin. Here biology is
Relaxed. It makes no effort to
Stick to rules. The aura of law
Has been sucked away by great
Souls who swopped theirs for a free
Ride into holiness. Notice
The popularity of the ground inside
The walls; it is teeming with birds,
Insects and mammals. See how
There is no fear. Even we are
Welcome. But nobody it allowed to spend
More than one night. In one night
Bridges can be crossed to
That next world. Dreams are made
Of messages and they have to get
Through as many as possible.
And many are off the beaten track."

Tarot

"I once inspired a writer
To think of a book called the Secret
Languages of Women. He researched
And wrote it in six months. It
Was rejected by feminist publishers
As being too condescending and by
Orthodox publishers as too unlikely.
He retained his manuscript, revising
It's here and there. Knowing his

Masterpiece would remain unpublished
He became depressed. One day
He burnt his manuscript and
Shot himself. Nobody else will
Write this book and the Secret Language
of women will remain Womens alone."

Arthur

"Although I'm not a legend
And have slain no dragon, as a
Poet I can follow Shelley and
Say I'm an unacknowledged vegetation
Of the world. Although to be
A vegetable is considered akin
To not thinking it is obvious
To the hapless onlooker that
The plant world is the happiest
In the world and can no more
Destroy it than one ant
Can eat through a ton of sugar.
The meaty eaters, particularly humans,
Not only encourage the Devils' own
Work but thwart the image of
Peace at every meal time. How can
Poets become vegetables and not
Fall prey to the mandibles of man?
Being one of the mandible crowd
I find it hard to escape the inbuilt
Conspiracy that is. I have eyes

Which roughly see what other
Humans see and not what a cat,
Or pigeon or butterfly or horse
Can see. As for what a cabbage,
A magnolia, a daisy, or weeds
Experience, that is almost an impossible
Case. So I am stuck with my luck
In being able to chop down
Trees but they can't
Chop down me.
I'm at the center, they'd better
Watch it. Carefully, softly, when
I become alone at the center,
The world could be out of stock.
So poets make bad vegetables
And are doomed to the bloom
Of humanity. When they eat meat

They are as happy as the next
Along the banquet table. Those
Who eat cellulose stew are thankful
For their B12 pills. However
Even if the theory of evolution
Kills you, your last chance
Might be to head for the hills."

Tarot

"It's no good talking to me
Like that, as if I was three
When the stones of goodnight
Have heated during the day

When the parchments of breakfast
Have been read
When the Duke of the Month
Has no cause
Do you regret the passing
Of tradition, silence, and sanity.
The breakthrough came
When Buddha discovered Zen,
He didn't think about it,
Plan or prepare it.
The invention fell from his hand
Like a chariot from a tree.
The momentum totem set
For a long run and its course
Was a delight to hand.
So proof has its dream
Sanctioned amid backbreaking
Work."

Arthur

"I have no desire
To be embalmed in a state
Of play; The word is out
You're here to guide me
To enlightenment anyway.
So I'll pounce upon your
Pomposity like a cat ox cathedra
And chew the mule pride
Till he's headless and once
Inside I'll knit the guts

And bail out the blood
My creation a boat and sail
To take me on a voyage
With a lotus flower."

Tarot

"I am Princess of the Night,
A Columbine who has come
To put cement into
The well of sadness,
Zero temperature into the fire
Of love, nails into the heart
Of kindness and shadow
Over the light of mercy.
Now the world is dying
You will pay for your deeds.
Revenge on the living will be sweet,
And the door of forgiveness
Barred by a giant.
When you journey to Europe
Be careful and don't quantify
The mind. I'll be there
Giving out punishment. Our
Specialties are bondage in dreams,
Scatology at breakfast, incestial
Necrophilia and acute pain
On contact with water. For lesser
Transgressions there is slow poisoning
By a delicious fruit or Wonderful
Meals in expensive restaurants;

Crippling by exercise in dance centers
And gymnasiums; deprivation of
The use of senses by electronic
Media. Lastly, mental terror brought
On by subversive writings
Which empty themselves of meaning
As soon as read. Those we
Rarely forgive are allowed to laugh,
Sometimes contagiously. Some even
Die of laughter and they have
A place in paradise."

Arthur

"I don't believe a word
Of it. It's time we moved

On. The Buddhist ruin
Has a mutinous influence
On our relationsgip. Our travels
From now on could take
A tragic trajectory. We are misslies
Who travelled too late. You are
The angel who can't pretend."

They halted on a crooked road
Stopping to eat fruits and flowers.
They waited for a traveler
To join them in conversation.
Along came a rabbit
Who was tired of the habit
And wished to become serene.

CHAPTER FIFTY-SIX

LAPAP THE RABBIT

Lapap The Rabbit.

"You two are shoe-shiners,
Rare birds in this matrix.
Like a spelling test for imperfects
I can see you would smile too wide
If you sat there too long.
With flowers and fruit
You'll become victims of vectors
Of the cosmic trapeze."

Tarot

"Yes, rabbit Lapap
I know you of old.
You almost had our blessing
But you went in for wrestling
And reproduced your crowd
Until it became safe
To kill you off with
Cotton socks, and then you
Had our blessing."

Arthur

"I know what you're on about.
It's curvature and servitude
All bound up in the Book of Books.
I prefer praise and censure
To test me on style and eat off
The plates of fashion until
The writer takes them away,
And presents a pleasing menu.
The waiter in his wisdom, waits

For the next order and then
He shows his acumen by
Slipping a finger up the arse
Of decorum. Guests at the table
Laugh and huff. If we are
Poisoned we'll call your bluff,

And rest our case in the buried body.
It is more peculiar to be
A ruler from a castle lying in state."

Lapap

"I know of a female executive
Who lets her lover
Carry her briefcase to work.
Every word has a number,
I write my books in
Numbers. Machines can read
Them much more easily.
I'll send you signed copies
Of my complete works.
Perhaps when you have returned
To the old country. I see
You are leaving, goodbye."

Tarot

"Yes, we are returning
To Our City to prepare
For a week-long feast
To celebrate our decision
To journey home."

Arthur

"Take this poem, Lapap,
And include it in your anthology."

CHAPTER FIFTY-SEVEN

DEFINITIVE POEMS OF THE UNIVERSE

"Definitive Poems of the Universe Part I."

The buyer of an ivory tower,
(Ten thousand elephants died
For the facing tiles)
Stood high above the clouds
Surveying the earth.
He was proud of his wealth
And the tower which contained
All magic formulae
Ever invented by shamans
And charlatans. Many formulae
Worked, and many were indecipherable.
They had been carved into word
Paneling in the six hundred rooms
By generations of magical scholars
Who had traveled from all over
To make their contributions
With a penknife. The rich man
Spent most of his waking hours
Using formulae to make money
And he felt as wonderful
As any human being could feel.
There was a problem with rising damp.
In the tower's base and some wood
Had suffered dry rot, obliterating
Many carvings. Other wood
Had fallen victim to the worm

And some formulae could be
Blown away by the slightest breeze.
The rich man thought it probable
That his most powerful magic
Was lost forever and therefore
The possibility of empire building
To rival Greece and Rome.
The time came to share his tower.
He employed the young son
Of the previous owner who had
To sell because of a lack of success
In the applied arts. It is necessary

To have the knowhow to make
The magic work.
The rich man knew the tower
Could be restored, and the knowledge
Contained published for the benefit
Of the world. It needed a fast
Reader and a good judge of priorities.
The youngest son would need help
And it was decided to employ
Fifty illiterate girls to make
Wax rubbings of all the surfaces.
Twenty-five girls started from
The top and twenty-five
From the base. Five rooms
Were reserved at the tower's center
To pile up the paper.

The young son began his reading
Of the universal knowledge.
As far as I know, the girls
Are old women with grandchildren
And the young son has a long white
Beard. The rich man died in
Ecstasy on discovering the secret
Of Atomic power. The young son
Still hopes for a solution to
All our ills. His vigorous approach
Allowed only minor works to be
Published. Their effect on
History, doubtful.
A week before he
Was due to die, he discovered
The formula for eternal life.
He hopes to save us all one day.
I was hired as caretaker
And will soon write an autobiography
'The dark side of the Ivory Tower'.

Our City was flourishing
As never before. Tarot and
Arthur married in the Temple
Of Janice, of Life's Fertility.
Janice was the first woman
To be wounded by a bullet
In a demonstration against Doomsday
Missiles. Before this, her books

Had sold in small numbers.

CHAPTER FIFTY-EIGHT

JANICE, POET

Janice was the Crème de Menthe
Of poets. Her passion for
The details of life enabled
Many a reader to solve
Idiosyncratic knots on their own.
Her Poems became manuals
Of the spirit and all its hide
And seek games. Fate, Luck,
Chance, Coincidence, Serendipity and
Synchronicity were all enhanced
By her words and charged with
The mission to work out the world.
Janice didn't become born again
Into the land of men, like most women.

An illegitimate daughter of a professor
Of Classics, she was raised in a women's
Commune in the heart of Scotland.
Science was banned from the curriculum.
Philosophy, languages, sympathetic magic,
Mother Nature, Arts and Crafts
Were studied in a ten-hour day,
Four days a week. Lesbian
Love was allowed at all ages
And when children were needed
A woman was sent to a male
Chosen by the group. They

Spread themselves amongst all races,
Amongst laboring men and professors.
Baby boys were immediately given
To adopting agencies in exchange
For a girl if available.
The commune had lasted ten years
Up to the war. Boredom, being a double
Negative of the spirit, usually leads
To action. At eighteen, Janice left
Her home to recite poems to
The world, waiting she thought
For her wisdom on a plate.
Errant days. Janice traveled

To every capital city to find
Similar spirited people. Her last
Stop L.A. She met Moon at
A reading. He whispered in her Ear.
"I love you." And her brain
Turned cold. Following him to the good
Ship 'Watchso' she felt under
A spell. Her old life seemed
To disappear. She knew about the war;
She knew she had to leave
During the great voyage. She tried
Many times to remember the story
Of her life; without fail she became physically
Sick, so after a few weeks she
Gave up. It was a self-imposed

Conditional reflex. Only after her
Return from the antibodies and
Away from Moon's influence did
Her memory flood back to help
Her write her autobiography.
On ship Janice's work produced
Many nature and ethnic poems
About Pacific Island people.
The Temple of Life's Fertility
Better known as Janice's Temple
Stood like a beacon of greenery;
A huge rock garden containing plants
Gathered from all over the land.
The Grotto, dug out from the earth
And supported by timber, held
Two dozen people. Around the walls
Miniature hand-carved statues;
Ideas of what local nature
Spirits looked like. They were
Embedded in plaster and painted white.
Eerie presences in a dark cavern
Whose only light traveled down
Glass tubes. These had been positioned
To direct light onto the granite
Altar. The grotto was also used to grow
Mushrooms, magic mushrooms used in
Ceremonies enabling free expression
To flourish at required times.

Janice employed four priestesses and
Three girls to run her operation.
Only women were allowed to participate

In intimate ceremonies, which usually
Ended in a sexual frenzy. Males were
Allowed in on open days and Sundays.

Janice, too, left Our City
To discover the hinterland and
The makings of her mind.

"O Janice,
Traveling over rocky roads
Over green bread hills,
Saddle the wind,
Rattle the clouds
You can outrun the fast hare,
Blowing leaves, rapids, and falling
Worlds. I found you working
On a tapestry of love as old
As life. At once, I fell in love.
Now you plunge through primeval forests
And tunnels of the night,
Skim across lakes and icy locks,
Shelter in caves from deluge
And drought. I can't keep up
This constant flight across nature's
Secular land. You couldn't be
Harnessed for the break of day,
Yet every day, you changed my life.

The pendulum had swung too far.
Now it was broken, and there was
No return. You had gone into
The lime of light. I rolled in
A ball of darkness from town to town
Wondering where the day had fallen
Down."

Janice trudged well-worn paths
Followed by other poets. She
Wasn't so impressed by their landmarks
Or the people they had met,
The words woven and carved
In rocks. As for writing in
Sand she saw folly in the easy
Hand. She found an outcrop
Of rock and climbed to check
The progress of roads, where they
Vanished on the horizon, numbers
Travelling and the prospects of ironic

Wit in their speech.She wanted
To find a happy tribe who could
Give their feet a miss. A tribe
Whose children didn't suffer
Whose music soothed the brain,
Whose food could be eaten without
Hearing the echo of pain,
Whose magic didn't brush with fear.
Janice looked for many hours,

Analyzing everything seen. Her vision
Took her to places which beat
The best. People were backward
And forward more than Mr Progress
Himself. There in a dapperland
Of praiseworthy names, people constantly
Searched for new words by which
To call themselves. A central
Bureau supervised distribution
And for a fee and an old nameplate
A new babel could be yours.
Status belonged to inventors and
All sorts of methods were available
To find star-status words.
Digging into the past, sifting
The stew of foreign languages,
Raiding the classics and far-eastern
Cradles. Libraries and thousands
Of books wore out by constant
Use. Some traveled far to seek
Out examples of linguistic
Treasure. Others resorted to nonsense
And poetic devices. Many learned
The great poets by heart, hoping
For an alchemy to conjure alphabets into
Gold. This land didn't hold
Janice's interest for long. It was
Doomed to die by the letter

And by the book.

At last, in the lowly south
An artery of sense seemed to pulse
Through a well-planned landscape.
Not rigid as a grid but designed
Along the banks of a river whose many
Controlled tributaries
Carried the wealth of ages.

Janice changed direction.
She needed a rest. To lie
In the sun and watch ants,
Butterflies, flowers, and bees brushing up
Pollen.
In the streets of Old Paradise,
The blind trip the blind,
The deaf ignore the hard of hearing
And cripples are treated like vermin.
Janice had made a mistake.
The river carried their dead
To the sea, to feed sharks
Fat rats and giant crabs.
Buildings crumbled into tributaries
And no one cared a damn.
Children worked like slaves while
Adults played out fantasies.
For all her tears, Janice
Knew this was the culmination
Of her wasted years. She had

To face up to the facts of
Her life and realized that being
A gifted being, a special vessel,
Was no big deal to the candid way
Of the world. She said a prayer
To her guardian God who sent
A message via a horse. Janice
Climbed on, the first time,
On a horse.

At first, it trotted
Along the road, avoiding potholes,
Then he stopped at a field
And Janice strapped herself
Around his neck. He worked
Up a gallop, across ploughed fields,
Through virgin forest, along lake
Shores, through deserted towns.
At night they rested. The magical
Horse had endless energy which
Only gave out when they reached
Their destination.

On a river's floodplain which
Wasn't of this world, a tall, elegant
Temple, pure white, stood unadorned
By outhouses, gates, moats, parapets

Or gardens. Its shape a truncated cone
Topped by a three-quarter sphere, topped
By an egg-shaped house. Here

Lived a wise woman who knew most
Things. She had trouble dispensing
Her knowledge because few people
Could find her although animals
Had no problem. And the fortunate
Souls who made it through the eons
Had difficulty understanding her oblique
Language. Hence this world progressed
Little and those messengers who
Returned arrived too late and were
Not thanked for being wise after
The event.

Janice didn't know what to expect.
Dismounting and arresting on the granite
Gravel ground, she watched tiny ants
Building their nest. The tower
With egg on top, about a hundred
Yards away kept changing size
And she knew the air had hallucinogenic
Qualities. The ground disappeared,
Re-appeared. The sky glowed gold,
Red and blue. No clouds, birds,
Wind or leaves. Far away she
Could see a silver river and faint
Mountainous shapes seemed to dance
On the horizon. She felt at peace
And slept for a night. When
She woke, the horse was watching

Her and she knew he hadn't
Much time.

Janice climbed up the tower's
Three thousand steps. The wise
Woman sat knitting, occasionally
Stopping to write down the next
Few lines of a play, she was
Composing or composting as the case
Maybe. She was well ahead of
The action having started a few
Million years before the first Homo
Sapiens evolved; she wasns't sure
When she first saw hombres.

Of late they had multiplied so fast,
Their actions increasingly manifold,
Her script writing had quickly lost
Ground. Now she was content
With a token script;
A few heads of state, great sinners,
Evil dictators, mad scientists
And a few outstanding artists
Of their generation. Even with
These she left huge gaps which
Were filled with ad lib and
Unexpected twists. When her guest
Arrived, she stopped all her writings.
Had she but known it, they weren't
Missed. She was one in a million

Such aces.

Her name Tell-Tale.
Once a cosmic dancer, spinning
Matter from her whirling veils.
Her tower higher than most and
Boasting a translucent tank
Filled with holy water.
Steps passed up into
The egg, a lightweight appendage
Capable of infinite flight, that is,
It could appear anywhere at
Any time instantaneously. Hundreds
Of blue spiders constantly wove
The fabric of the egg over a skeleton
Of microscopic crystal. The machine
Was powered by zero thought.
A form only open to the chosen.
It couldn't be learned or imitated.

Tell-Tale

"Come in my dear.
Sit down by the window.
Admire the view.
Watch for subtle changes.
Tell me your problems."

Janice

"I would like to return
To a fireside and book,

This land or place you
Live in, I don't want
To stay. The quiet,
And under this sky

I find a claustrophobia."

Tell-Tale.

"Where do you want to return
To? As you must know
There is no going back.
If you returned in this machine
And I let you outside
You would vanish into the present
And events would take
Their course. It's better you stay
And rest. Meditate on the colors
Of life outside. I will summon the horse.
It can take you back to Our City
Where no doubt your temple
Will need your support."

Janice

"I'll take your word for it.
I'll swallow it whole.
And ride to Our City
To resume life. You sit
There knitting away our troubles.
Don't you find it lonely
Away from the world,
Away from love
And the tremors of hope?
Stitching anguish and resting
Tears, turning over bodies
Of the past, inventing the future

As if it was your next meal.
Why don't you ever look
Straight at me. Why don't
Your eyes register contact.
Sometimes they flicker like a fire
Just lit. Yet your body is
Cold, colder than dead flesh
In a frost. If I tried to warm
You, it's impossible. I would die
Like a babe in arms."

Tell-Tale

"Now you are rested
And color has returned to
Your skin. Descend the tower's
Thousands of steps. You will sleep
Well on the horse's back."

Janice's journey home held no fear.
Before strapping herself to the horse's
Neck she looked back at the tower
For the last time. She fell very
Quickly into sleep without dream
Or nightmare. The magic horse
Flew the forever journey. Janice
Woke by a stream in bright sunlight.
Over the hill rested Our City.
Her temple had become overgrown
And needed rescuing from troubled
Decay.

CHAPTER FIFTY-NINE
RACHEL

Rachel the youngest of the crew.
Still only eighteen. She met
Gas Jenny Falcon at a London
Party. Her parents were publishers.
Gas liked her conversation and
Invited her to L.A. for a
Short summer holiday. Good ship
'Watchso' had just been bought.
Gas told Rachel of their project,
Inviting her to join. Rachel wrote
Poetry and had won prizes in
England. She wrote home saying
She wanted to spend all summer
In L.A. They understood.

During the voyage Rachel
Wrote very short poems and fell in
Love with the sea and island
People who saw her golden blonde
Hair as a sign of hope, her blue
Eyes as jewels from heaven.

Rachel's temple was a simple affair.
A temple without foundations or roof.
It was named Temple of the Forms
Of Life or Temple of Forms. She
Decided the whole world was her temple.
All creatures
Must take their turn in having
Her followers worship their form.

Some days they would climb trees,
Meditate, celebrate by eating fruit.
Birds would come and feed with them.
On other days fields of sheep,
Anthills, cliffs, swamps, and forests,
Seashores and marshes would play
Host to her small and enthusiastic
Group, mostly young people and
Children with a few fit older folk. All
These were the happiest of the people

In Our City. They loved life
And each other more easily
Than most and statistics proved
They lived longer and raised
Hopeful generations. By the time
Other temples had been completed
Rachel's activities in the temple
Earth had exhausted her body
And her inventiveness. Praying
In pond water up to her neck,
In damp caves with the bats,
Digging tunnels to be with the worms,
Acqua-diving to pray with the sharks;
All this and more weakened her.
After initial
Ventures reaching out to the hearts
Of the most secretive creatures
Rituals became more symbolic

And sights chosen reflected
The wishes of a stable group who
Desired less difficult but more
Frequent worship. Drawings in sand
Of tropical, creatures overcame the problem
Of symbol. Sometimes clay was brought
In and models made during the service.
Rachel, at this point, like others before
Needed to leave and find out
The true makings of her mind.
It would have been easy for her
To leave Our City, look for some
Spiritual companion, whether old man,
Dog, snake or another woman.
Rachel felt this would be too
Predictable a course with predictable
Results. Either a premature enlightenment
Or time off from the world in some
Transcendent capacity. 'No thanks'
She thought to herself. Better
To stay here and dig deep
Into the pit of humanity.
She became a street walker
Picking up men from all walks
Of life. From richer settlers
She asked higher prices for
Her long golden hair and emerald
Blue eyes. From laborers, she asked

For less than half a week's wages
For thirty minutes in her small room
On the edge of town. Within eight
Months she had been with every
Man between eighteen and sixty.
She felt worn out, and gave up
Prostitution.

What had she learned
From the men who had fucked her.
That each one fucked in a different
Way. Few were happy with
The women they'd married. Each
Moaned about getting old.
The young were awestruck
At the sight of an open woman.
She made them kiss it
Before anything else. Altogether
The male of the species was
Loaded with crap. They had
Substituted virility for sensuality
And the death wish for wishful life.
They were scared of women
So had them enslaved
By marriage, harems, and
Secretarial work. Rachel knew
Men had won when the missiles
Started to fly. The female
Brain had mysteriously atrophied

Allowing the final assault,
The big bang on Mother Nature,
The great revenge for being bort.
The day she returned to Europe
To see the remains and start
Again, she grew old quickly
And slept without dreaming.

To recover from prostitution
Rachel visited thermal pools,
North of the city, run by nuns.
They healed victims of radiation
With their magic waters.
These vegetarian nuns prayed
While they worked and rumor
Had it, their urine was so pure
It was added as one secret ingredient
To the holy volcanic waters, recently blessed

By remnants of the Vatican Church.

Some simple folks thought
That the forty nuns were angels of
The Lord come to cure the world.
Plane loads of people would come
Once the knowledge of their success
Spread. However it would take many
Lifetimes to cure everyone so they
Gave preference to the young. Animals
Had their own pools. Many a farmer's
Livelihood was saved. Wild animals suffering

From sickness used a lake hidden
By bushes and bamboo.

For two years, Rachel took
The waters, eventually helping
Out with administration as business
Grew.

The Mother Superior
Was the most beautiful woman
Rachel had ever seen. About
Thirty years old, she hardly ever
Spoke; talking was generally avoided
Anyway. Her height five feet ten inches
With a curvaceous figure. These nuns
Didn't wear old fashion habits,
Instead beautiful gowns donated by
Fashion houses just before the war.
All were as desirable as models or
Film stars. Their radiant skin and
Infectious smiles, light laughter
And long glossy hair helped their
Cures as much as air, water, flowers
Or the total knowledge they seemed
To possess about the human body.
At the end of her stay Rachel
Had decided they were angels
Earning their place in heaven.
Before leaving the thermal nuns, Rachel
Had a last meeting with Mother Superior.

Her name is Miss Longhi

CHAPTER SIXTY
MISS LONGHI AND RACHEL

Rachel

"What did you do before
Being stuck here nurturing babies
And psyches back to health?"

Longhi

"Before civilization, I watched
Many generations live substantial
Lives in richly living lands
Of abundant wildlife and forestry.
Slowly but surely, you grew in
Numbers as you become more confident
About knowledge and its possibilities.
Before long, many animals were being
Killed for food and clothing.
I wasn't happy with the human race.
In all my travels, I haven't seen a more mean
Cunning creature than Man.
How happy I would have been
To see you perish in a global disaster.
No such luck. You grew from strength
To strength. Then civilization
Appeared, and from past experiences I
Knew that entertaining though such
Developments had been they had always
Ended in downfall."

Rachel

"Down but not out.
Line no time.
Watch the clock.
Spread your wings.
Chew the cud.
Crap on ice.
Starch a cliche:
Dig for victory.
Dance on juice.

So humans are crazy to face up
To laws of nature."

Longhi

"Dear Rachel, I know
You are a great feminine
Who has come to this planet
To save its soul,
To dance on the hot irons
Of love placed across
The gates of paradise.
Your mission was seen as
A necessary failure.
Only through anguish
Could victory come."

Rachel

"I know I am a lemon turd,
A good girl oligarch,
A tremor on the cream,
A note on a harp,
A negligee up to my neck,
Beauty on a rosta,

Make-up for a matchmaker.
But, dear Longhi, you have
Bought this postwar world
Cheaply at a knockdown price.
Now you exploit the wronged
For a place in heaven,
A place few have a chance to win."

Longhi

"We are beauties, not beasties.
Our good deeds will soften ravages,
Give hope a peace of mind.
The other day I met a family
Who had taken our treatment.
Completely recovered now they plan
An Empire. That's progress.
From a subliminal to an empirical
Calculus. It makes me happy."

Rachel

"You use words the same way
You used the Great God Pan."

Longhi

"Pan had it all his own way
For many thousands of years.
Civilization put paid to his power.
A sad case of obsolescence.
I have heard he lurks
In deserted olive groves and
On ghostly moonlit shores,
Wallowing in self-pity."

Rachel.

"I remember some of the time
I fell in love. It was like

A catechism in the depths
Of the soul, a whirlwind
Drawing in the all of life,
A torment of desire,
A longing to enter the gates of
Happiness that grew until
Every breath was the chasing
Of death. In that moment
When love was requited.
The empiric unified with the idyllic
To give birth to the romantic.
What are words worth
After the fall?"

Longhi

"I was a prima donna
Of paradise when I fell in love
With Pan. We met on a bridge.
He leading a group of Bacchants
And I a group of Lotus-eaters.
Pan seemed to have a permanent
Erection, so no female within
Running distance was safe.
And he was the fastest runner
Whoever lived. He fell in love
With me and loved me.
On mountainous trails,

In ancient forests,
On deserted islands,
In luminous caves,

Behind temple altars,
In haystacks and cornfields.
Elemental Pan had an insatiable
Sexuality. He needed on average
A fuck an hour, and if
There wasn't a female around
He'd dig a hole in the ground
And fall upon. It. Such sperm
Production, such a metabolism.
No wonder his followers soon left
For the harbor of marriage
And husband fucks."

Rachel

"In our City
My temple of Form
Successfully set up anywhere to
Worship a particular creature.
Direct sexuality had no part
In the ritual. By the time
I was ready to leave, the worship
Sequence had began to use the
Principle of Christian Sacraments
To take us through the ceremony. For example
In the case of snakes, we didn't
Have time to differentiate between
Types, so we took as representative a humble
Grass snake. Once a location had been
Found we sprayed it with blessed water,

Communed with the grass snake by eating
Grass, confirmed our intentions by
Wriggling around, married the snake
By mock snake-like copulation, forgave
Ourselves past snake hate with some
Gentle flagellation. Death was
Met with dignity.
We kissed each other on the cheek
And buried a clay model
Of a snake on a grassy slope."

Longhi

"It is time you left
These waters of life.
Our magic minds mimic the past,
Masquerade as the present
And mutilate the future.
It is too long to be a conscience
Being. To rest, I turn to meditation,
Hoping to miss the deceits of dreams,
Entanglements of nature, vices of pleasure
And trivialities of work.
You are as good as new
As they say.

When I was young and
Hadn't a human body,
I was a happy panoply,
An unirritable spirit,
An untethered ether,
A cosmic osmotic,

A galactic act,
A light year ahead
As fancy took me
The matter became
What's the matter
And slowly, free spirits
Were drawn to the new fashion.
Take it and shape it.
That was the game
Like children dressing up.
The game was overpowering.
Form took over, self-perpetuating,
Everchanging. Too complicated
To unravel, too ingenious to upset.
Some, like me, could come and go,
Given certain circumstances;
Change in the cosmic weather,
Change in-tile microclimate.
Some became tied into more
Abstract phantasy and waited
For changes in history,
Changes in thought or
The coming of a new species.
Others went even further into form
In desperate attempts to devise
A way out, inventing astrology,
Palmistry, the Tarot, and many
Other toxic divinations. Some became

Mad. Some became tyrants.
Others craved sexual omniscience.
All to no avail.
After service here, I will
Leave for Heaven,
Having had my permission.
Goodbye Chinese, goodbye passion,
Goodbye flesh, goodbye leash of life.
Eternity is protein to the soul."

Rachel rampaged through
The water gardens kissing everybody goodbye.
The Temple of Form had become
The most fashionable in Our City.
Eventually, its members bought some
Prime land and built a house
Of worship for the increasingly
Large congregation. Rachel wandered
In a stranger and wandered out.
This isn't what she had wanted
To happen, preferring small groups
To remain separate in their worship.
She wandered off to find Low and
Plan a return to Europe.

CHAPTER SIXTY-ONE

DIANA, TOO BEAUTIFUL TO LOOK AT

Diana had suddenly appeared at
The gangway of the ship Watchso.
Moon saw her from the top deck
And his sixth sense knew
Here was his last passenger.

The mystery he had dreamt of.
She didn't speak at first.
Too beautiful to look at,
A voice as seductive as a warm night.
Hair as dark as the ashes
Of a thousand dead,
A figure hidden by golden robes,
For the whole journey, she hardly
Spoke, wandering the decks
Deep in thought. At poetry sessions
Her contributions came in long
Non-stop readings from hand made
Paper in a language nobody
Had heard of. During island
Stops she went ashore
And disappeared for the whole visit,
Usually into the hills. She didn't
Eat meat, fish, or eggs but existed
On fruit, vegetables, seaweed and
Water. Nobody had even a glimpse
Of her body under the golden robes,
And few dared to try and speak
To her, in case they came under
Her spell. In the founding
Of Our City, she was given
A prime site for her temple. For
The first time she spoke.

"My temple will be dedicated

To the Goddess Moon. I will
Build it out of straw every year.
It will be seen to by my followers
Who will be no more than nine?
They will be taught my secret

Arts; the art of bringing
The dead to life; the art of
Taking the living to death,
The art of shaping the edge
Of mind, the art of making
People fall in love, the art
Of war and of peace.
With this knowledge, I will
Set them free and send them
Out to conquer the world.
Only women will be chosen.
In batches of nine, every three years.
Intensive study in a straw hut.
Under the power of hypnotic dream,
Through my eyes, I will wash
My protege clean and plant
The seeds of a new world.
Gone will be the dominant male
Cruising over virile wasteland.
The new woman will replace
His vices with a virtuous understanding
Capable of stamping out layabouts
And dog eaters."

At the end of each summer
The old straw temple was burnt
And rebuilt after the harvest.
Diana said "All is illusion"
And proceeded to shit.
A few students dropped out
Unable to take the truly psyche?
Busting teaching.

Diana remarked

"If you catch yourself
Smiling at a man,
Spit in his face."

And continued

"If you feel a yearning
To bear his child
Go and kill the nearest lamb"

It was a long quiet summer
And Diane had trained as many
Students as she thought necessary

To carry out her undivided task.
It was her turn to leave
After sending off the new women
To four corners of the earth.

In a long dark valley, Diana meditated
Upon the black rushing water. Her mind
Disappeared first into the moon's bubbling
Reflection.
Here she saw the shape of her soul

And knew the beginning of time was hard
Work. Down through the liquid harness
To pebbles and weeds. An entanglement
For logic. She knew she could float
Faster than the sound of light traveling
From the nearest star, yet dared
To keep a snail's pace along the waterway,
Well into the depths of a forest.
The stream flowed through its neglected
Valley whose fields had become overgrown.
Domestic animals had gone wild and felt
Free of the fear of being hunted down.
Diana of the fearless earth chewing
The cud and bathing in mud.
The long valley had lost its way
And ended at the sea. In the silent
Forest Diana trod between the poles
Of fear and shackled her mind
To the house on the hill. If
All she had known was the way
To go she would have thanked
The Lord with all her heart.
As it was her legs were shaking,
Her lips quivering, her hands
Trembling, they dropped food.
Her heart beat the sleep from shadows.
She had a cold sweat all down her back.
Her throat was dry, she tried to pray aloud,

Her voice disappeared in a whisper.
Broken back of courage. Where can Diana
Gain new hope, a resource to take her
Out of this passionless loop? She noticed
Luminous fungi growing underneath
The lowest branches. She picked one
Out of hope. Tasted a nibble, didn't
Fall sick. Here was a hope in hell.

She ate one and knew she couldn't
Go wrong. The forest disappeared
And Diana stood high on a cliff
Watching fierce waves battering
Shattered rocks. She looked back at once
And could make out the valley
Covered in mist and steaming song:

A very large man tapped her shoulder,

"I want to talk with you.
You're Diana, supernatural servant
Of the Goddess Moon,
Revolutionary reveler with a silver spoon,
Riotous raven, terror of time,
A philosophic shadow who cannot
Be grasped. I want to speak
Till the sun sets, till we have
Sorted out the order of masque.
You have the choice of words
And the shape of argument under
Your skin. There are no blemishes

Or rough patches, which could distract
The eye. Undress and begin.
We haven't all day."

CHAPTER SIXTY-TWO

LORD ABAPPLE, FIRST SON OF MOTHER NATURE

"My name is Lord Abapple,
First son of Mother Nature.
I bring the seasons, gamble with evolutions,
Have no regrets about lemmings or lice.
The shapes of surfaces and forces
On structure, I leave to my other brothers.
It is your presence
I find a challenge to my chair.
You come from another world to interfere
With a game of chance which has
Brought more entertainment than justice,
Yet more form and content than
All the inventions since time began.
And it works, even though the radiation
Spread and upset nature below.
You are here to cast out and usher
In, to measure the rightness of life
And death if it has to go. You want
A blessing from me which won't
Arrive because I am here until
The sun gives out."

Diana

"Abapple, long in the tooth
Evolution booth, how we live
In a post-bomb world,

Where butterflies are extinct
And birds are rare; your time
is over number one son.
Mother nature gave to you
Many loves, and you failed to take
Into account the make of mind.
What is left we will call our own.
Short term will be ours too.
We will change this game
And shape the heart,
Unite the brain, extend the hand.
Fix wings and increase vision.
Hearing will extend to the slightest

Murmur. Fifth sense and sixth sense
Will defeat pain. Everybody will be
Free to take the path of the informed
Life. Where will you stand in
This new world Lord Abapple?
Burden of ages, burden of science,
Bruiser of art and organ grinder."

They fought a cosmic battle
Out in another time, through
Space and galaxies to the end of the universe,
And consumed vast energies
In the pursuit of victory.

CHAPTER SIXTY-THREE

MOON, GESSO, LOW, AND GAS GO TO THE TEMPLE OF THE DEAD

Moon, Gesso, Low and Gas
Two horsemen and two horsewomen
Of the Apocalypse
Rode to the Temple

Of the Dead or Temple of
Barbed wire outside Our City
And forbidden to non-members.
Inside this tangled mess
Connected by a tunnel to the outside
World,
A single magic stone which had
Written on it the names of everybody
Who had ever lived. This list was
To be updated by a mason
Connected by telephones to different parts
Of the world.
A brick wall encompassed the complex.
The four friends who had started
The journey knew their speculative time
Was coming to an end. Laws
Had been made. Ordered democratic
Life seemed secure. The temples
Had woken up the spirit in people.
The Temple of Death had many
Members all dedicated to the task
Of carving on a piece of granite
The name of all the dead. To encode
A granite stone with new information
A mason used a laser and electron
Microscope. Helping him with his task
He had a computer, a replica
Of Daedalus. The mason showed

The way.

The good ship
'Watchso', had been
Rebuilt and updated. Daedalus
The Computer had been given extra
Capacity; his experience being counted

Upon for a safe return home. It
Was time to pick a crew and
The four Apocalypsos went searching
For their new guests.

In the far north of the country
Is a strange city called Quagmire.
It was founded by a hunchback
And his wife with slaves imported
From all over the world, paid for
With gold. On arrival slaves
Were sent to work for two years
Then set free to build homes
And raise families. All this was long
Ago. Now Quagmire City is an ancient
Shell only inhabited by a core
Of hangers-on. Moon and friends
Arrived to look for a likely crew.
They decided to choose children
Of about fourteen, train and teach
Them all manner of things,
Strengthen their bodies for the hard work
Ahead. Six boys and six girls
Chosen for great intelligence

And magic. How were they
Selected? Each candidate (five hundred
In all) had to capture a devil
And his shadow in order to win
A place on the voyage. Only a handful
Succeeded, but a brilliant selection came through.

He took them to a secret place
And for a year, they were instructed
By a Buddhist monk.
The Good Ship 'Watchso' was filled with many
Foodstuffs, flowers, domestic creatures
And fruit trees in wooden tubs.
The children returned from education
Changed young people. Instead of snivelling
Malcontents used to grubbing around
Ruins, fighting on waste ground
And stealing from neighbors, back came
Subtle dialecticians, contemplatives,
Right action activists, nature lovers
And artists of life.

The journey home is another story
Told in another book.

CHAPTER SIXTY-FOUR

JOURNEY HOME

Moon, Gesso, Low and Gas
Found peace and happiness
Living in the ruins of Venice
Until the end of their days.

CHAPTER SIXTY-FIVE

POSTSCRIPT

Mr Nicest, Monster and mannequin
Of divine proportions was kind to his remarried
Wife Mrs Thankyou, yet had
Trouble in telling her of the sacred
Journey that had been undertaken
By their imperial friends.

"You have been flattered by moonlight
While copulating,
You have been washed by spring
Water while sleeping in afternoon sun.
I fed you the rarest fruits
Whose tastes are prized by Kings
And Queens. On your wedding day
I gave you gifts unseen by
Ordinary mortals and brought from
Lands whose names travelers have yet to hear.
Listen while I tell you a story.
Long ago, four travelers settled
In the ruins of a city called Venice
Which was deserted by its inhabitants
After the war. Their only companions
In the watery city, tramps, dogs,
Cats, occasional artists rediscovering
Through remnants, a glorious imagination."

Moon said -

"It is time to survive,
Look through the eyes of statues
To the heart of marble.
Carve out a skull,
Carve out a brain;
The morning mist carries the wave.
Rummage among the ruins.
Dig out paintings and artifacts
Of a thought which gave
Philosophy to the people.
Let us imitate as best we can,
Sharpen the senses, cudgel
The man. Carry off prizes

With their flawed promises,
Translate their message into the present.
Preserve tombstones and harpsichords,
Columns and domes, balconies
And fountains, piazzas and frieze.
Welcome a church rediscovered,
A pathway of shrines, tunnels for lovers.
We will build a living museum
And with our hands revive
Those properties which have
Made this place Heaven's state."

Lightning Source UK Ltd.
Milton Keynes UK
UKHW031004090223
416652UK00005B/1015